Autumn Sonata

Autumn Sonata

Noreen Riols

This edition published in 2014 by:

Thistle Publishing
36 Great Smith Street
London
SW1P 3BU

www.thistlepublishing.co.uk

ISBN-13: 9781910198254

To

Louis and Chloe
with my love

To Rachel,
with my besh
wiches

Mullen Ritts

Life begins at 50!!!

ACKNOWLEDGEMENTS:

My grateful thanks to my sister-in-law Sylvie Baxter for giving me an insight into the life and work of an international conference interpreter.

To my cousin Dr. Sarah Linacre for sharing me with her medical expertise and her sister Melanie Weild for her help and advice on diplomatic protocol.

To my agent Andrew Lownie for always being available.

And lastly to my husband Jacques for his encouragement and his endless patience.

PROLOGUE

One of the most daring clandestine operations undertaken during World War II was the arming and supplying from England of Resistance groups fighting the Germans in occupied Europe. These were organised by SOE, the Special Operations Executive (Churchill's Secret Army) and greatly contributed to the successful Normandy landings in June 1944, thereby saving thousands of Allied soldiers' lives.

These operations were carried out by fishing boats, feluccas, submarines and RAF planes flying at high risk at night without lights to infiltrate and rescue SOE'S secret agents, and to parachute arms, food, money and equipment to the Resistance groups.

As the attached note shows, in France alone SOE organised 329 such landings and pick-up operations by RAF planes - out of which 105 failed. 'Autumn Sonata' is story of an operation which failed. Behind dry statistics lie the tragedies of captured air crews. This wartime love story attempts to revive the little known drama of one of them, a pilot reported 'missing believed killed' who fell into a German trap, fights for survival in a devastated Europe and the heartbreak he faces when he unexpectedly returns.

Although fiction, the novel is based on truth. The failed landing described and the German reactions are drawn from actual historical facts.

PART ONE
LONDON 1943

———

CHAPTER ONE

Big Ben's chime echoed in the distance as the air raid siren's mournful wail sounding the "All Clear" broke over London's smouldering ruins.

In the BBC studio, Julien Fourcade cleared his throat, took a sip of water and leaning towards the microphone, fixed his eyes on the green light above the plate glass window separating him from the control cubicle. The signature tune slowly faded and the green light turned to red.

'Ici..... Londres,' he announced, introducing the first news bulletin of the day from London to German occupied France.

Twenty nine minutes later, Julien glanced towards the Studio Manager, still fiddling with the controls on the other side of the glass panel, and raised his eyebrows enquiringly. The "S.M." smiled, gave the thumbs up sign and, as the red light turned back to green he pressed the intercom. button. 'Everything went smoothly,' he announced, 'no fluffs.'

Julien put down his bulletin, tilted backwards in his chair, stretched and gave a cavernous yawn. 'God, I'm tired,' he groaned, as another yawn rose to the surface.

'*Don't,*' pleaded Fleur de Rosny his co-announcer, sitting opposite him at the microphone, 'you're starting me off.' Shuffling her papers together, she rose wearily to her feet. '*What* a night! I'm going straight home to bed.'

'No breakfast?' Julien enquired, rocking his chair back into an upright position.

'Can't face the canteen.'

Rounding the table to join her, Julien threw an arm around her shoulder. 'Neither can I,' he confided. 'How about splurging and going over to the Waldorf?'

Fleur hesitated, hunger and fatigue fighting for supremacy.

Julien pushed open the door separating them from the Studio Manager's cubicle. 'Thanks Brian,' he called as they went through. 'Your night over?'

'Almost. Got to put the Dutch on the air in ten minutes, then Nan arrives and I'm off to bed, hopefully to sleep. The Luftwaffe certainly had a good innings last night. At one point I thought the building was going to collapse about our ears.'

Julien grimaced. 'So did we. Sweet dreams,' he called, as he and Fleur walked into the deserted basement corridor and headed for the lift. The smell of frying floated towards them from the canteen. 'Definitely the Waldorf,' Julien declared.

The lift doors slid open and two immensely tall Dutchmen clutching sheafs of paper nodded as they stepped out and made for the studio.

The early morning team were already hard at work when Fleur entered the newsroom and handed in her bulletin. The news editor popped his head round the door. 'Everything went well I hear. Glad you managed to squeeze in that last minute flash I sent down.'

'Five of our aircraft failed to return from last night's bombing raid over Berlin,' Julien intoned, putting on his announcer's voice. He sighed, and reached for his coat. 'Just another cheery bit of news to add to the rest.' Knotting his scarf around his neck he turned towards the door. 'Fleur and I are going across to the Waldorf for breakfast, Edward. Why don't you join us?'

The news editor's eyes swam round the room; everyone was typing furiously. 'I think I might. They've got enough to keep them busy for another hour, and if there's a crisis they know where to find me.'

Julien and Fleur walked down the steps of Bush House into a changed city. As they crossed the street dust from the raid mingled with flecks of soot hovered in the air over the Aldwych like an enormous mushroom cloud.

'A lot of the newspaper offices in Fleet Street seem to be down,' Fleur remarked, seeing firefighters still battling to direct hoses onto the flames rising high into the sky. She glanced across the road. 'But the Waldorf's still there.'

'For the time being.' Julien added grimly.

They entered the hotel and walked across the hall to the dining room. It was deserted, except for a young airman sitting alone in a far corner.

'He's wearing pilot's wings,' Julien noted, pulling out a chair for Fleur, 'I wonder if he's one of those who got away last night? Let's ask him to join us, he looks lonely.' He strode over to where the young man was studying the menu. The pilot looked up in surprise when Julien approached him, then putting down the menu, followed him back to his table.

'Hugh Cunningham,' he smiled, when Julien introduced Fleur.

'And this,' Julien announced, as Edward joined them, 'is our news editor, Edward Adams. Though whether there'll *be* any news to-night is anyone's guess: Fleet Street's practically destroyed.'

The airman looked enquiringly from one to the other. 'Are you journalists?'

Julien laughed. 'No, Edward is the only real journalist, he was the Times correspondent in Paris before the war. Fleur and I are only playing at it. We work across the road at Bush House, BBC World Service, French Section. Fleur and I have just come off the night shift, broadcasting the first news bulletin of the day to occupied France.'

'A voice of hope in the darkness,' Edward put in. 'Listened to by several million patriots, all of them risking arrest and probably worse for tuning into the BBC.'

Hugh nodded. He appeared to understand. 'So you two are French? he queried.

'We're mongrels. French fathers and English mothers.' Julien lifted his cup of coffee and pointed it in Hugh's direction. 'Your very good health'

Hugh laughed and returned the salute.

'I should be getting back,' Edward announced, when Fleur shook the last drops of coffee into his cup. 'I'd like you to come with me Julien, there's one or two matters I want to discuss.'

Julien groaned. 'Can't they wait till to-night? I'm all in'.

'Fraid not.' Edward caught Julien's eye and jerked his head towards Fleur and Hugh, deep in conversation. Julien frowned, then suddenly understood.

'No don't rush, Fleur,' Edward said, when she got up to leave as her two colleagues said goodbye to Hugh. 'I don't need you. Stay and keep our pilot friend company.' Fleur hesitated, uncertain what to do.

'I'd love you to stay if you have time,' Hugh said shyly.

'Sorry I was so slow on the uptake, Edward,' Julien grimaced as they walked out of the Waldorf and crossed the street. 'Do you *really* want to see me?

'No, of *course* I don't, it was merely an excuse to leave those two together. Didn't you see, he couldn't take his eyes off Fleur. The poor girl has had a tough time since France fell, she needs a break: a little romance in her life will do her a world of good.'

Julien glanced at his companion, a wry smile on his face. 'For a hardened old bachelor Edward, you're remarkably perceptive.'

Fleur stared at her plate, her fingers crumbling a roll.

'Would you like me to order more coffee?' Hugh ventured. The silence between them was becoming uncomfortable.

Fleur shook her head.

He smiled. 'I think you need to go home and get some sleep. Let me find you a taxi.'

'No, the coffee has revived me. I've been cooped up in Bush House since midnight, I need some fresh air. I'll walk along the Embankment and catch my 'bus in Parliament Square.'

'May I walk with you?

Fleur looked at him in surprise. 'Don't you have any plans?'

'None at all. I got back in the early hours of the morning and am free for two days. My squaddie was going to see his wife in Kent and offered me a lift; he's picking me up at 6.30 on Wednesday morning.'

'Julien announced on the dawn bulletin that five of our aircraft failed to return from a bombing raid over Berlin last night,' Fleur said hesitantly. She paused. 'Were you one of the lucky ones who did?'

'No,' he answered briefly, and rose from the table. He seemed disinclined to continue the conversation.

Fleur slung her gas mask over her shoulder and followed him through the swing doors into the Aldwych. The early morning rush had started. Crowds of office workers were scurrying past: others patiently queuing for the red buses which lumbered by, packed tight, a sea of heads jammed against the taped-up windows: less fortunate passengers swayed as they clung to the overhead strap hangers. The bus platform was crammed with people who had either squeezed themselves on at the last stop or were desperately trying to push their way through the crush in order to jump off at the next one.

'Glad I'm not in a hurry,' Fleur remarked, as they dodged through the traffic. 'Let's go down to the Embankment and walk along the river. I often do that when I come off duty.'

They cut across the Strand into Surrey Street. Weary mothers carrying blankets and the remains of last night's picnic were emerging from the Temple Tube Station dragging bleary-eyed children or attempting to soothe crying babies as they headed for the lengthening bus queues. Hugh steered Fleur round an enormous bomb crater.

'That must be the one we thought had our name on it last night,' Fleur remarked grimly.

The Embankment was littered with rubble from the night's raid. Further down the river fire barges bobbed in the water and ambulances, their bells ringing furiously screeched past them as they picked their way along the bank.

'Shall we sit down?' Hugh suggested when they entered the gardens below Charing Cross Station. A lone whistle split the air as they took their seats and above them a train rumbled past. The early morning mist veiling the river had evaporated leaving a silvery grey sheet of water brimming with reflections, and the sun now rising high left the sky awash with a clear green light giving promise of a fine Autumn day. It looked so peaceful. How *could* England be at war. Fleur brushed her hand across her eyes as painful memories crept into her mind, and she knew that the fatigue of a heavy night was beginning to overtake her. From a long way off, she heard Hugh's voice.

'Are you on duty to-night?'

'No, thank goodness,' Fleur replied, jerking herself back to consciousness. 'I'm free till midnight to-morrow.'

'So am I,' he smiled. 'I was thinking of going to a theatre. It would be wonderful if you could come with me.'

Fleur looked at him in surprise. 'Haven't you any friends you want to see in London?'

Hugh shook his head.

'But what about your family?' she probed.

'My home's in North Yorkshire. Rather a long way to go for two days.'

Fleur nodded thoughtfully. 'In that case I'd love to come.'

'Anything special you'd like to see?'

'Theatre tickets are like gold dust nowadays,' Fleur laughed. 'You'll have to take what you can get. But please, please nothing dramatic, daily life is dramatic enough.' She raised her hand to stifle a yawn and got to her feet. 'I must get some sleep, I'm dropping.'

'Pick you up at half past six,' Hugh confirmed, when the No. 11 bus trundled along the Strand and rumbled to a standstill.

'What are you going to do now?' Fleur enquired, dodging a large hole in the road and jumped on.

'Same as you,' he grinned. I've been up all night too!' And with a cheery wave he was gone.

Fleur thoughtfully climbed the stairs and sat down beside an elderly woman with a large basket balanced on her knees. Hugh's parting shot had puzzled her. 'He said he'd been up all night too,' she mused. 'But he wasn't part of the bombing mission over Germany, so what *was* he doing?' She yawned. 'It's none of my business,' she concluded. 'He's only a passing acquaintance, I'll probably never see him again after this evening.' But oddly enough that thought gave her a pang.

Hugh was smiling broadly when Fleur opened the door to him that evening.

'You'll never guess what I've got tickets for,' he teased, walking into the hall and throwing his cap onto a chair.

'Jack and the Beanstalk?

He shook his head, his eyes dancing with mirth.

'Puss in Boots?'

'Not quite. A Ralph Lynn-Robertson-Hare farce.'

Fleur gasped in amazement. 'How on earth did you do it? It's one of the most popular shows in town. People are *fighting* for tickets.'

'I fought,' he replied, following Fleur into the sitting room. 'What a *charming* room,' he murmured, looking round.

'The flat belongs to Claudine, my godmother who has remarkably good taste,' Fleur explained. 'She's living in the country for the duration and has lent it to me.' She held up a decanter. 'A glass of sherry?

'A quick one. We're booked for the early performance.' He hesitated. 'I took the liberty of reserving a table at the Hungaria for after the show. I hope you don't mind'.

Fleur looked at him quizzically. 'For a North country boy all alone in London you seem to know your way around extremely well.'

Hugh grinned and raised his glass.

They laughed themselves silly.

'*What* a tonic,' Fleur spluttered as they left the theatre, laughter still bubbling up inside her. 'I didn't realise how grim life has been these last months, and how rarely I've actually *laughed*'. She took a small gold powder compact from her handbag and peered in the mirror. 'But it does play havoc with one's make-up.'

'You look wonderful,' Hugh whispered. Taking her arm, he hailed a taxi.

The Hungaria was crowded, but Hugh's wings got them a floorside table. It was when they sat down that Fleur noticed his Distinguished Flying Cross ribbon. She raised her eyebrows enquiringly.

'They were giving them away,' he shrugged. 'I just happened to be passing.'

A young man stepped from the band and clutching the microphone cradled it to his lips.

Shall we dance?' Hugh smiled.

They rose simultaneously and wriggled their way through the couples on the crowded floor. Hugh folded her in his arms, her head nestling itself naturally against his shoulder. 'You'd be so nice to come home to,' crooned the singer, his voice wobbling between a sigh and a moan.

'He's *so* right,' Hugh whispered, his lips brushing lightly across her hair.

Fleur felt a blush creep across her cheeks. She pressed her face into his jacket, afraid that her feelings would betray her. She had felt a strange sensation zig-zag through her body when he took her in his arms: it had been intoxicating and terrifying at the same time and Fleur knew she was teetering on the edge of a precipice. It would be so easy to fall in love with this handsome stranger. She could not deny the erotic emotions he aroused in her: emotions to which she longed to surrender. Yet she was afraid. The war had brought her nothing but pain. All she wanted was to remain safely cocooned in the web she had spun around herself: she couldn't face being hurt again. She stiffened and drew away.

Hugh looked down at her, puzzled by her abrupt change of mood.

The crooner broke into "The nearness of you" as they returned to their table, and an awkward silence fell between them.

Hugh put down his knife and fork. 'Fleur have I done or said something to upset you?'

Fleur shook her head, not trusting herself to speak. 'I'm sorry,' she blurted out at last. 'It's this blasted war.'

He nodded sympathetically. Reaching across the table, he took her hand. 'Tell me about yourself, 'he coaxed. 'All I know is that you're a mongrel working for the BBC.'

Fleur laughed.

Hugh noticed that her eyes were an unusual colour, tawny with flecks of green dancing in them. They were almond shaped and turned up at the corner like a gull's wing. His gaze travelled down to her lips which were soft and shining and he caught his breath. He had been bewitched by her beauty that morning at breakfast, but now in the half-light wearing a simple emerald green dress which emphasized the unusual flecks in her eyes, she was breathtaking. He smiled encouragingly.

Fleur shrugged. 'There's very little to know.'

'But I know *nothing*' he pleaded.

'I could say the same about you.'

'You could. But you're much more interesting.' His blue eyes twinkled. 'I'm not a beautiful mongrel, only a boring old Brit.'

But Fleur seemed disinclined to talk.

Hugh glanced at his watch. 'Almost midnight. Fritz seems to be giving himself a night off.'

Fleur looked up at him slyly. 'I imagine that's what the Germans say about you when you fail to appear over Berlin with your bombs.'

Hugh gave her a strange look. 'I don't fly bombers,' he said curtly, and rose to his feet.

Fleur resisted the temptation to ask him what he did fly, realising that as far as Hugh was concerned the subject was closed. He smiled and held out his hand. 'I'm going to take you home, you look all in.'

When they entered the vestibule the night porter stumbled sleepily out of his cubby-hole and crossed the hall to summon the lift.

'Thank you Sydney,' Fleur smiled when the lift ground to a halt. 'Hope you manage to get some sleep.'

'Hope we all do,' Sydney replied gloomily. '*If* those blasted Jerries will give 'emselves a night off.' He gave an approving look at Hugh as the lift door closed on him and Fleur. When it stopped at the third floor Hugh held out his hand for her keys.

'It's very late so I won't ask you in for a nightcap,' Fleur blurted out, her heart beginning to pound erratically when he unlocked the door of the flat.

Hugh hesitated on the doorstep. 'If you have nothing better to do to-morrow I'd love to take you to Kew or Richmond. I'm sure we could find a country pub serving lunch.'

Fleur bit her lip. It would be so easy to crawl back into her shell and stamp out those disturbing emotions now racing through her body. All her senses seemed to join forces and scream no. She looked up and saw the eager expression on his face. How *could* she refuse his invitation. He was a pilot. He might be dead before the week was out. 'Thank you,'she heard herself saying. 'I'd love to.'

A broad smile flashed across Hugh's face. 'Splendid,' he enthused. 'I'll call for you at eleven.' Planting a kiss on her cheek, he ran swiftly down the stairs.

Fleur entered the flat and closed the door. Leaning wearily against it, she asked herself what she had done. But after the heavy night's work at the BBC and the short rest she had had during the day, fatigue suddenly claimed her, and throwing off her clothes she fell exhausted into bed. She was just drifting off to sleep, in that state of limbo before oblivion finally captured her when the air raid siren burst into its high-pitched lament: footsteps pounded past her door on their way to the shelter, and even in her semi-conscious state she knew she should get up and follow them. She half rose, but sleep overcame her and she fell back among the pillows. Pulling the blankets over her head, she snuggled beneath them and, in spite of the hum of approaching aircraft, the bursts of ack-ack fire from the guns in Hyde Park and the distant thud of bombs raining down on the city of London, she slept.

Fleur was relaxed and happy, refreshed after a good night's rest when she opened the door to Hugh the next morning. The fears which had gripped her the night before replaced by a feeling of joy and well-being.

'You look a million dollars,' he murmured. 'I ought to take you to the Ritz not to a country pub.'

Fleur's eyes sparkled. 'I adore country pubs.'

'Have you ever been to Knole?' he enquired as they walked to the lift. 'I thought it might be an interesting place to visit.' He glanced at his watch. 'There's a train from Charing Cross for Sevenoaks at half past eleven, I checked on my way here and bought the tickets to save time.'

'Last night you mentioned Kew or Richmond,' she said provocatively.

'I did. And if you'd rather go there we'll go.'

'But you've bought the tickets,' Fleur protested.

'I'll buy some more.'

A taxi drew up at the entrance to the flats and a young woman carrying a sleeping toddler in her arms alighted. Hugh signalled to the driver. 'Well, where's it to be?' he teased, holding the door open for Fleur.

'Charing Cross,' she said contritely.

When they arrived at Sevenoaks and walked up the hill to the town the pale early morning sun was now high in the sky, filtering through the banks of clouds.

'The pub where I thought we'd lunch is at the other end of the town, after the church,' Hugh explained.

The White Hart was crowded when they entered, but once again Hugh's wings got them a favoured seat in a secluded alcove. A haze of tobacco smoke drifting in the air mingled with the smell of beer and smouldering pipes. Fleur sniffed nostalgically. The last time she had been in a country pub was with her father.

She gasped when after lunch they entered the park and she caught sight of Knole. 'It's *magnificent,*' she enthused. 'But it will take ages to visit it properly.'

'Probably a day,' Hugh answered.

Fleur frowned thoughtfully. 'It seems a shame to waste a beautiful autumn afternoon inside, let's walk in the deer park and come back when we *have* a whole day.' She stopped abruptly. And they both knew why. Hugh was a pilot: would he *have* another whole day?

He took her arm and winked. 'We'll come back when it rains.'

They walked in silence. But it was a comfortable silence, broken only by delighted cries from Fleur when she saw a doe peeping shyly out at them from behind a clump of fern, or a stag leaping gracefully through the trees.

'Do you realise we've been walking for almost two hours,' Hugh exclaimed, glancing at his watch. 'What do you say to tea? There's a little teashop at the entrance to the town, just after the Saddlers. I noticed it when we came in.'

Fleur stretched her arms in the air luxuriously. 'It's so beautiful here,' she exulted. 'I could go on walking for ever.'

'No regrets for Kew?' he teased, taking her hand and swinging it between them as two horsemen cantered past and raised their caps in salute.

'Do you ride?' Hugh enquired.

'I used to ride a lot when we lived in Hungary.'

He looked down at her. 'When was that?'

'When I was nine. My father was at the Embassy in Budapest, then he was posted to Berlin. We only arrived in London in the spring of '38.'

'You must be quite a linguist.'

'No, just lucky, with a natural gift for languages. I was born in Moscow, but we left when I was four so I've forgotten almost all my Russian: but my German's fluent.'

The bell jangled as Hugh pushed opened the door to the tea-shop. 'You're a revelation,' he said softly. 'How many more hidden layers are there to discover in you?

'If we leave now we can catch the six five train back to London,' Hugh announced, peering at the grandfather clock ticking in the corner.

By sheer chance, they found an empty compartment. Hugh closed the door and sat down beside her. 'Fleur,' he said earnestly, as the train rattled through the Kent countryside. 'I've never met anyone like you and..... you fascinate me.' He fondled her hand. 'You told me a little about yourself as we left the park: I'd so much like to know more.' He paused, seeming embarrassed, as if not knowing how to continue. 'You and Julien,' he ventured hesitantly. 'You seem very close.'

'Julien and I are great friends. We did have a mild flirtation when he first arrived at the BBC, but it wasn't serious. He had left his mother and two younger sisters in Paris and had an horrendous time crossing the Pyrenees on foot in the snow before finally reaching London. I had just lost my mother. It was our mutual misery which threw us together.'

'And now?' Hugh probed.

Fleur's face broke into a smile. 'Julien married a very beautiful secretary in the BBC's Polish section last November. They're expecting a baby in the New Year.'

Hugh leant back in his seat, her hand still in his. 'I'm so sorry about your mother,' he said gently. 'I understand a little of what you went through because I lost my mother from cancer just after I came down from Oxford. She was there to see me graduate, though I don't know how she made it.' He paused and looked through the dirty taped-up window. 'She died a month later.'

'When was that?' Fleur said softly, her eyes clouding as her memories surged.

'June '37.' He paused. 'And your mother?'

The tears overflowed from Fleur's brimming eyes, roaming in little rivulets down her cheeks. Hugh took a handkerchief from his pocket and gently wiped them away.

'My mother was killed during a daylight raid over London. And... you may as well know the rest. My father went to Paris in June '40 when his father refused to leave. My Grandfather was convinced France would never surrender. Unfortunately by the time my father arrived the exodus had begun, the roads to Calais were blocked with refugees so he drove south and managed to get my grandfather and my aunt on to the last boat to leave Bayonne. It was overcrowded: my father gave up his place to a woman with two young children, and that's the last we heard of him. I imagine he joined a resistance group and is hiding out somewhere in the mountains.' Fleur paused and took a deep breath in an attempt to control her emotions. 'My mother was killed five months later.'

'You poor darling' Hugh whispered, folding her in his arms.

The train ground to a halt and an elderly couple pulled back the door and entered the compartment. They looked sympathetically at the two young people locked in each other's arms, the girl's face streaked with tears. The whistle blew and the train shunted off again.

'And you?' Fleur whispered.

Hugh kissed her wet cheeks then gently stroked her hair 'Very little to tell. Born and raised in a Yorkshire village can hardly compete with your exotic background.'

Fleur looked fixedly out of the window. 'Hugh,' she stammered at last. 'Are you married?'

'Not yet. And you?'

She shook her head.

'Not even engaged?

'No.'

'The men you meet must be blind,' he said drily.

The train pulled up at a busy station and three people joined them.

'Clapham Junction,' Hugh remarked, peering through the chinks in the taped-up window. 'Charing Cross next stop.'

A packed suburban train lit only by a dim blue light was drawing away from the opposite platform as they arrived. The autumn evening had faded and a chill wind arisen, chasing the papers strewn all over the station as they headed for the taxi queue, already snaking round the corner into Villiers Street. A convoy of weary women and children armed with blankets and carrier bags of food together with elderly couples and office workers was making its way down the street to spend the night on the platforms of Charing Cross Tube Station in an attempt to escape from Hitler's bombs. Two elderly buskers, strumming ukuleles and singing popular songs accompanied them as he and Fleur joined the straggling taxi queue. 'You said you were free till midnight,' Hugh remarked.

'That's when the first edition of the morning papers is delivered,' she explained, turning up her coat collar against the chill. 'They still arrive even though Fleet Street was almost bombed out of existence a couple of nights ago.'

'*Then* what do you do?'

'Prepare the dawn press review: that takes till about five. The news team and the night editor arrive around half past three when we all rush down to the canteen for an early breakfast. We need it by then.'

'Sounds worse than being a pilot,' Hugh remarked. He paused. 'If you're not too tired would you come back with me to the Waldorf for dinner, then all you have to do is pop across the road.'

'I've got a better idea,' Fleur announced, as they shuffled their way forwards. 'Why don't you have supper with me at the flat?'

'I couldn't steal your meagre rations,' Hugh protested.

'Don't worry about *that*,' Fleur laughed. 'I have so many meals in the canteen rations are hardly a problem. And anyway, my godmother brings me eggs and other farm produce whenever she comes to town.' They had reached the head of the queue. 'Kings Court South,' Fleur told the driver when their taxi drew up beside them. 'It's just behind Chelsea Town Hall. There,' she announced triumphantly when Hugh sat down beside her. 'All settled.'

It was dark when they entered the flat. Fleur threw her gas mask onto a chair in the hall and, peeling off her jacket hastened to draw the blackout curtains before switching on the lights. 'Make yourself at home,' she called over her shoulder, heading towards the kitchen. 'I'm going to forage around the cupboards to see what I can find. Pour yourself a glass of sherry.'

Hugh poured two glasses of sherry and carried them both to the kitchen. Fleur was enveloped in a flowered apron furiously beating eggs. Setting one glass on the table beside her, he leant against the doorpost watching her. 'It's true what the crooner said last night,' he remarked. 'You'd be *so* nice to come home to.'

Fleur hurriedly took a sip from her glass. Then in an attempt to hide her embarrassment, picked up a peeler and attacked a carrot.

'Here, let me do that,' Hugh said, taking the peeler from her hands.

'I prefer to have supper on our knees in here,' Fleur explained, preceding Hugh as he pushed a laden trolley into the sitting room. 'The dining room is cold and formal.' She sat down on the sofa and placed the frothing omelette on the low table in front of them. For a while there was silence except for the clicking of cutlery against their plates.

Hugh wiped his mouth and throwing down his napkin leant against the cushions, resting his arm along the back of the sofa. 'Isn't this cosy?' he smiled, 'just like an old married couple.'

Fleur's blush began to creep up from her neck. She bent her head willing it to disappear, but Hugh had noticed. He drew her into the cushions till her head rested on his arm. 'You've no idea how enchanting you are, especially when you blush.' He bent down and lightly kissed her cheek. 'It's strange,' he mused as if he were talking to himself. 'I only met you yesterday yet I feel as if I've known you all my life.'

'I feel that way too,' Fleur whispered, leaning back against his arm.

His arms closed around her. He slowly bent his head towards her and she quivered with excitement as his lips brushed hers. Holding her with a grip which caught her breath, he kissed her eyes, her neck, her cheeks until finally his lips found hers again. 'Fleur,' he groaned, 'oh..... Fleur.'

She clung to him, her hand caressing the back of his head as his kisses increased in intensity. Her body trembled, suddenly alive with passion. She pressed his mouth harder against her own and felt his body stiffen with suppressed excitement as he drew her even closer. Then picking her up in his arms, he walked towards the door. The shrill ring of the telephone split the air as they reached the bedroom. They looked at each other helplessly, each willing it to stop. But the ringing continued.

'You'd better answer it,' Hugh said tightly. 'It's obviously going to go on until you do.'

Fleur looked up at him, her eyes pleading, but he avoided her gaze and lowered her onto the bed. She grabbed the receiver and the piercing ring ceased. 'Hallo,' she said tersely, not bothering to announce the number. 'Oh..... Hélène, yes, what is it?'

A rapid exchange in French followed. Through the open bedroom door she could see Hugh standing in front of the oval mirror hanging above the fireplace, smoothing his hair and straightening his tie. She replaced the receiver and waited, but he didn't return. Climbing slowly off the bed, she went to join him on the sofa, but the moment had passed: the magic had evaporated.

'Nothing serious, I hope,' he queried, turning to smile at her.

'Just a colleague wanting to change shifts.'

Hugh's eyebrows rose in surprise. 'Strange time to ring. Couldn't it have waited?'

'Not really. She's been off for two days and was supposed to come back to-morrow night, but she's just received a telegram from her husband - he's in submarines - saying he's got four days leave and is arriving at midnight. She's asked me to take over.'

'And will you?'

'Of course, she'd do the same for me. It just makes a rather a long week that's all. I shan't be free now till Sunday morning. 'They lapsed into silence, both lost in their own thoughts. 'Will you be flying to-morrow night?' Fleur ventured at last.

Hugh switched off the shaded lamp on the table beside him and, striding across to the window pulled aside the blackout curtain and stood looking out. The night was dark, the roofs on the houses opposite a wet tapestry of oblong tiles. Neither of them had noticed the rain. A three quarter moon like a broken yellow soup plate sailed by. Hugh dropped the curtain back in place and switched on the light. 'Very probably.'

Fleur frowned. 'Why did you do that?'

'I wanted to look at the moon.'

'But why? What's the moon got to do with it?'

'Everything.'

Fleur got up, irritated by his enigmatic answers.

He walked across and playfully tweaked her nose. 'Careless talk costs lives,' he teased. 'Don't you read the posters?'

Fleur shrugged in exasperation.

The little gold clock on the mantelpiece tinkled and gave eleven rapid chimes.

'Isn't it time you were thinking of moving,' Hugh enquired, piling the empty plates onto the trolley.

'I don't have to leave for half an hour,' she whispered, her eyes pleading, longing to be in his arms again.

He looked at her. Her eyes were large and luminous, almost filling her face, her lips parted in expectation, her body now close to his, soft and yielding. His heart began to beat like a tam-tam thudding against his chest, his breath thundered in his ears as he felt her trembling with passion at his side. His eyes travelled down her slender body: she was exquisite: but she was also an enigma. Behind that outward veneer of sophistication there was an innocence about her, an almost virginal purity. Suddenly Hugh realised that that beautiful body had never been penetrated: had never known a man.

'I'll make you some coffee,' he said tightly, abruptly turning away and steering the trolley towards the kitchen, not daring to give way to the feelings now catapulting crazily through him. 'You've got a long night ahead of you.'

Fleur walked slowly to the bathroom, biting back the tears. Angrily tearing off her blouse, she turned on the taps full force and viciously scrubbed a flannel around her face before changing into a comfortable skirt and warm sweater.

'Coffee's ready,' Hugh called. 'Then we'd better be off.'

The dark road was gleaming like a shiny black macintosh when they left the flats and headed into the drizzle. A taxi cruised by in the King's Road. Hugh put two fingers into his mouth and whistled. The driver slithered to a stop then turned and drove to meet them. Neither spoke on their drive to Bush House. Hugh helped her down then walked up the steps and pushed open the door into the deserted hallway.

'Shall I see you again?' Fleur asked hesitantly, when he pressed the lift button.

He looked at her and the expression in his eyes reminded her of her mother's spaniel, warm and loving, yet bewildered. 'Fleur,' he said softly, 'of *course* you'll see me again, as soon as I can possibly make it.' He looked at her quizzically. 'Unless you'd rather not.' The lift came to a standstill and the doors opened, but neither of them noticed. 'Well?' he faltered. Her eyes met his. She nodded her head and smiled. He bent and kissed her gently on the lips. The lift doors closed and with a whirr it rose again. As they clung together the air raid siren split the air.

'What happens now?' Hugh asked, pulling himself away. 'Do you go to the shelter?'

'No,' Fleur replied tightly, 'we carry on. If people risk their lives to listen to us the least we can do is the same.' She looked up at him. 'And you?'

'I've dodged enemy planes up till now: I'll go to bed.' He put a finger under her chin forcing her to look at him. 'Pilots have charmed lives, didn't you know?' The lift descended. The doors opened and several people got out and rushed down the stairs to the basement. 'I'll call you very soon,' he promised.

'When?' Fleur asked anxiously. 'You've got both my numbers, here and at the flat?'

He nodded. 'I'll probably call to-morrow,' he assured her, pushing her into the lift as the doors began to close once again. 'Certainly before the end of the week.'

But Hugh did not call.

Fleur slept with the telephone beside her on the pillow, afraid she would not hear its piercing shrill. But no call came. By Friday evening she was beginning to despair. She had no idea where he was stationed, no idea how to get hold of him and with a shock she realised that she knew very little about him. When she dragged herself to Bush House on Saturday for her last night shift, she had come to the conclusion that he had never intended to contact her. He was just another glamorous playboy, taking advantage of his pilot's wings to seduce as many women as possible. And her spirits sank to zero.

'My idea that the airman would do Fleur a world of good doesn't seem to have worked,' Edward remarked to Julien on their way back from early breakfast on the Sunday morning.

'She's probably overtired,' Julien replied. 'She's had one hell of a week taking on Hélène's night shift on top of her own. Kristina had tea with her on Thursday and said she'd never seen her in such splendid form, she was positively sparkling.' He frowned. 'Though she did say Fleur seemed edgy every time the telephone rang,' he went on thoughtfully. 'Perhaps the blighter promised to call and didn't.'

'Could be,' Edward said philosophically. 'How is Kristina by the way?'

'Blooming,' Julien grinned. 'Only a couple of months to go now.'

The night dragged on.

'Aren't you coming with us to the canteen for breakfast?' Julien asked in surprise when Fleur handed in her bulletin and reached for her coat.

'No,' she replied shortly. 'I'm going home to bed.'

'Come on Fleur,' he coaxed, taking her coat from her and hanging it back on the peg. 'You've got the next four days to sleep. I don't know what's biting you, but it won't go away by burying your head in the sand.' He took her arm and led her to the lift. But the smell of sizzling bacon didn't seem to lift Fleur's spirits. She moodily broke a piece of dry toast into small pieces and pushed it round her plate. Edward and Julien looked at each other and shrugged helplessly.

The tannoy clicked into action. 'PBX calling Miss de Rosny. PBX calling Miss de Rosny.'

Fleur looked up without any great show of interest, then ambled over and picked up the receiver.

'There's someone to see you at Reception, Miss de Rosny,' the telephonist's voice came down the line.

'Wonder what's happened?' Julien frowned, when without a word Fleur walked out of the canteen and up the stairs. 'Hope it's not more bad news: that's the way she heard about her mother's death.' The comparison had not escaped Fleur. Dragging herself wearily up the stairs, she relived that winter evening three years before. She had been laughing and joking over supper in the canteen with Edward and Julien and other members of the team when she had heard that same announcement. Running up the stairs to meet her unknown visitor, she had come face to face with a policeman. 'Miss de Rosny?' he had enquired.

Puzzled, Fleur had nodded.

The policeman cleared his throat. 'I'm afraid there's been an accident.'

'An accident?' she frowned. 'I know there was an air raid this afternoon, but it can't be my mother. She *always* goes immediately to the nearest air raid shelter.'

'I'm afraid it is......'

'But.....' Fleur interrupted.

'The shelter near Marble Arch received a direct hit. Your mother's body was one of the first to be brought out.'

Fleur had leant against the Reception Desk for support, unable to believe it. She had said goodbye to her mother at two o'clock before leaving to come on duty; she couldn't be dead. But she was. The Receptionist had rushed round the counter and caught her as she fainted. The pain of loss had never disappeared: until she met Hugh. When he had kissed her she had suddenly felt alive again, liberated from the pain which had imprisoned her. Now with the memory of that winter evening, coupled with Hugh's apparent desertion, the pain came back in full force. She was on her way to that same Reception desk to hear.... what? Rounding the corner of the stairs, she wearily began to climb the last few steps.

Hugh was standing at the top. Fleur blinked. She closed her eyes and blinked again: he was still there. Fatigue must be making her hallucinate.

'Fleur,' he called. He leapt down the few stairs which separated them as Fleur stood rooted to the spot. 'Fleur,' he breathed, his voice hoarse with emotion. He grasped her hands in his. 'Fleur darling........ will you marry me?'

Fleur's tawny eyes widened, dark with shock. She opened her mouth to speak, but no words came.

'Will you?' he pleaded. 'Oh *please* say you will.'

'But..... I'm having breakfast,' she stammered.

Hugh relaxed and smiled. 'Then afterwards?'

Suddenly they both realised the ridiculousness of their conversation and burst into peals of laughter: wave after wave engulfing them.

'Does that mean yes?' Hugh gasped, when the hysteria subsided.

Fleur nodded, still unable to speak.

Hugh held out his hand and pulled her up from the top step where they had collapsed. 'Then let's *both* have breakfast,' he grinned.

Holding hands, they literally danced back down the stairs.

'Oh hallo, Hugh,' Edward said, peering at him over the edge of his glasses when they collided in the doorway to the canteen. 'We seem to specialise in breakfast meetings.'

Julien got up from the table where he had been anxiously waiting to hear what news Fleur's unknown visitor had brought. His fears now calmed, he walked over and shook Hugh's hand. 'Nice to see you again, Hugh. Must dash, I promised to take my wife breakfast in bed. See you at the end of the week, Fleur.' He winked at her as he passed. ''Enjoy your days off.'

Walking out of Bush House into the Aldwych, Fleur noticed a shiny red sports car parked in front of the steps. Hugh opened the passenger door and, with a flourish, ushered her in. She looked at him in astonishment when he walked round and jumped over the door into the driver's seat.

He grinned sheepishly. 'My squaddie lent it to me on condition I returned it by this evening.' He turned and looked at her. 'I've been in a state, these last few days,' he confessed, 'ever since I got back on Wednesday morning. I couldn't get you out of my mind. I've never known anyone like you Fleur, and I knew that you were the woman I wanted to marry, but I didn't know whether you felt the same.' He carefully studied his nails. 'Last night I told my squaddie. He said he understood, he'd met his wife during the Battle of Britain and married her a few days later. Then he told me to take his car and get the problem sorted out because I was no adjectival use to him or anyone else as I was.' Hugh smiled shyly. 'Now where?'

'To the flat please.' Fleur answered weakly. They drove in silence through the Sunday early morning calm of London's deserted streets leaving behind the empty craters and jagged outline of bombed out buildings for the relative peace and normality of Sloane Square, almost untouched as yet by Hitler's bombs. When they entered the silent flat, Hugh took her in his arms and kissed her with an intensity which left her gasping. 'I've got five days leave next week,' he whispered into her hair. 'Could we use them for a honeymoon?'

Fleur stepped back from his arms, her eyes wide with astonishment. 'Next *week*,' she stammered.

'I know it sounds crazy,' Hugh pleaded, putting a finger over her lips to stop her protests. 'But the whole world is crazy at the moment. In peacetime, I would never have suggested such a thing. But this isn't peacetime darling, we're in the middle of a bloody war and no-one knows how long it will go on.' He drew her back into his arms. 'I want to know you're mine, and that you'll be there for me to come back to. Is that terribly selfish?'

She nestled against him. 'No, Hugh, it isn't,' she whispered.

'I could be here by mid-afternoon next Thursday week,' Hugh continued eagerly. 'I'll get a special license and we could be married on Friday morning.'

She looked up at him her eyes shining, the green lights dancing. 'Claudine and my grandmother are expecting me at Marchmount for my days off: I said I'd be there in time for lunch.' She slipped from his arms. 'I'll ring and tell them there'll be two of us.'

Hugh wandered into the kitchen and put on the kettle. Through the open bedroom door he could see Fleur talking animatedly. 'Around twelve thirty I imagine. No, we don't need a taxi, I'm bringing a friend who has a car.' She looked across at him and grinned. 'No, *not* a BBC friend. He's an airman. A pilot.... my fiancé.' A torrent of words he couldn't hear catapulted down the line. 'I couldn't tell you before, Claudine, because I didn't know myself.' Fleur took a deep breath. 'We've only been engaged a couple of hours and we're going to be married a week on Friday.' Fleur put her hand over the receiver. 'I expected an outburst,' she reassured him, 'but Claudine'll have recovered by the time we arrive.' She smiled across at Hugh coming out of the kitchen carrying two steaming cups.

'I've made some tea,' he mouthed.

'Yes, *do* invite grandfather and Tante Clothilde,' she went on, removing her hand from the mouthpiece. 'There,' she said, replacing the receiver. 'Now you'll meet what's left of my family.' Planting a kiss on his cheek, she took her cup and danced across the hall into the bathroom. When she walked back into the sitting room, Hugh looked up from his newspaper. She was wearing a plain navy blue coat with a multi coloured scarf at her throat. It was tied as only a Frenchwoman could tie it and once again, he was overwhelmed by her beauty. 'Come here,' he said softly. And drew her into his arms. 'Close your eyes.'

'But....' Fleur began to protest.

'Just *close your eyes.*'

She heard a rustle of paper and then a soft plop as something was placed on the low table by his side. Taking her left hand, she felt him slip a ring onto her third finger. Unable to contain her curiosity any longer she opened her eyes and looked down at her hand still lying in his. Three identical Ceylon sapphires surrounded by an oval of small diamonds winked up at her. 'Hugh,' she gasped, 'it's *beautiful*. But..... where did you get it?'

'It was my mother's. My father chose sapphires to match her eyes, they were blue, like mine. My mind was in such a turmoil when I left you on Tuesday night I couldn't sleep, so at two o'clock I got up and telephoned him.'

'At two o'clock in the *morning,'* Fleur gasped.

'Oh, Dad's a country doctor, he's used to it.' Hugh smiled sheepishly. 'I told him I'd finally met the woman I'd been waiting for and wanted to get married as soon as possible, and asked if I could have Mother's ring. It arrived yesterday afternoon.' He paused. 'She wanted it to be given to the first of her sons to marry.'

'But didn't you tell me you had an older brother?' Fleur demurred. 'Shouldn't he be given first chance?'

'John?' Hugh queried. 'I doubt he'll ever marry. He's a cryptologist, working somewhere secret on something even more secret. He's wedded to his codes.' He picked up his cap. 'Hope you know the way to where we're going, because *I've* never been to Buckinghamshire.'

'Head for Windsor,' Fleur smiled, 'then I'll guide you to Fulmer. Marchmount, my grandmother's place is off the road, just after the church.'

⚜ ⚜ ⚜

'I'm feeling weak at the knees,' Hugh grimaced, when they entered Fulmer village. 'Do you think they'll accept me?'

'*Accept you.* You'll *captivate* them.' She looked up at him. 'Like you did me,' she said softly.

He glanced down at her and planted a swift kiss on her upturned face.

'Claudine, my godmother was astounded when I told her over the 'phone,' Fleur went on. 'But she's pretty resilient, she'll have bounced back and marshalled the troops. By now she's probably written out the guest list and organised the wedding breakfast.' The car turned in at the wide open gates and swept up the drive. At a bend behind an enormous rhododendron bush the old stone house came into view bathed in a late autumn sun which suddenly appeared from behind the clouds.

'You were right about your godmother, 'Hugh smiled, as they rounded the bend in the drive and the waving group on the steps of Marchmount disappeared. 'She'd already got the wedding organised before we arrived, even to raking through trunks in the attic to find your grandmother's wedding dress.'

'Both my mother and my grandmother were married from Marchmount,' Fleur said dreamily. She snuggled up to him. He took his hand off the steering wheel and put his arm round her shoulders, drawing her close. 'I had thought of a quiet wedding in London,' Fleur continued, 'but the old church in Fulmer is so beautiful.' She sighed deeply. 'Oh Hugh, in less than two weeks I shall be walking down that aisle to be with you forever.' His grip tightened on her, but he didn't reply. It was October1943. War raged everywhere. And he was a pilot. 'I *do* like Claudine,' he reflected, changing the subject. 'And what a charming old lady your grandmother is.'

'They're both adorable,' Fleur smiled. 'So are my grandfather and Tante Clothilde. But what's more important is *they* like *you*.'

Hugh smiled mischievously. 'I did my best. The lady with the delightful French accent, your Tante Clothilde .... where does she come in?

'She's my father's twin sister. There was an elder brother Antoine, but I never knew him. He was killed at Ypres.'

Hugh slowed down as they came to a traffic light. He turned and looked intently at Fleur. 'Darling,' he said gently. 'Are you *sure* you wouldn't rather be married in the French church in Soho?'

Fleur looked up at him, her eyes shining. 'No,' she whispered. 'I'm marrying an Englishman and I want to be English from now on.'

'Please don't,' he pleaded, as the lights changed from red to green and they weaved into the traffic. 'It's because you are so different from all the other girls I've met that I fell in love with you.'

'It's so kind of your grandmother to invite my father and John to stay at Marchmount on the night before the wedding,' Hugh said, following Fleur into the lift at King's Court. 'I'll ring him to-night. The local babies will just have to hang on till he gets back.'

'But you've been banished to the "Black Horse",' Fleur giggled as they walked along the corridor to the flat. 'Grandmother wouldn't allow the bridegroom to sleep under the same roof as the bride on the night before the wedding. Isn't it sweet?' She sighed. 'The only people missing will be my parents and your sister.'

'Bit difficult for Elizabeth to race over from Ceylon even if the Wrens would allow her to,' Hugh smiled. He looked down at Fleur as he put the key in the lock. Her face had suddenly clouded over. 'Hey,' he laughed, tipping a finger under her chin and forcing her to look at him. 'What's this? We've just become engaged and we're to be married next week, this is supposed to be a happy occasion.' He stepped into the flat pulling her with him and swiftly closed the door. Wrapping his arms around her, he hungrily showered kisses on her upturned face, finally enclosing her lips in a long, lingering embrace. 'Fleur,' he groaned. 'I love you so much.' She was limp in his arms, sighing softly as he led her to the sofa. 'How I wish I could stay,' he said hoarsely. 'At this moment, I'd give anything to be in civvy street and able to do as I liked, and to hell with the consequences. 'I love you darling *so* much and...... wanting you is almost a physical ache.'

She looked up at him appealingly. 'Can't you stay?' she whispered. The longing in her eyes almost broke his heart. 'Just for a little while?' she pleaded.

'I can't darling,' he groaned. 'I've got to get the blasted car back this evening and also report at the base, otherwise I'll probably be court-martialed for being absent without leave. And then where would we be? I'd be behind bars and you'd be waiting at the church!' He glanced at his watch. 'Oh Lord, it's already half past seven.' Fleur looked up at him, fear in her eyes, as he bent to kiss her. 'Hugh,' she stammered. 'Will you be flying before our wedding.'

'I don't know sweetheart.' She put her hands over her face and burst into tears. 'I couldn't bear it if anything happened to you and we'd never.....' Her body convulsed in sobs. He sat down on the arm of the sofa and held her close. 'Spent the night together,' he said gently. 'Is *that* what you mean?'

She nodded. 'Couldn't you.... couldn't you *please* stay a little longer?' She looked up at him through her tears, and his heart melted.

'Darling, if only could,' he whispered brokenly, 'but I can't. It's more than my life's worth. I dread to think what might happen if I did: I've already overstepped my time.'

Fleur's shoulders shook with silent sobs and she clung to him desperately. 'Hugh, I won't have a moment's peace. Every time a flash comes through saying one of our aircraft failed to return I'll go to pieces, wondering if it's you.'

Pulling himself together, he eased her firmly back into the cushions. 'Now listen to me Fleur,' he said sternly. 'I don't fly bombers. It will *not* be me.'

'What *do* you fly?' she persisted.

But he didn't answer. 'I promise you that if I don't return you will be informed before the flash arrives. So stop worrying.'

'How?' she asked truculently.

'My old school friend Peter Drummond, you'll meet him at the wedding, will let you know. He's ground staff in charge of ops.' He glanced at his watch. 'Heavens, it's eight o'clock: darling, I *have* to go or I'll never get back in time.' But she clung to him. 'What if....' she protested.

'What if, what if,' he interrupted, a slight edge to his voice. He suddenly smiled. 'What if the war ended next week, wouldn't that be wonderful?' He gently released her arms from around his neck.

'No, don't come down with me. I'll see you in eleven days' time at Marchmount for the pre-wedding dinner.' Grabbing his cap from the chair where he had thrown it, he ran swiftly to the door. She heard his steps racing along the corridor and taking the stairs two at a time. Running to the window she caught a last glimpse of him as he jumped the door of the car, and with sound like a thunderbolt hurtled towards the King's Road.

—ooo-O-ooo—

Chapter Two

Fleur slowly turned the knob and peered round the door. Claudine didn't stir. In her early fifties and asleep, she still looked elegant. Fleur hesitated, but the soft click had roused her godmother. Claudine opened her eyes and smiled. 'Come in darling.' She patted the bed. Fleur crept in and perched on the end, cushioning her back against the old fashioned footboard 'You're awake early.'

'I couldn't sleep,' Fleur grimaced. 'I'm too excited.' She looked across at her godmother. 'Were *you* excited on your wedding day?'

Claudine pushed herself up against the mound of pillows. 'Oh, it's so long ago. But yes, I think I was. I was only nineteen and all London was there.' She smiled dreamily. 'It was at the Guards chapel. George looked so handsome in his blues, booted and spurred with his sword clanking at his side.' She pensively smoothed the sheet. 'Your mother was one of the cloud of bridesmaids. Even at ten she showed signs of the beautiful woman she was to become.' Claudine looked fondly across at her goddaughter. 'You're very like her darling.'

'My father always called her his English rose,' Fleur mused. A lump rose in her throat as the memories surged. 'Now he's missing somewhere in France and she's *dead*,' she blurted out bitterly, a sudden burst of anger sweeping through her. 'It's so unfair. She was only forty four.'

'Life can be unfair Fleur,' Claudine replied. 'I felt like you're feeling when George was drowned. I couldn't believe it when they brought me the news. George was an experienced yachtsman and to perish in a stupid accident which should never have happened.' Claudine sighed. 'We'd had fifteen very happy years together and suddenly... there was nothing. But one adjusts darling. The memories eventually stop being like a knife turning in a wound and become sweet. It will happen to you, especially now that you have Hugh.' She leant across and squeezed Fleur's hand. 'To-day is your wedding day Fleur. Let's enjoy *it.*'

There was a tap at the door and Ivy entered with a tray of tea. She looked the picture of gloom.

'Whatever's the matter?' Claudine enquired, reaching for her bed jacket, when Ivy crossed the room to draw the curtains.

Ivy turned round, one hand on the tasselled cord. 'It's *raining,* Madam,' she wailed, as if announcing the end of the world. With a melodramatic gesture she tugged at the cord swishing back the curtains and a leaden sky, hung with sullen clouds sprang into view. A white layer of mist lying over the garden pressed against the wet window panes.

'Oh is *that* all,' Claudine remarked, pouring her tea.

Ivy stood rooted to the spot, her mouth wide open like a question mark. 'But madam,' she mooed, 'it's Miss Fleur's *wedding day.'*

'Ivy,' Claudine cut in briskly. 'To-morrow is the 1st of November, we can hardly expect a heat wave.'

Fleur slipped off her godmother's bed and ran along the corridor to her own room. When she drew the heavy blackout curtains the rain slashed angrily against the window panes. But she didn't care. Her grandmother's wedding dress, hanging on the door, gleamed in the grey dawn. In a few hours she would be wearing it, walking down the aisle to become Hugh's wife.

The grandfather clock in the hall whirred then gave three mellow chimes. Starry-eyed, Fleur walked carefully down the stairs, a posy of white rosebuds clutched in her hands.

She saw the little group gathered at the bottom to greet her. Her grandmother, leaning heavily on her stick. Claudine who had become a mother to her since her own mother's death. Clothilde, elegant as ever, a swathe of feathers wreathing her head. Her family. Only her parents were missing. With a bow her grandfather, magnificent in his French cavalry general's ceremonial uniform, offered her his arm.

The village had turned out in force and the old stone church was full.

When Fleur entered, radiant on the her grandfather's arm, it seemed to her that the entire BBC French Section together with a mass of airforce blue was standing smiling at her. The old general, who had abandoned his silver topped cane for his sword hanging stiffly at his side, marched upright and firm-footed looking neither to right nor left till they reached the altar where Hugh was waiting for her.

Fleur realised later that she remembered very little about her wedding. She was so overcome with emotion she had been unable to join in the hymns. Her vows were uttered in such a low whisper that the vicar had to bend his head to hear them. But Hugh's responses rang out loud and clear. Once or twice Hugh had glanced anxiously down at her but she gave him a reassuring smile. Then, as if he were speaking just to the two of them, in his address the vicar said that even the terrible carnage of man fighting man could not separate us from the love of God.

When she left the church on her husband's arm, the drizzle which had greeted her arrival had turned into a downpour. But she hardly noticed. Hugh had put his mother's wedding ring on her finger, making her his wife. She had gladly, if inaudibly, promised to love, honour and obey him until death should part them. And he had promised to love and cherish her. Nothing else mattered. As they stood in the porch, guests and family crowding round, smiling, congratulating, embracing, Fleur suddenly felt overwhelmed with joy. Then with the rain lashing down in great sweeping brooms,

Hugh caught her round the waist, and heading into it, ran swiftly to the waiting car.

Leaning forward to wave when they splashed away from the church, for a brief moment as the waving crowd in the porch disappeared from view her heart lurched and missed a beat. The happiness which had engulfed her only minutes before was abruptly replaced by a terrible anguish. She saw the reality, the poignancy of their brief time together. Soon they would be torn apart, perhaps never to meet again. Hugh would return to his base, soar into the sky, be lost behind hostile clouds.

Sensing her change of mood, Hugh looked anxiously down at her. He took her in his arms and in that moment the future vanished and only to-day remained. Nothing mattered beyond the fact that they were married. They were together and Hugh had been given five days leave during which no-one could separate them. No-one could tear them apart. When there would be no good-byes. Five days and nights of perfect happiness. Of unclouded rapture made all the more precious because it was snatched out of the ugly mire of blood and fear and slaughter which ravaged England.

Fleur looked down at the shiny gold band on her finger and knew that those beautiful unforgettable moments in the church, heavy with emotion and meaning had been engraved on her heart whatever the future might hold.

'Do you intend to spend the night sitting at that dressing table?' Hugh enquired. Fleur looked up and caught his reflection in the old-fashioned mirror. He was lying on the turned down bed, his hands locked behind his head, an amused smile on his face.

'Well?' he queried.

A blush crept up her neck suffusing her face with a pink glow. She bit her lip in annoyance. 'I feel shy,' she whispered, avoiding his eyes.

Hugh swung his feet over the side of the bed. Walking towards her, he put his arms round her neck. 'With me?' he said softly. He leant his cheek against hers and looked at their reflection in the mirror. She reached up and lovingly touched his face. He slid his fingers beneath her hair and undid the clasp of the double strand of pearls which Claudine had taken from around her own neck the evening before and fastened around Fleur's. They snaked downwards and coiled sensuously into her hands. Lifting her gently to her feet, he drew her to him. His hands caressed the back of her neck then slipped down to her shoulders and released the flimsy negligée. It slithered down her body and lay in a pool of satin and lace at her feet. Suddenly, Fleur was no longer embarrassed. No longer shy. His touch had sparked that same thrill and it shuddered voluptuously through her. She felt as if she had known Hugh all her life and was already part of him.

Hugh's eyes wandered down her body lingering on her firm breasts, the nipples already peeked by desire. He realised again that her exquisite body had never before known the passion which was now inflaming her. 'You're so beautiful, 'he said hoarsely. 'and you're wholly mine.' Picking her up in his arms he laid her on the bed and climbed in beside her. Her heart began to beat erratically, her breath escaping in short gasps when his hands caressed her body. She closed her eyes, winding her arms tightly round him as Hugh slowly aroused her, awakening sensations which she had never known, never even dreamed of, prolonging the ecstasy until she arched towards him, his muscular body closed over hers and she felt herself floating away on a sea of sparkling delight. And a new love blossomed between them.

Dawn was breaking when Fleur, warm and replete in the afterglow of love slipped out of bed. Drawing aside the heavy blackout curtain, she sat on the window seat gazing dreamily across the garden of the small country hotel where Hugh had brought her the evening before. She looked across at her husband, sleeping peacefully one arm stretched out towards her empty place, and a surge of happiness rippled through her. Hugh had led her into an enchanted garden, a place of beauty where there was only the two of them. She shivered with excitement remembering his embrace, knowing they still had four nights and days of love. Shutting her mind to the future, she refused to think beyond Wednesday when the gates of their paradise would clang behind them and they would be outside in the war torn world again. For now she was content to know that he was there. That she could touch him, watch him as he slept. And hear his voice when he awoke.

Drifting in and out of sleep, Fleur stirred. In the distance she heard the low rumble of traffic in the King's Road and was momentarily confused. Where was the melodic gurgle and splash of the fountain below their window? Stretching out her hand to her husband, she felt a warm empty space where Hugh should have been lying. Then she remembered. She was back in the flat. And it was Wednesday morning!

Fumbling for the bedside light, she noticed a glimmer coming from under the bathroom door. It opened and Hugh appeared, shrugging himself into his jacket. She thrust aside the bedclothes, but Hugh quickly crossed the room and gently pushed her back against the pillows. 'No darling, stay there.' He sat down on the bed and took both her hands in his.

'But I want to come to the station with you,' she pleaded, now fully awake 'I want to stay with you till the very last minute.'

'I don't want you to come. Railway stations are ghastly places especially in the early morning. Anyway, there's not time.'

'What time is it?'

'Almost five. The taxi should be here any minute.' Hugh took her in his arms.' I'd much rather kiss you goodbye here,' he whispered. 'Remember you as you are now, warm and rosy from sleep.' The telephone rang shrilly. 'That'll be the taxi, 'he said picking up the receiver. 'Thank you Sydney. I'm on my way down.' He drew her back into his arms. She clung to him as he gave her one last lingering kiss.

'When shall I see you again?' Fleur cried desperately when he turned to go.

'I may not have leave before Christmas.'

'*Christmas,*' Fleur shrieked, sitting bolt upright in bed.

He turned in the doorway, adjusting his cap, mouthed "I love you" and was gone.

Fleur heard the taxi start up and head for the Embankment. Flopping back onto the disheveled bed she closed her eyes. But she couldn't sleep. Rolling over she hugged Hugh's pillow, breathing in the distinctive scent of his hair cream which lingered on it like the scent of a beautiful perfume lingers after the person has gone. 'Hugh, oh *Hugh,*' she cried brokenly rocking miserably backwards and forwards, his pillow clutched in her arms. 'Why did you have to leave me? Why did you have to go? I don't want to wait for a won-derful post-war world. I want you here in my arms *now.*' The sudden blare of the air-raid siren's dreary wail followed by the distant drone of approaching aircraft split the air. Doors opened and closed and footsteps hurried down the stairs on their way to the shelter as the drone drew nearer. But Fleur took no notice. With the boom-boom of anti-aircraft fire pounding in her ears, she pulled the bedclothes over her head and hugging her husband's pillow even tighter sobbed herself to sleep.

The "All Clear" woke her. Switching on the bedside light she squinted at the clock. Half past seven. She felt exhausted, but she knew further sleep was impossible. Dragging on her dressing gown, she crossed to the kitchen and lit the gas under the kettle. Pulling up the blackout blind, she looked out at the grey November morn-ing: it matched her mood, and she wondered what to with the rest of the day. She couldn't stay in the flat. Everything reminded her of Hugh, his presence was everywhere, yet without him it was just an empty shell. The kettle came to the boil, whistling loudly and she decided to go to Marchmount.

Claudine was in front of the house dead-heading the last of the roses when Fleur's taxi drove up the drive and stopped at the front door. 'Darling,' she cried, dropping the shears and running to greet her. 'How lovely to see you.' Her godmother hugged her warmly. 'Has Hugh left?'

Fleur nodded. 'We got back last night and I'm not on duty till Friday afternoon.' She smiled sadly. 'I couldn't stay in the flat without him.'

Claudine slipped an arm through hers and squeezed it sympathetically. 'Victoria,' she called, walking into the hall. 'Mrs Cunningham's come to visit us.' Her grandmother appeared at the drawing room door, her face wreathed in smiles. She held out her arms and as Fleur ran into them, the gloom and despair of the early morning lifted and she breathed a long sigh of relief. She was no longer alone. She was home and secure, surrounded by love.

That evening Hugh rang.

'I'm moving to a new base,' he announced. 'Much farther north which means I won't be able to snatch the odd day to come to London. But the good news for you is that I won't be flying, or very little, so you can stop worrying.' He paused. 'Christmas might be a problem though.'

'Oh Hugh.'

'I'm sorry darling,' he consoled. 'But things are hotting up. I don't think it will be long now, then there'll be no more goodbyes.' The pips went and the telephonist's voice came over the line. 'Love you,' Hugh said quickly, as the line faded. 'Love you, love you, love you, love.....' The line went dead. Fleur replaced the receiver and walked slowly back into the drawing room, her husband's voice ringing in her ears.

It was late February before Hugh announced his long awaited leave.

'I've got five days beginning the 1st of March,' he announced. 'Do you think we could meet in Edinburgh, otherwise I'll waste two of them travelling.'

'Where on earth are you?' Fleur gasped.

'In the north of Scotland. I've looked up trains. If you could take the one which arrives at Waverley Station at half past three, I'll be on the platform to meet you.' The line crackled ominously, threatening to go dead. 'This is hopeless,' Hugh sighed. 'See you on the first. Love you dar .....' But the line carried out its threat.

The crowded train slowed down and rumbled into the station. Fleur saw Hugh anxiously scanning the compartments as hers passed by and she struggled to open the window. A soldier came to her aid and she leant out, waving frantically. 'Hugh', she screeched. He turned and ran towards her. As the train drew to a standstill Hugh wrenched open the door and she fell into his arms. 'Darling,' he breathed, holding her tightly. 'Darling, darling Fleur. At last.' He kissed her with a passion which left her breathless. Taking her arm, he picked up her suitcase and made for the exit. 'I've booked us into an old inn outside the town,' he explained, hailing a taxi. 'It's in a cove on a deserted sea-shore, wild and beautiful. Only seagulls for company.' Driving away from the station he looked down at her and took her hand. 'Fleur,' he said softly, his voice almost a caress. 'I can't believe you're really here. It's been so long.'

'Tea is served in the dining room till half past five', announced the buxom woman who led them up the creaking stairs to their low ceilinged room. She patted the bed. 'I hope ye'll be comfortable.' Closing the door she creaked back down the stairs. Fleur wandered to the window and looked out on the scene below. Waves were lapping against the shore, rushing in then rippling back in a froth of foam.

Hugh dropped his greatcoat onto a chair and came to join her. 'Are you hungry?' he asked. 'Shall we go down to tea?'

Fleur looked up at him her eyes dark with love. 'Are *you* hungry?' she whispered. He shook his head. 'Not for tea,' he whispered back hoarsely. She reached up and pulled his head down until their lips touched. Leaning into him, she felt his heart beating rapidly against her breast. She closed her eyes, her body trembling, every nerve alive and throbbing with love for him as he kissed her, slowly, lovingly, his mouth moving in small circles against her own in what seemed like an endless embrace. Gathering her up into his arms, he carried her to the wide old fashioned bed.

Fleur awoke to the gentle swish of the sea receding from the shore. It reminded her of the splashing fountain at their honeymoon hotel. 'Heavens,' she exclaimed, stretching luxuriously as the smell of bacon sizzling drifted in through the open window. 'I haven't had a cooked breakfast in years.

'Then let's go down and have one,' Hugh replied, throwing back the bedclothes. 'I can't believe our good luck with the weather,' Hugh remarked. 'How about having a long stroll along the shore, then just lazing the rest of the day away? That suit you?' Anything would have suited Fleur. Had he suggested they hang by a bootlace from the flagpole on Edinburgh Castle she would have agreed.

The weather held for the next three days. They picnicked by a frozen loch and wandered hand in hand through the glorious countryside.

'How much longer do you think you'll be up in the wilds?' Fleur enquired, walking in from the bathroom on their last night together.

'I've no idea darling. But you've no need to worry, I doubt that I'll be flying.'

'Then what *are* you doing up there?'

'Oh, this and that.' He patted the bed and she climbed in beside him.

'Darling,' she whispered, when he gently stroked her thighs. 'I want a baby.'

Hugh propped himself on one elbow, gazing down at her. 'Sweetheart it's not reasonable,' he said gently. 'Not now.'

'Why not?' Fleur flamed. 'Is *anything* reasonable? Is it reasonable to start married life in bite size pieces, always being torn apart, not knowing if we shall ever see each other again?' Hugh gathered her in his arms as she burst into tears. 'I want our child as much as you do,' he whispered. 'But I want to be there when it is born, not hundreds of miles away, waiting for a telephone call, only catching glimpses of our baby when it starts to grow.' But Fleur refused to be comforted. He realised that she was under a strain, already anticipating their parting. 'Fleur,' he murmured his hand wandering sensually down her body. 'I promise you that the minute this war is over we will start our family. Until then, don't let's spoil our last night together.' He tentatively kissed her lips. She slowly turned and putting her arms round him held him close.

The taxi drew up at Waverley Station and Hugh handed her down. He glanced at the departure board. 'Platform five. And my train goes from platform eight half an hour later. Good timing.'

He propelled her along the crowded platform. Stark evidence of war was everywhere. Weary soldiers and sailors, some with soiled kitbags slung across their shoulders slouched past, many with tearful girls clinging to their arms. Others were locked together in what might be their last embrace. People were hanging around open carriage doors laughing too loudly, saying stupid meaningless things, anything that would keep away the spectre of their imminent parting, longing for the train to go, yet dreading the emptiness the back of its clacking carriages would leave behind. Threading his way through the crowd, Hugh peered into overflowing compartments in an attempt to find Fleur a seat. 'Here we are,' he said at last, throwing open a door. 'Just one seat left.' A crusty old Colonel furiously rustling the pages of The Scotsman glared at them.

'He didn't look very pleased,' Fleur whispered, when Hugh jumped back onto the platform after placing a magazine on the empty seat.

Hugh grinned. 'I don't think he was. Perhaps he'd reserved that seat for his feet.' They stood facing each other, oblivious of the crowds rushing past, the porters' raucous shouts, the hisses of steam from the panting engine. All either of them could see was the other's face. A hoarse voice shouted 'All aboard', and the hissing became more insistent.

Hugh kissed her hungrily, with hard almost cruel passion. But the guard had blown his whistle and was now raising his flag. Dragging her arms from around his neck, Hugh bundled her into the compartment just as a porter was about to slam the door. The train snorted then slowly moved away from the platform, its windows crammed with heads and furiously waving arms. Fleur leant out and reached for his hand. He grabbed hers and ran a few steps along the platform holding it tightly. But the crowd, blank misery etched on most of their faces, was too dense and he was forced to let go.

The train gathered speed, its engine belching out acrid black smoke which coiled backwards, then fanned out. As it enveloped him, she caught a last glimpse of her husband, his hand raised to his cap in a half salute.

In April, Hugh telephoned to say that he had been promoted to Squadron Leader and was moving back South. 'Isn't it wonderful darling,' he enthused. 'I'll be able to pop up to London for the weekend. I'll try to make it early in May.'

'Will you be flying again?' Fleur asked anxiously.

'Yes,' he answered. 'But don't worry, I'm a survivor.'

'Oh hallo Hugh', Julien said. He handed the 'phone to Fleur. 'It's "you know who",' he grinned.

'Darling,' Hugh shouted delightedly. 'I'm free next Friday and Saturday. I'll be in London late Thursday evening.'

'Wonderful,' Fleur enthused. 'Do you want to do anything special.' There was a slight pause. 'Let's just stay in the flat and play house.'Fleur replaced the receiver and looked appealingly at Julien. 'Hugh will be here on Thursday evening till Sunday and I'm on night shift. Could you.....?'

Julien threw his eyes upwards in a gesture of mock despair.'O.K., O.K.,' he sighed. 'I get the message.' He shook his head resignedly, then smiled and winked at her. 'Of course I'll stand in for you.

The two days passed in a haze of happiness.

Shortly after five on the Sunday morning, on his way to the station Hugh dropped Fleur off at Bush House, her eyes puffy from lack of sleep. She was on the "Dawn Shift".

'I'll be back as soon as I can,' he assured her, accompanying her up the steps and through the swing doors. He took her in his arms and gave her a last lingering kiss. 'See you soon,' he called over his shoulder, turning to wave before he jumped back into the taxi.

It was two weeks later that the call came.

Chapter Three

Hugh looked down from the cockpit and saw pinpoint lights from the maquis reception committee's flashing torch signalling G, the pre-arranged signal. He dipped his wings, signalled back and slowly circled. Immediately four bonfires blazed into a flare path guiding him to his target. He began the descent, and carefully negotiating his way between the flames cruised almost to a stop. The engine throbbed as the despatcher threw open the door. A machine gun pointing directly at Hugh was thrust into the cabin. And he knew he had fallen into a trap. It was no use trying to take off, that would be certain death. He switched off the engine as hands reached in and roughly dragged him out. 'What a pleasant surprise.'a suave middle-aged man said, raising one eyebrow sarcastically.

'I'm a British officer,' Hugh said, struggling to get out of his cumbersome flying suit to reveal his uniform underneath. 'In uniform. I demand my right to be treated as a prisoner of war.'

The man looked at him contemptuously. 'You demand your right,' he sneered. You can demand nothing, you have no damn rights. You're a bloody *spy*.'

'Do spies *usually* arrive in uniform,' Hugh asked, unflinchingly meeting the man's eyes.

The man smiled sardonically. He nodded towards a guard who raised his rifle and dealt Hugh a vicious blow on the side of his head. Hugh put up his hand, blood was pouring down his face. 'You will learn to cooperate, you son of a bitch' the man menaced. And.... you're beginning to bore me.' He jerked his head towards the guard standing at the ready with his rifle. 'Take the bastard away. Hugh was roughly seized and his hands manacled behind his back. His despatcher, held between two armed guards, stared in horror. The man half turned and looked the despatcher up and down. 'The sod's no use to us,' he shrugged. 'Get rid of him.'A guard shot the despatcher in the head.

Seeing him crumple and fall to the ground, a blind fury suddenly blazed in Hugh. The sergeant had received news just before they left that his wife had given birth to their first child: he was due to leave as soon as they returned to be with her and meet his baby son. Now she was a widow and her child fatherless. 'You bloody *murderer,*' he hissed. A second blow from the rifle butt sent him staggering, almost unconscious. He was dragged from the landing ground and roughly pushed into the back of a lorry, landing on the floor. Two armed guards climbed in and sat with their guns pointed at him as the door was slammed shut and the lorry began to bump its way across the uneven ground. Hugh's head throbbed excruciatingly, the jolting sending bolts of lightning through his skull, the blood clotting on his cheeks tightened the skin, making any facial movement painful. The lorry's erratic jerking made him roll uncontrollably from side to side on the hard, dirty floor until pain and fatigue took over and he drifted into unconsciousness. He was dragged to his feet when the lorry entered a paved yard and roughly prodded into a large building and up the stairs. The early morning sun was streaming through the windows when Hugh stumbled into a pleasant room.

An Abwehr officer rose from behind a large desk. 'My poor friend,' he commiserated in almost perfect English. 'What *have* they done to you.' 'Release him,' he said curtly. 'Then leave us alone.' He indicated a chair and Hugh gingerly sat down. Every bone in his body ached. The man pushed forward a box. 'Cigarette?' he enquired. Hugh shook his head. The officer took one, lit it and leant back in his chair. 'I'm sorry about this,' he said pleasantly, pointing at Hugh's face. 'I'll have it seen to as soon as we've had a little talk.' He inhaled deeply. 'Now,' he went on, placing his smouldering cigarette in an ashtray. 'We're both officers and, I hope, gentlemen. Let's be civilised. Perhaps you'd like to tell me about yourself.'

Hugh's face hardened: he'd been warned of their tactics. 'My name is Hugh Cunningham. I'm a squadron leader in the Royal Air Force. My number is....' 'Yes, yes,' his interrogator interrupted, 'I know all that.' He picked up his cigarette and flicked off the ash.'As a matter of fact, I know a great deal about you all.''Then why do you ask? Hugh said coldly. He shrugged. 'I'd like to know more.'

'My name is Hugh Cunningham. I'm a squadron leader.......'

The German smiled slyly. 'I had hoped you would be more cooperative,' he cajoled, stubbing out his cigarette. 'Now, let's start again.'

'My name is Hugh Cunningham. I'm......'

The man's fist crashed down on the desk. 'Enough,' he shouted. His face hardened and an angry glint came into his eyes. 'We have ways and means of *persuading* bastards like you,' he gritted.

'I'm a British officer. In uniform. I demand my right to be treated as a prisoner of war.'

His interrogator banged a bell on his desk and immediately two guards entered, rifles at the ready. 'This son of a b itch demands his *rights*,' he sneered. 'Take him away. and give him his bloody rights. He smiled maliciously. Give him the *treatment*.' As Hugh was dragged from the room, the German rose and spat contemptuously out of the window.

'I'm fed up with that censor,' Fleur exploded, crashing into the News Room and tossing her bulletin on to the table.

'What's he done now?' Edward enquired, an amused smile on his face. Fleur and the censor had been at loggerheads for some time.

'He keeps pressing down the key and hissing, "change this, insert that," pulling out bits of my bulletin and shoving in others willynilly till I'm completely put off my stroke and don't know what I'm doing. *Then* he books me for fluffing.'

'It's his job I'm afraid,' Edward shrugged. 'You know as well as I do that important snippets of news often arrive once the news-reader has gone down to the studio, and its the censor's job to see that they get on the air.'

'Yes, but he's *impossible*,' Fleur exploded once more. And,' she added 'he's a pervert.' Edward glanced up over the top of his half moon glasses. 'Oh, and how do you work that out?''He always books *me*, never Julien,' she snapped.

'I think you mean a sexist,' Edward said calmly, picking up his pen and slashing a red line across a document on his desk. 'Perhaps Julien doesn't fluff. The telephone rang cutting short any further recriminations. Furious, Fleur turned to leave the newsroom. 'Hang on,' Edward called, 'that'll probably be for you Fleur. He called while you were in the studio, but wouldn't leave a message '.

Fleur's anger vanished and her face lit up. 'Hugh?' she queried.

'No. At least I don't think it was him.'

'Newsroom,' he announced picking up the receiver. 'Yes. She's just arrived.'

Fleur eagerly took the telephone from Edward's hands. 'Yes, Mrs. Cunningham speaking. Oh Peter, how nice.....' Her voice faltered, then slowly trailed away. She fumbled for a chair, remembering Hugh's words."My friend Peter Drummond will tell you if I don't return".'

'It's Hugh... isn't it?' she whispered hoarsely. 'He's.......'

But she couldn't pronounce the word. Couldn't bear to hear it out in the open with all it implied.

Julien looked up from a discussion with Edward. Fleur's face was like parchment, the receiver shaking in her hand. He grabbed it from her. 'Fleur seems to be in a state of shock.....' he said. 'I see.... yes if you could. Don't worry, I'll look after her until you arrive.' He slowly replaced the receiver.

Edward looked at him enquiringly and Julien nodded. 'Oh my God,' Edward breathed. 'The poor girl.'

'Can you spare me for a couple of hours?' Julien asked. 'I'll take her home and stay with her until Hugh's friend arrives. She can't be left alone as she is.'

Fleur was sitting dry-eyed, staring into space. Julien gently eased her from the chair, but a heavy weight seemed to be tugging at her feet, anchoring her to the floor, refusing to let them obey her. Like a zombie she allowed him to propel her along the corridor and into the lift.

Peter Drummond and the telegram arrived at the same time.

'I've doped her with brandy,'Julien confided when he opened the door.

Fleur was lying on the bed drifting in and out of a restless sleep, interspersed with nightmares and beautiful dreams. Hearing Peter's voice she got unsteadily to her feet. 'Fleur,' he said softly, when she walked into the the sitting room. He hugged her warmly.

'I'll leave you,' Julien whispered. 'Her godmother's on her way here. But Fleur if you need me.....' She nodded and gave him a weak smile. He silently handed her the telegram and slipped out of the door. Fleur tore it open. 'It says missing, believed killed,'she said hoarsely.' It doesn't say he's *dead.*' She looked at Peter, a glimmer of hope showing in her eyes, now dark with pain. 'Does that mean?......' she pleaded.

Peter took her arm and led her to the sofa. 'I'm afraid it's a formula they use when there's no absolute certainty', he replied sadly.

'So he could be.....' she whispered, trying desperately to hold back the tears. But he didn't reply. 'Peter, 'she cried pitifully, 'I don't understand. I was on duty all night and there was no report of any aircraft failing to return. What happened?'

'Fleur,' Peter said gently. 'Don't you *know* what Hugh was doing?'She shook her head. 'I did ask him but he always changed the subject.''He was bound to secrecy, though some did tell their wives,' Peter went on. He sat down beside her. 'Hugh is one of our most experienced pilots. He flew light aircraft, Lysanders mostly, parachuting secret agents into enemy occupied Europe at night: and also at times landing the 'plane to bring them out. Only highly skilled pilots can do it. They have to fly without lights and navigate by moonlight.'

'So *that's* why he looked at the moon when I asked him if he would be flying,' Fleur interrupted.

'Of course. They can only fly during the moon period. Hugh flew into France last night to pick up a wounded agent and bring back two other members of the team who were in hiding.' Peter shrugged sadly. 'Unfortunately, the 'plane didn't return.'

'So he could still be alive?' Fleur said hopefully.

'He *could* be........' He took her hand and held it tightly between his own. 'I'm so sorry Fleur,' he murmured. 'I promise you if there's any news I'll let you know immediately.' He squeezed her icy fingers. 'You can be proud of your husband. He was a very brave man.'

Fleur caught her breath. Peter had said 'he was'. In his mind had Hugh already been written off as dead?' She looked straight at him, daggers flashing from her eyes. 'I don't *want* a dead hero,' she muttered through clenched teeth. 'I want *Hugh.*'

Hugh came to shivering and disorientated. He was lying on a cold stone floor, still manacled. His head throbbed unbearably and his shirt was sticking to his back with congealed blood causing searing pain to shoot through his body every time he tried to move. Then he remembered 'the treatment' *and* the severe beating he had received. His face was swollen, one eye completely closed: he imagined the other one must be black and bruised. His lips felt as if they were two blown-up balloons glued together. And he had a raging thirst.

In the dim light from the high barred slit of a window he saw just inside the door a metal bowl with a layer of grease clinging to its surface. In agonising pain, he rolled from side to side, then sliding onto his belly slithered across the filthy floor like a snake till he reached the unappetising concoction and began to lap up the cold watery soup like a dog.

His eyes becoming accustomed to the semi-darkness, he made out an iron bed with a palliasse of straw in a corner, and he longed to lie down and rest his aching body. Crawling like an animal, then pushing up with his chin he managed to get to his knees and finally by a series of excruciating movements flopped onto the bed. Total exhaustion claimed him, and he slept.

He was awakened by heavy footsteps tramping down the passageway and the rattling of chains as cell doors were opened and banged shut. He heard cries and screams and lay trembling, afraid he might break down under another 'treatment'.

But the steps passed his door and he was left in peace for a few days..... Until the torture began again.

'I know how you're feeling darling. I've lived through it.' Claudine reassured Fleur holding her tightly in her arms while Fleur, wooden faced and dry-eyed remained stiff and unresponsive, as if unaware of the world around her. 'I felt exactly the same when George was drowned.' Claudine sighed. 'They didn't find his body for ten days. The agony of waiting was terrible, so I can understand what you're going through now.' She paused. 'Your parents were both wonderfully to me kind at the time. Now perhaps I can repay them a little by trying to help you darling, if only you will let me.'

Without waiting for any response from Fleur she had bundled her into a taxi and taken her to Marchmount, hoping that the peace and security she had always found between those old stone walls would do its magic and restore to her a semblance of serenity amidst the turmoil of bewildered and terrifying thoughts now churning round in her brain.

Fleur was grateful for Claudine's love and concern and she tried to be positive, not to give up hope, to cling to the fact that Hugh had only been reported 'missing, believed killed': there was no certainty of his death, he could still come back to her. But that niggling doubt kept returning to haunt her.

Whenever they were alone she found her grandmother's gaze on her, longing to help her but powerless to counter the emptiness she saw in her granddaughter's eyes. Victoria's troubled gaze worried Fleur and she tended to retire to bed early, ostensibly to sleep, but once in the semi-darkness of her room, she would draw back the blackout curtains and sit at the window staring at the moon, willing it to shine on a lone Lysander, bursting through the cloudbank, bringing Hugh safely home.

'I'm afraid the spark has gone out of her,' her grandmother remarked sadly one evening after Fleur had climbed the stairs to bed leaving her and Claudine alone to continue knitting balaclava helmets and yards of khaki scarves for the troops. 'What *can* we do to help her, Claudie dear?'

'Not very much,' Claudine had replied, 'except be here for her. Each person has to come to terms with grief in his or her own way. It's early days yet, Victoria. She managed to survive her mother's death; give her time, she'll come through'

Her days at Marchmount, tended with love and care by her grandmother and Claudine, helped Fleur regain some sort of composure. Claudine's positive attitude and eternal optimism had given her hope even in her darkest moments, but it was true what her grandmother had said: the spark had gone out of her. When after a week she returned to the BBC she threw herself into her work, willingly taking on extra shifts and duties when any of her colleagues needed time off. Anything to stop her from thinking: anything to dull the pain.

She heard from Peter Drummond occasionally, but it was always the same story. No news. She sensed he was trying to tell her there was no hope.

Hugh was a remnant of his former self, his clothes in tatters when one morning he was taken before his first interrogator.

'So my friend, we meet again,' he said, raising one eyebrow sardonically. 'What a bloody fool you are. We know all about you and your sodding accomplices. We have "taken care" of the colleague you came to rescue.... along with his companions.' He leant across the table, and his eyes narrowed. 'Do you *still* want to play the little British hero?'

Hugh did not reply.

'Well?' he hissed menacingly.

But Hugh said nothing.

The German got up and coming round the table gave Hugh a resounding blow across his face which sent him reeling. 'Take the bastard away,' he fumed to the two guards standing with rifles at the ready just inside the door. 'He's no use to us. *I* haven't been able to get a b loody thing out of him. We've tried everything, but nothing will make the bugger talk.'

Hugh was seized, bundled from the room and pushed into a narrow passageway filled with other scarecrows like himself. They stood for hours. Then suddenly the barred doors clanged open; they were pushed into a yard and sent tumbling into a large van which rocked its way out through the heavy doors and into the streets of the town.

The doors of the van were opened at a station. There was already a crowd of frightened people of all ages, some with suitcases, some with children, queuing to board a train. It was overflowing when finally Hugh stumbled up the steps. Shovelling twenty of them into a compartment designed for six, the guard slammed and locked the door.

Hugh closed his eyes trying to ignore the hunger which gnawed at him as day after day the train rattled through the countryside with the sun beating mercilessly down on the blistering roof. Whenever the door opened, there was a fight for the meagre rations which were pushed in. Thirst became an unbearable torment and the stench of urine and sweating, unwashed bodies was overpowering. At last, the train stopped at a siding and the doors crashed open. Guards shrieked at the terrified passengers stumbling down the steps to run as best they could between their double line of rifles the short distance towards a heavy metal gate. Passing through it Hugh looked up at the inscription written boldly on the top. "Arbeit macht Frei".

And he knew where he was. He had arrived at a concentration camp.

Hugh hadn't prayed since compulsory prayers in the chapel at school. But, running with the crowd towards the rows of drab huts, his thoughts returned to those carefree days. 'Lord, 'he cried in his heart. 'If you exist and you hear me *please* let me see live to Fleur again.'

There was no reply.

But he felt comforted.

—ooo-O-ooo—

Chapter Four

D-Day finally arrived and Julien with others of his male colleagues went off to France to cover the news on the spot. Towards the end of August Paris was liberated, but after the hysterical rejoicing life suddenly went flat in the BBC French Section. The war was winding down, victory was in sight, there was no longer that sense of urgency Fleur had known for the past four years. New people were coming to work in the Section, people who had never known the strain, the comradeship, the togetherness that had united them as exiles fighting for a common cause. To the newcomers it was merely a job. In September Fleur heard that her father was alive and well, fighting with General de Lattre de Tassigny's First French Army in Alsace before it broke through into Germany. But of Hugh still no news. Fleur's positive attitude which she had struggled to keep alive against all odds began to falter, and in her darkest moments she almost gave up hope.

From the officers' mess rose maudlin voices massacring "Silent Night".

'A merry Christmas to you all, you sodding bastards' mocked the Gestapo sergeant supervising the distribution of thin soup which constituted dinner.

It was Christmas Eve at Flossenburg. The last Christmas Eve of the war. Hugh had been moved from Dachau to this extermination camp together with a truckload of political prisoners two weeks earlier. Conditions, if possible, were worse than at Dachau.

The exhausted group of skeletal men shuffled forward with their tins before facing the barrage of baton weilding soldiers waiting outside the kitchen to club them as they ran shakily through their ranks to their squalid huts. Making for the door, a prisoner tripped and bumped against the sergeant, spilling soup over his boots.

'Schweinhund!' the sergeant yelled hysterically, raising his baton and striking him a vicious blow which sent the him crashing to the floor. He struggled to his feet, but not quickly enough: the sergeant seized his revolver and shot him in the head. 'Another pig for the bonfire,' he sneered at the silent group waiting in line.

Hugh's fists clenched at his sides, but he had become used to such barbarity and knew that any show of anger would produce dire results. As he left the kitchen hut and ran trying not to spill his meagre ration, he heard a voice close to his ear, but he dared not look round.

'I'm in hut 3, 'the voice hissed. 'I know you, we met in Scotland. Let's try to get together on the working party to-morrow.'

When the line divided to go to their different huts, Hugh stole a glance at the man behind him running towards hut three. He was tall, but that was all Hugh could deduce. He prayed that they might be able to exchange a few words on the following day. 'What a wonderful Christmas present,' he breathed. He'd found a friend. Perhaps he could give him news of Fleur. Then doubts crept in. Why had the man risked his life by contacting him? Perhaps he was a German plant put there to glean information. His English was accented, but Hugh couldn't place it. It didn't sound German. And suddenly the light which had momentarily shone at the end of the dark tunnel went out: and Hugh decided to have nothing to do with him.

The following morning he watched warily as hut 3 inmates were pushed down the steps of their hut and prodded into line, but he couldn't see his so-called friend. It was 5.30., dark, snowing heavily and bitterly cold with a sharp wind whistling through their threadbare garments. They stood motionless in serried ranks for almost two hours, drenched and shivering, watched over by two muffled-up soldiers who had obviously enjoyed their previous night's celebrations and were suffering hangovers: with tempers to match. Before the Commandant arrived to hear the roll call, several prisoners had collapsed from harsh blows or exhaustion They were left where they fell.

Hugh was one of the party sent back to the huts to bring out those who had died in the night, or were dying, too ill to roll out of their bunks. Pushing the cart piled high with bodies to the crematorium to deposit them on the frozen heap waiting outside, the man from hut 3 slid up beside him with his grisly load. 'You're English, aren't you?' he hissed out of the side of his mouth. 'I was in the truck from Dachau and recognised you.'

Hugh did not answer. But he noticed that the man, like him, was placing the bodies carefully, almost reverently on the pile, not slinging them like carcases of meat as others were doing. That was not the attitude of a German 'plant'. Perhaps he *was* a friend after all. But Hugh was still wary.

'You're a pilot aren't you?' the man whispered when they turned back to the stiffening pile.

But still Hugh didn't reply.

'I'm a Dane', he breathed almost inaudibly, his lips not moving. 'Recruited in London by SOE's Danish Section. You dropped three of us over Jutland in March '44.'

Hugh softened. In Scotland, he had trained many prospective agents to identify suitable landing grounds for future 'drops'in the Alps, the Jura and the Norwegian mountains once they themselves had been dropped. But he had done only one 'drop' during that time and it had been over Western Denmark. He remembered it very well.

But still he was afraid.

They were reaching the bottom of the pile.

'I'll try to keep in touch,' the man whispered, as they bent towards the cart. 'The Allies are advancing rapidly. Ever considered escaping from this hell hole?'

Hugh had. Several times. But he had also seen the results of those who'd tried. Electrocuted as they attempted to climb the barbed wire fencing, machine gunned by sentries from their lofty lookout towers or flogged and, hung by piano wire if the other two options didn't get them first.

It was several weeks before he saw the Dane again.

One morning after roll-call, they were marched to the execution block to witness two hangings and he discovered the Dane standing tight-lipped and motionless beside him. In front of him was a young boy, his eyes wide with fear. Hugh's mouth set in a hard bitter line: his stomach churned and threatened to expel its meagre contents when two emaciated manacled men were led to the flogging post before being dragged, half dead, to the gallows: he recognised two Russians who had been in the truck from Dachau. The "show" over, the prisoners picked up their tools and assembled for another gruelling day of forced labour in the granite pits. The Dane shuffled up beside him. 'They've moved all the political prisoners,' he hissed through closed lips.

'Where to?' Hugh hissed back, looking steadily ahead.

'Special extermination block. Nacht und Nebel, sent there to disappear without trace. They've probably been hung by now. Our turn's coming. The bloody bastards are panicking, hanging and shooting everyone, especially those connected with SOE. We'll be moved or executed very soon.'

In spite of himself Hugh was desperate to know more. 'Where did you learn all this?' he enquired suspiciously, still gazing steadily ahead.

'One of the guards in my hut comes from a town on the German-Danish border. His mother's a Dane: he's fed up and damned disillusioned and is willing to help us if we try to escape.' A heavy blow on the back of his head from a rifle butt sent the Dane reeling. He was dragged from the line and savagely whipped. Hugh knew that their conversation had been discovered.

Two weeks later, they were marshalled into line and marched to a railway siding where a series of cattle trucks were waiting. With the help of his half Danish sergeant, his unknown friend managed to squeeze in beside him, but neither he nor Hugh gave any sign of recognition. Day after day, they shunted through the late winter landscape. The rations became more and more meagre ending in fights for the few crusts occasionally thrust into the wagons by the guards. Every morning inert bodies were collected and thrown out to 'fertilise the soil'. The deaths became more and more numerous until one morning the convoy was halted and working parties were formed to dig mass graves.

'This is our chance,' hissed the Dane as they sweated and heaved, hacking through the hard ground. We'll have to carry out the bodies. There's a line of b loody guards beside the train but the bastards can't watch everywhere at once. My guard will give us a signal, then we run like hell for those woods over there.'

Hugh nodded. 'Why is he doing this?' he whispered, still suspicious.

'He knows Germany's finished and he wants us to speak in his favour when the war's over.'

The digging completed, they began to carry the bodies out of the trucks. When there was a steady line of carriers packed behind them, the Dane looked up, threw in the corpse he and Hugh were carrying and stopped as if to get his breath. 'We may get separated,' he hissed. 'In case you ever need me my name's Svensen, Knud Svensen. I'm from Helsingfors.'

The line of guards in front of the train all seemed to be looking in the opposite direction.

'Run,' the Dane mouthed.

At once, there were shrieks of 'halt' followed by the whizz of bullets singing past their ears.

Hugh ran, mustering his last ounce of strength, ducking his head as the bullets in increasing numbers whistled past his ears. His breath was coming in short sharp gasps : his chest felt as if it were about to burst and his legs threatened to buckle under him when he reached the wood. He heard the sound of heavy boots crashing through the trees behind him. Gasping for breath, a harsh rasp escaping from his lungs Hugh suddenly felt he could go no further when a hand shot out and grabbed him, and he collapsed into a hedge of brambles on to the crouching body of his Danish friend. The footsteps got nearer. He heard shouts and through the brambles saw a pair of jackboots racing towards them. The brambles were roughly parted and his bloodshot eyes looked up into the face of Knud's guard. The brambles snapped together again, enclosing them.

'There the buggers are,' the guard shouted, pointing in the opposite direction. 'They've just disappeared into that clump of trees.'

The jackboots changed direction. The two fugitives held their breath until they heard them disappearing in the distance.

Knud helped the exhausted Hugh to his feet. 'Better push on,' he whispered, the bastards are bound to come back this way and we may not be so lucky next time.'

They had neither maps nor compasses so decided to plunge out in the opposite direction from the search party.

'We're not *that* important,' Knud said reassuringly, 'I doubt they'll hold up the bloody convoy for days looking for us. All the same, we'd damn well better put as much distance as possible between the buggers and us.' He set off at a trot, pushing his way through the dense undergrowth. Hugh, at the point of exhaustion, summoned what little strength he had left and followed him.

After about an hour, they came to a stream. Tearing off his tattered prison tunic and tying it around his head in an attempt to keep it dry, Knud plunged into the icy waters and swam swiftly to the other side: he seemed to have summoned a reserve of energy which Hugh was unable to command. Taking a deep breath, Hugh plunged in after him: but on reaching the other side, he collapsed. 'I can't go on,' he gasped.

His head felt as if it were about to explode with the tremendous effort he had put into swimming across the narrow stream. His torso was heaving, his heart thumping wildly, beating a tattoo against his chest as if about to burst through his rib cage. Each breath he took was agonising, like a sharp knife slicing through his lungs: and his legs felt as if they were stuffed with cotton wool.

Knud looked down at him sympathetically. 'Come on, old chap., he coaxed. 'We made it so far. Just one last effort. We can't be far from the Czech border, or the Allied line of advance. Don't let those bloody bastards get the better of you.'

Hugh attempted to get up, but the effort was too much. Even the thought of seeing Fleur again which had kept him going through the long agonising months was not sufficient to help him stagger to his feet. He shook his head and fell back onto the bank.

'You go on, Knud, 'he whispered. And closing his eyes, he lapsed into unconsciousness.

—ooo-O-ooo—

CHAPTER FIVE

The letter arrived when Claudine was standing on a ladder in the library checking the books and calling the titles down to Fleur, stationed below. The two of them were busy making an inventory of the contents of Marchmount which was now on the market. Lady Percy had died a few months before the war ended leaving the house to her only grandchild, but Fleur had no desire to keep it, there were too many memories, too many ghosts.

Ivy walked in and looked anxiously at Fleur before reaching up and discreetly handing the envelope to Claudine. It was addressed to Madame Hubert de Rosny, Fleur's dead mother. Claudine recognised the handwriting immediately. Climbing down from the ladder, she put her arm in Fleur's and drew her onto a sofa.

'This letter has just arrived from your father,' she ventured.

'Papa?' Fleur exclaimed. 'How wonderful! News at last.'

Claudine hesitated. 'I'm afraid it's addressed to your mother, darling. Hubert obviously doesn't know about the accident.'

Fleur's face dropped. Taking the letter she tore open the envelope and glanced down the page, the flimsy sheet trembling in her hands.

'My darling,' she read out aloud. 'I shall shortly be travelling to Paris to finalise my release from the 1st French Army (you didn't know you'd married a soldier, did you?). As soon as that is settled I'll pull all the strings I can to get a visa (doesn't this sound ridiculous!) and then as quickly as possible a passage to England and race down to Marchmount to fetch you and Fleur. I cannot wait to see you both again. The thought of at last being able to hold you in my arms, my precious Julia, makes the waiting almost unbearable. It has been so long. Till then my darling, your ever loving - and very impatient! - Hubert.

Fleur looked at Claudine. 'However are we going to tell him that mother has been killed?' she pleaded, 'it'll be a terrible shock.' She paused and scanned the page again. 'Do you think I should write and let him know?'

Claudine frowned. 'It might be kinder, he'd be able to absorb the shock before he arrives.' She pursed her lips. 'Or he may not want to come once he knows that Julia will not be waiting for him.'

Fleur put her head in her hands the tears not far away, the surge of joy she had felt when she heard that there was a letter from her father abruptly extinguished. Claudine leant across and removed Fleur's hand. 'Would you like me to write to him darling? It might be easier for your father to receive the news from a third party: it would be less personal and he wouldn't feel he needs to comfort me as he would if it were you.' She sighed. 'Though I don't imagine he's the only soldier to return to such a sad situation, he may have come across some other cases in his regiment already.'

Fleur raised her head. 'Won't Papa think it strange if he hears the news from you and not from me?' she queried, relief flooding through her.

'I don't think so, darling,' Claudine replied reassuringly. 'I know Hubert. He'll understand.' She frowned thoughtfully. 'Perhaps he even suspects that things might not be the same as when he left. After all, he'll have heard about the terrible pounding London received from German bombers, and wonder whether you and Julia survived.' She squeezed Fleur's hand. 'It may not be as dramatic as we think. And.... if he does decide to come, you'll still be here.'

Fleur gave her godmother a strange look. '*And* you,' she said quietly.

Claudine smiled sadly. 'Poor Hubert, I don't know whether that will be much of a consolation. But at least I can try to help him in the way he and Julia helped me when George died. They were a tower of strength, I don't think I'd have survived without them. Hubert coped with all the nasty sordid details and Julia never left me.' Claudine's eyes misted over. 'She was *such* a comfort.'

Fleur thoughtfully slipped the flimsy sheet of airmail paper back into its envelope. 'You're very fond of my father aren't you?, she said without looking up.

'I've always been very fond of both your parents,' Claudine replied simply.

'But you have known Papa since you were a child.'

'Our two families have been neighbours and friends for many generations: Hubert and I were practically brought up together.' She gave a mischievous smile, making her look almost girlish. 'Many people expected us to marry, but I fell madly in love with George and Hubert with Julia.'

Fleur picked up her inventory and thoughtfully jotted down a few items. 'Perhaps now that you're both alone,' she ventured, without looking up, 'you and Papa will end by marrying.'

Claudine laughed, relieved that Fleur had taken the news so well. 'Stranger things have happened. But I don't think so, we'll just go on being wonderful friends.'

'Your grandfather and Clothilde are getting ready to go back to Paris,' Claudine said later as she closed the library door, and she and Fleur walked across the hall to attack the drawing room. 'Why don't you go with them? Your father said in his letter he would pass through Paris, you could be there when he arrives.' She sucked the end of her pencil thoughtfully, checking down her lists. 'Or come down to St. Raphael with me. I've got to go and see what's happened to my house, though goodness knows whether I still *have* a house. There was a terrible battle on the beach at Le Dramont after the Allies landed there and it's only a stone's throw along the coast from Boulouris.'

She raised her eyebrows enquiringly.

Fleur met her godmother's gaze unflinchingly. 'When Hugh comes back Claudine,' she answered quietly, it's here or in London that he'll expect to find me, not in Paris or Boulouris.'

'Darling, 'Claudine said softly, mentally noting that Fleur had said 'when' not 'if'. 'I know it's hard, but you've heard *nothing*, and it's over a year since Hugh was reported missing. You can't spend the rest of your life hoping..... and grieving.' She put down her lists. 'I promise you that if ever there is news of Hugh, we'll make very sure the authorities know where to find you.'

Hugh slowly returned to consciousness, shuddering with fear, and cautiously looked up through half closed lids. A man was kneeling beside him, his fingers on his pulse. He placed a stethoscope on his chest then rose to his feet, a grim expression on his face and shook his head at an old priest wearing a faded black beret and dusty cassock, looking down at Hugh on his other side. 'Very little hope, 'he sighed. 'I doubt he'd even make the journey.'

The priest smiled down at Hugh, sending lines in little rivulets crisscrossing his face. His eyes were deep grey and full of compassion.'Let's try to get him to safety, doctor,' he pleaded, 'we can't leave him here to die. If we found him still breathing I believe God sent us here to rescue him. Who are we to argue?'

'If you're willing to take the risk Father,' his companion said grimly. 'It's after curfew, and there are German patrols everywhere.'

'I promised his friend we'd do out best,' the priest coaxed. 'A Sister is waiting with a convent van in the shadows at the edge of the forest'.

The doctor shrugged and began tossing the foliage covering Hugh's body into the undergrowth. Making a tremendous effort as he drifted in and out of consciousness, Hugh raised his head slightly. He realised that he and Knud must must have crossed the border into Czechoslovakia when they swam across the stream and that Knud must have dragged or carried him into the undergrowth and camouflaged him with broken branches. He noticed a young boy standing beside the priest holding a wheelbarrow.

The two men lifted him gently into the wheelbarrow and covered him with a blanket and more forest camouflage. Dusk was creeping through the trees, the darkening sky almost devoid of clouds as they jolted through the undergrowth. Hugh raised his eyes appealingly to the priest. He hadn't the strength to speak, but the priest seemed to understand.

'The good doctor and I are friends, 'he said gently. 'And this is Vaclav his grandson. You are safe for the moment.'

But still Hugh's eyes clung to his face.

The priest smiled kindly. 'Your Danish friend managed to get to my back door unobserved: the presbytery is at the entrance to the village. He told me where to find you.' He placed his hand reassuringly over Hugh's. 'He is safe, hidden with people who organise escape routes.'

Hugh smiled his gratitude and breathing a sigh of relief closed his eyes and fell into a deep dream haunted sleep.

He awoke with a start. Loud raucous shouts were coming nearer. Hugh heard the clatter of jackboots on a tiled floor and the rattle of brass rings as curtains were thrust roughly aside. A young woman was pleading with the soldiers, but to no effect.

'There's an escaped British spy and his damned accomplice hiding somewhere in the area,' a man shouted angrily, 'and we b loody well intend to find the buggers.' He lowered his voice adding menacingly. 'They're *very* dangerous.'

Hugh began to tremble. Half opening his eyes, he realised that he was lying in freshly laundered sheets in a hospital bed, bathed and clothed in a white night shirt. A heavily built middle aged woman wearing a wimple was standing beside him. She appeared to be unperturbed by the shouts and threats. The rings jangled angrily as his curtains were torn open.

'There are *no* spies *here,*' the nun said authoritatively.

The soldier seemed taken aback by her self assurance. 'Sister,' he stammered, 'I need to check.'

'By all means,' she answered coldly, standing aside to allow him to pass.

Hugh's heart began a staccato beat, then leapt into his throat threatening to choke him. His hands felt damp and clammy and sweat broke out on his forehed. Despite himself his teeth began to chatter with fear.

'But I must warn you,' the nun continued, 'that this patient has typhus and is highly infectious.'

The soldier drew back, a terrified look on his face.

She shrugged. 'If you think it is worth risking catching the disease for a man who is not likely to last the night..... then go ahead.'

The soldier gave her a sidelong glance then slyly drew his gun and aimed it at Hugh. But the nun had seen his manoeuvre. Swiftly drawing the curtains, she stood like a flagship in front of them.

'Only God takes life here!' she thundered.

The soldier fell back; he seemed terrified by her words. Those coming behind him stopped dead in their tracks. Abruptly he crossed himself and hurried from the ward.

Hugh opened his eyes, but the light was too bright. He closed them and lay quite still. Suddenly the room heaved and swayed from side to side. His bed turned upside down, his feet on the ceiling, his head dangling in mid air.

He opened his mouth to call, but no words came. His throat was parched and raw and his head felt as if it were being rythmically beaten with a hammer. The bed now started to swirl and turn in circles. He felt sick and dizzy. Suddenly it righted itself. Daring to open his eyes, he stole a glance through the window. A dazzling sun almost blinded him: it danced onto a field of cowslips where Fleur was running barefoot towards him, smiling and holding out her arms. He tried to raise himself in the bed, but it began to swirl again. Fleur flew in through the window and perched on top of a cupboard. His bed heaved and he was once again upside down. His foot shot out and dislodged her. She turned into a hawk. Squawking throatily and angrily flapping her wings, she flew off her perch and out through the ceiling.

He tried to call to her, but the meadow had disappeared: the sun had gone and the room was in shadow. The bed swayed from side to side then floated off into the darkness.

When Hugh opened his eyes the matronly nun was standing beside him.

'He's still delirious,' she whispered to a small man with a beard wearing a white coat and a pince nez, standing on the other side of the bed, holding his wrist. 'It's been nearly a month now.' She glanced at the thermometer in her hand. '42. We've *got* to get it down.'

The doctor nodded. 'Complications I'm afraid,' he whispered back.

Hugh felt a cool hand take his arm and a soft prick as a needle was inserted. He opened his eyes: the matronly nun was still standing beside him holding his wrist. The room was now almost dark, deep shadows crisscrossing the walls. He shut his eyes and Fleur reappeared. She took his hand and he felt himself gliding with her over the walls, wrapped in a warm mantle of happiness till they merged with the shadows and floated together into oblivion.

Lost in the mists of consciousness, Hugh heard the strains of 'Silent Night' drifting through the curtain which separated him from the corridor, and he began to shiver with fear. He was back in Flossenburg. And it was Christmas Eve. He broke out in a cold sweat, tensing in anticipation of the blows he would receive. Shaking with fear, he awaited the bullet which would send him reeling lifeless to the floor. But no blow came. No bullet. He realised that it was not the maudlin singing of drunken officers he was hearing, but sweet angelic voices approaching and he cautiously opened his eyes.

As if by intuition a nun appeared. She looked down at him and smiled. 'Fetch Mother,' she hissed to a passing nun.

The voices came nearer. The nun drew back the curtain separating him from the corridor. In the semi-darkness, he saw a double row not of jeering guards, but young novices carrying lighted candles walking past, singing the well-loved carol.

Within seconds the matronly nun was standing at his bedside. 'Call Dr. Schneider,' she whispered to the nun still hovering by the bed.

'He's on his way,' she whispered back.

At that moment, the man with the pointed beard and the pince nez hurried into his cubicle pulling on his white coat.

'Temperature and pulse normal,' the matronly nun informed him.

The doctor looked down at Hugh and smiled. 'So you've finally decided to wake up,' he said, taking his wrist. 'You gave us quite a scare young man.'

Hugh looked from one to the other and tried to speak, but only croaking sounds came from his throat.

'Don't worry,' the doctor reassured him, 'it's quite normal. Your speech will gradually come back.' He released his hold on Hugh's wrist and gently put his arm back under the bedclothes. 'He's soaking wet,' he frowned.

'I think he had a difficult time when waking up,' the young nun explained. 'He was very agitated and screaming in fear. I imagine he thought he was back in the concentration camp.'

'Quite possibly,' the doctor nodded. 'That's all behind you,' he reassured Hugh. 'The war has been over for nearly eight months, you've nothing to fear. All you need to do is rest and get better. You've been in a coma since the end of April,' he explained. 'But don't worry, the good nuns will nurse you back to health.' He smiled down at him. 'Then perhaps we'll be able to find out more about you and help you get back to your own people.' He patted Hugh's arm reassuringly. 'Now, if you'll excuse me, I'll go back to my family.

It's Christmas Eve: we're celebrating Jesus' birth. What a wonderful night to come back to life. I'll look in on him in the morning,' he said to the matronly nun as he drew back the curtains and walked out into the dimly-lit corridor.

Hugh was vaguely aware of gentle hands bathing him and changing his linen: of his head being carefully lifted and a feeding cup placed between his lips. The warm liquid trickling into his mouth comforted his body and made him feel drowsy. He drifted off into a dreamless sleep.

Why don't you stay here?' Hubert de Rosny asked his daughter when she and Claudine stopped off in Paris on their way back to London. 'Like me, you've now nothing to keep you in England, it holds only unhappy memories for both of us.'

They were sitting together on the deep sofa facing the wide open window. He took her hand and fondled it gently. 'Now that I'm back at the Quai d'Orsay, I have to do a lot of entertaining: I'd be very happy to have you as my hostess.' He smiled sadly. 'Your mother did it so well.'

Fleur was tempted by her father's offer: but she was torn. Julien and Kristina were now living in Paris with Felix, her little godson and many of her former BBC French Section colleagues were here. It was true, she had nothing to keep her in London except her crazy hope that one day Hugh would return. But this was 1946. The war had been over for almost a year. It was nearly two years since Hugh had been reported missing, believed killed. And there was still no news.

She got up and strolled across to the door leading on to the terrace. Propping her elbows on the stone balustrade, she gazed out across the Champs de Mars to where in the distance the top of the Eiffel Tower glistened in the afternoon sun. The air was like champagne. It was one of those rare winter days heralding the Spring which sometimes surprises in February. 'April in Paris can be a magical time,' she murmured to herself.

Below her children were calling to each other as they bowled their hoops along the alleyways: elderly couples were sunning themselves on the benches: young lovers wandered across the grass hand in hand, and she longed to be one of them. To be loved again, no longer to be blanketed by this fog of misery. No longer to be alone.

'Perhaps I should take everyone's advice,' Fleur mused. 'Face reality and accept the fact that Hugh is *not* coming back. Turn the page and get on with my life.'

But still something held her back. She turned and walked thoughtfully through the open French windows into the sitting room. Her father looked up from the evening paper.

Claudine, flicking through a magazine, smiled encouragingly, and suddenly Fleur's mind was made up. Crossing the room, she perched on the arm of the sofa. 'Thank you Papa,' she said softly, 'it's very sweet of you.' She smiled down at him. 'I'd love to stay.'

It was some months before Hugh was fully aware of the world around him. One morning, he was helped out of bed and settled in an armchair by the window. 'Thank you,' he whispered. They were the first words he had spoken.

He looked out of the window. The sun was beaming down on a sunny courtyard where nuns were walking purposefully backwards and forwards. Flowers were blossoming in the surrounding beds and a tree in the middle was heavy with young green leaves.

'It must be Spring,' he mused. His mind went back to last Spring when he had left the death camp, and he shivered. He realised that he had lost a whole year of his life, and he wondered what Fleur had been told. Was he still "missing believed killed" or had he been written off as dead. At the thought he became agitated. He called for a nurse and instantly a nun appeared. 'I have to leave, 'he said urgently. 'I must get back to England.' He tried to rise from his chair, but he did not have the strength.

The nurse helped him back to bed. He could hardly walk. 'You must rest,' she soothed.

He attempted to get up, but she urged him back onto the pillows. Sinking wearily into them, he realised that he was in no state to go anywhere, and tears began to trickle down his emaciated cheeks.

The doctor reappeared. 'Now what's all this?' he asked sternly. 'You've made wonderful progress. You have finally spoken and you've even been up for a while. You *must* be patient,' he went on, sitting down beside Hugh's bed. 'You've been very, very ill, you cannot go anywhere until you are fully recovered. Do you realise that at one point we thought we had lost you?'

Hugh turned his face to the window. He was grateful for all they had done for him. They had given him back his life. But Fleur. Where was she? What did she think? And again the tears began to flow.

'My wife,' he managed to stammer, but that was all. He closed his eyes in despair.

The doctor signalled to a passing nurse and whispered something. A few minutes later he felt a soft prick in his arm, peace slowly invaded his body, and he slept.

—ooo-O-ooo—

CHAPTER SIX

'Fleur,' Hubert de Rosny called, crossing over to the terrace where Fleur was chatting with a group of other guests. 'I want you to meet someone who says he remembers you in your cradle.'

It was May. The Paris social season was just beginning and Fleur and her father were attending a reception at the American Ambassador's residence. Excusing herself, she turned towards a tall very blond young man standing beside her father.

'Arvind Kristensen,' he murmured, bending over her outstretched hand. 'My mother took me to tea with Madame de Rosny when we lived in Russia and I remember we visited you in the nursery. You were about three months old; a beautiful baby.' He smiled.'You haven't changed.'

In spite of her outward appearance of sophistication, Fleur still had not managed to control that blush which had enchanted Hugh. It now crept up her neck and suffused her magnolia cheeks with a soft pink glow. The blush seemed to have the same effect on this young Dane as it had had on her husband.

'Arvind's father was my opposite number at the Danish Embassy when we were in Moscow,' her father explained. 'He's now Danish ambassador to London, and Arvind appears to be rapidly following in his footsteps.'

'*Fleur,*' a middle aged woman squealed from across the room. 'I've been looking for you *everywhere.*' She hurried towards her, arms outstretched and embraced her warmly.

Fleur had no idea who she was. She supposed she must be someone from the past or more probably a 'hopeful' for her father's hand. Hubert de Rosny was a very attractive, eligible widower. And in the few weeks since Fleur had returned to Paris this was not the first woman who had tried to ingratiate herself with his daughter.

Arvind tactfully faded into the crowd.

They were saying goodbye to their hostess when Fleur noticed Arvind standing head and shoulders above a group of admiring middle-aged women.

'Husband hunters for their debutante daughters,' her father remarked with an amused smile as they crossed the impressive hallway and down the steps into the courtyard. 'And Arvind's quite a catch!'

It was on May 17th, Fleur's 25th birthday, that she met Arvind again. She and her father had been invited to a reception at the Norwegian Embassy to celebrate their National Day. When she took her place at the elaborately decorated dining table, Arvind was standing on her left.

'What a pleasure to meet you again Mademoiselle de Rosny,' he smiled.

Fleur smiled back as he pushed her chair into position. 'Actually my name is Cunningham. Fleur Cunningham.'

He glanced down at her hand resting on the table. And noticed her wedding ring.

'I'm a widow,' Fleur explained. 'My husband was a pilot, killed in the war.' Fleur's heart jumped and began to beat in staccato leaps, and she suddenly went cold. It was as if an icy hand had gripped her intestines and twisted them into a hundred loops. She realised that she had pronounced the dreaded word. Had admitted out loud something she had never admitted even to herself. That Hugh was dead. She bit her lip and looked down at her plate.

'I'm *so* sorry,' he said softly.

Fleur looked up at him. There was genuine concern in his violet blue eyes. They were darker than Hugh's, but just as arresting. And she could almost believe he meant it. Not wishing to continue the conversation, she turned to the elderly Belgian on her right.

'Do you remember living in Russia?' Arvind enquired joining her on a sofa after dinner.

Fleur's brow puckered. 'Not *really*. Just occasional flashes. I *was* only four years old when we left.'

'Then perhaps I can refresh your memory There's a wonderful Russian restaurant not far from the Trocadero, the 'Nitcheva'. It's run by impoverished Russian aristocrats working as waiters or playing the balalaika and singing mournful songs. Would you care to dine there with me one evening?'

'I'd love to,' Fleur smiled.

'I'll ring you in he morning and you can tell me when you are free.'

'What a delightful restaurant that was, 'Fleur enthused when Hugh accompanied her in the lift up to the flat after their dinner at the Nitcheva. 'But how terribly sad for all those people who have known such luxury to be reduced to waiting on tables.'

Arvind shrugged. 'We none of us know what the future has in store.'

Fleur's lips tightened, her mind swivelling back to the war and the brief moments of happiness she and Hugh had shared.

Arvind noticed her abrupt change of mood, but did not comment, though he couldn't help wondering whether it had something to do with her lost husband. He inserted her key in the lock, but made no attempt to enter the flat. 'I hope you've enjoyed this evening as much as I have,' he said quietly. 'Perhaps we could do it again? Paris is full of the most fascinating little restaurants.'

'Thank you, 'Fleur murmured. 'I'd like that very much.'

He raised her hand to his lips, and was gone.

Summer was far advanced before Hugh was strong enough to leave the convent. He was still painfully thin, but he had regained a certain amount of strength. The day he left he was given a collection of very German clothes.

'I'm afraid we cannot provide a British uniform,' the matronly nun smiled, 'but I don't think you should have a problem establishing your identity once you get to Nuremburg. The war criminals trials are coming to an end and the town is bristling with British and American troops. Here is a train ticket: as soon as you get to Nuremberg make for the courthouse where the trials are being held and ask for the British base. Your German is good, you shouldn't have any difficulty finding your way around.' She handed him a small knitted purse. 'But if ever you do have a problem, here is a little money and the address of one of our nearby Bavarian convents. I'll warn them you may be coming'

Hugh was confused and embarassed by their kindness and generosity. He tried to express his thanks, but no words seemed adequate to show the gratitude he felt. Now, thanks to their dedication he was on his way home. To Fleur. He almost burst with happiness at the thought that very soon he would hold her in his arms again. There would be no more goodbyes. They would grow old together.

Impulsively, he bent and kissed the matronly nun's cheek. She smiled and shepherded him towards the door where a car was waiting to take him to the station.

'May God be with you, my son,' she said softly. And made the sign of the cross over him.

'This is a lovely surprise,' Arvind exclaimed when he and Fleur bumped into each other at the Elysées garden party on Bastille Day. 'Had we tried to arrange it we'd never have made it in this crowd.' He grinned down at her. 'Must be fate.'

Fleur had seen Arvind at various Embassy functions and they had dined together once or twice in the past two months, which was all their busy schedules allowed. It was the 14th of July: The Paris season now over and everyone was drifting towards the coast.

'Are you leaving soon?' he enquired.

'Yes. I'm joining my godmother at Boulouris, near St.Raphael. And you?'

'Only briefly. I'm going to Bornholm, an island in the Baltic off the coast from Copenhagen where my parents have a house, but I'll be back mid-August. I'll contact you then. We must get together again before the Autumn merry-go-round begins.'

Hugh had no difficulty finding the courthouse: Nuremburg was buzzing with British and American troops. But the guards on duty were suspicious of this emaciated "British officer" dressed in a collection of Bavarian peasant clothes. It was useless his trying to explain that he was wearing a German workman's clothes because he was an escapee from a concentration camp: they refused to believe him.

'After nearly two bloody years?' one asked sarcastically. 'Them camps were all liberated and the Brits. in 'em repatriated in April '45 mate. Wocha bin doing in the last eighteen months? Fratting with the local German bints?'

''E ain't a British officer,' his companion interrupted, 'e's a bloody Nazi.' He jerked his head in the direction of the courthouse. 'E should be in there being tried with the rest of them bastards. Call the Sar' Major.' The sergeant-major put him in the guard house.

Hugh was furious. He had imagined that once he got to Nuremberg and contacted the British, he would immediately be repatriated. He had even dreamt of being reunited with Fleur within a few hours. Now he saw his dream slowly fading. He looked up. There was a small window: if he could push a chair under it he could perhaps escape and get to the convent. But what then? The nuns couldn't repatriate him, and he couldn't stay there indefinitely. He put his head in his hands. He had been afraid of the Germans, now it was his own people who had put him behind bars: and he almost gave way to despair. He heard a key turn in the lock, but he was too tired and dispirited to look up. He hadn't realised how little energy he had. A plate of food was brought in along with a steaming mug of bright orange coloured tea.

'Ere y'are chum,' a cheery private announced. 'Good old British bully beef and spuds.'

Hugh looked up and his eyes brightened: he had never thought the sight of bully beef could give him such pleasure.

'Eat up mate,' the soldier went on cheerily. 'May be yer last bloody chow. Them trials are over and most of yer chums are for the 'igh jump: perhaps you'll be joining 'the bastards to-morrow.' He grinned and Hugh heard the lock click as he closed the door.

He picked up the mug and gratefully drank his first cup of tea since his 'plane was shot down in May '44. Over two years before. He turned to his meal, but soon pushed it away, his emaciated body no longer allowed him to absorb much food. Lying down on the narrow bed he looked up at the ceiling. It was now dark, but a bright naked bulb shone mercilessly down on him. He closed his eyes, weary and despondent, then exhaustion overcame him. He dreamt of Fleur, but she was always just out of his reach, tantalisingly appearing and reappearing: turning round to laugh at him, the green lights in her beautiful almond eyes shining more brightly than ever. As a grey dawn seeped through the barred window he awoke unrefreshed.

The lock turned again in the door. A different soldier walked in with another steaming cup and a plate with thickly cut slices of bread plastered with butter and marmalade.

'When are you going to release me?' he asked.

'Release yer mate?' the soldier replied incredulously. 'Yer must be bloody joking. Eat up quick, they'll be coming for yer soon.'

Before he could enquire further the door had clicked shut. Hugh had barely had time to rub the rough towel round his face before two armed guards appeared. He picked up his few belongings and followed them. 'Where are you taking me?' he enquired wearily.

'Dunno chum. Probably for the 'igh jump along with the rest of yer lot.'

'But I tell you I'm a British officer,' he replied angrily.

They laughed. 'Oh yeah? Tell that to the sodding Marines! But I must say you speak our lingo bloody well.'

He was ushered into a bare office where a major was sitting behind a huge desk. He did not rise when Hugh entered, merely indicated a chair with a jerk of his head. 'So,' he said after a few minutes, without any great show of interest. 'You say you are a British officer.'

'I *am* a British officer,' Hugh replied firmly.

The major balanced a pencil between his two forefingers. 'Which regiment?'

'I was a pilot in the RAF.'

'I see. Name?'

'Hugh Cunningham.'

The major nodded to a corporal sitting at a desk in a corner. He got up and left the room.

'Rank?'

'The same as yours,' Hugh said steadily.

The major's lips tightened and his eyes narrowed. An angry flush tinted his cheekbones. Hugh realised that his provocative reply had done nothing to advance his cause, rather the reverse. But the major's scepticism as to his identity on top of all the other humiliations he had suffered at the hands of his compatriots had been the final straw.

'I was promoted from Flying Officer to Squadron Leader a few months before I was shot down,' he added.

'A mere *squadron leader*,' the major sneered. 'I'm surprised you didn't make yourself an Air Commodore, or even a bloody Air Vice-Marshal while you were at it.'

Hugh's lips closed in a tight line, but he refused to allow himself to be provoked further.'

'Number?'

The little reserve of strength Hugh possessed abruptly left him, and his mind went blank. He tried to concentrate, but his brain refused to function.

'I-m sorry, but..... I'm afraid I can't remember my number.'

The major looked at him contemptuously.'And you expect me to believe your story? It's bullshit"

Hugh's eyes narrowed, but he didn't reply.

'Where are your papers?' the major asked coldly.

'I don't *have* any papers,' Hugh said in exasperation. 'They were taken from me by the Gestapo. I was in a concentration camp, then escaped from the death march.......'

'So what have you been doing in the meantime? The bloody war's been over for eighteen months.'

Hugh told him his story. But the major was sceptical.

The corporal came back into the room and placed a folder in front of him.

'A Squadron Leader Hugh Cunningham......'

'I told you I was a Squadron Leader,' Hugh interrupted.

The major picked up the report, ignoring Hugh's interruption. 'The Squadron Leader's 'plane disappeared over France in May '44,' he read aloud, his eyes scanning the pages.

'It *did,'* Hugh,' stressed. 'I landed the 'plane and fell into a German trap.'

The major looked up. 'You *landed the 'plane?* he said scornfully. *'In enemy territory.* 'He raised a sardonic eyebrow. 'What was it, a bloody social visit?' He didn't appear to have heard about Special Operations. Hugh glanced at his impressive array of medal ribbons, but they were all "mickey mouse", none of any real worth. He concluded that the major must have spent the war pushing a pen in a government office and earned his rank because of his knowledge of German.

'And of course,' the major went on sarcastically, 'there are no witnesses, no-one to verify your cock and bull story. You were having a fucking joy trip all on your own I suppose.'

'My despatcher was shot by the Gestapo when they dragged him from the 'plane.'

'How very convenient,' the major mocked, 'and you of course were spared. What saved you, your beautiful blue eyes?' His lips curled contemptuously.'Nice try Herr?......' he ended scornfully.

'I'm not Herr *anything,*' Hugh shouted, as his two guards seized his arms and practically lifted him out of his chair. 'I'm.......' But they were dragging him towards the door. 'Where are they taking me *now?*' he asked desperately.

'To the cells. We shall investigate you further and if we find nothing against you you will be released to return to wherever you came from.' The major smiled maliciously. 'But I can assure you, it *won't* be England. *I'll* bloody well see to that.'

Once again, Hugh heard a door slam shut and a lock being turned as he was thrust into another bare cell, and he remembered the Sister's parting words.

'Once you get to Nuremburg you will be all right, there are plenty of your own people there.'

A wry smile flitted across his cracked lips. His "own people" were proving to be almost worse than the Germans had been. And in spite of himself, Hugh laughed.

Three weeks later he was told his description had not appeared on any of the "Wanted" lists. He was free to leave.

'To go where?' he enquired.

'That is your bloody problem', the major replied, shuffling his papers together to indicate that the interview was over.

'But if only I can get to England, 'Hugh said desperately, 'I can *prove* my identity.'

'Then I suggest you try,' the major said coldly, taking a pen and languidly writing. 'But don't expect any sodding help from *us.*'

It was early September before Fleur was able to tear herself away from the Riviera.

'A Monsieur Kristensen has telephoned several times,' Marthe announced when she arrived back in Paris. 'He's ringing again to-morrow.'

She and Arvind dined together the following evening at a small intimate restaurant in the Latin Quarter. The food was delicious.

'How do you know about all these wonderful places?' Fleur marvelled as they walked out into the magic of a late Summer evening.

Arvind laughed. 'Word of mouth. Danish food isn't exactly exotic, so whenever one of us is lucky enough to be appointed to Paris we pass on the gourmet addresses to our successor.' He looked down at her. 'I've still got a few up my sleeve. If you have time we can work through the list.'

Autumn seemed to go on forever that year. Winter was almost upon them when one evening dining at yet another one of Arvind's 'discoveries' he was unusually quiet. Fleur was surprised. He had always been so full of life and she couldn't help wondering whether she had said something to upset him. 'Arvind,' she ventured tentatively. 'Is something the matter?'

For a moment he kept his eyes fixed on his empty coffee cup. Then, raising them he reached across the table and took her hand. 'I've been recalled,' he said flatly. 'It was too good to last. I've *so* enjoyed being here with you, just the two of us. And now..... I have to leave for Copenhagen very soon.'

'But just a routine visit,' Fleur consoled. 'You'll soon be back.'

He shook his head. 'No,' he replied sadly. 'I've been appointed First Secretary at the Embassy in Washington, to take effect in the New Year.'

'But Arvind,' Fleur exclaimed, 'that's wonderful news.'

He smiled briefly. 'I know it is. A big promotion. But......' Looking up he squeezed her hand tightly in his. 'I'd much rather stay here with you.'

Fleur slowly withdrew her hand, embarrassed by his outburst.

'Fleur,' he said desperately. 'Don't you know I'm hopelessly in love with you? I realised it when I was in Bornholm in August and I couldn't wait to get back to tell you. I've been trying to tell you ever since, but you've always been so remote. I thought if I was patient you would end up seeing how I feel.' He shrugged. 'But now there's no more time.'

She looked down at her plate, and didn't know what to say. Her thoughts went back to that balmy day last February when she had watched young lovers crossing the Champs de Mars and longed to be one of them. Longed to be loved again. She had decided then to turn the page on the past. Could Arvind be the fulfilment of that vow? The answer to that longing? Her mind in a turmoil she raised her eyes. 'Arvind,' she stammered. 'I'm so sorry. I had no idea.'

'Fleur,' he pleaded. 'Do you think you could learn to love me?'

She looked intently at him. He had everything a woman could desire in a man. He was handsome, charming, amusing, kind. Many women would have jumped at the chance he was offering her, she had seen the way they flocked around him at the receptions they had attended during the Summer. What was holding her back?

'I'm very fond of you Arvind,' she said hesitantly. 'And I enjoy being with you. But is that enough? I'm not sure I *love* you.' She did not add: 'Not in the way I loved Hugh'.

His face lit up. He grasped her hand again and held it tightly in both of his. 'For me,' he said breathlessly, 'it's enough to start with. I know you've been terribly hurt and I understand how you must feel. But let me try to heal the wound. Marry me Fleur and we'll begin a new life together in Washington.'

Fleur's head was in a whirl. Events were taking over and submerging her. She felt as if she were trapped inside a snowball rolling uncontrollably downhill. 'Arvind,' she whispered, rising unsteadily from the table, 'I need to go home.'

Neither said a word as the taxi manoeuvred its way through the narrow streets and out onto the Esplanade des Invalides. When they reached the door of the flat Arvind took her in his arms. 'Do you think you can give me an answer before I leave?'

Fleur nodded.

He bent and gently kissed her lips. Then folding her more tightly in his arms he kissed her with a passion which lifted her off her feet, leaving her gasping and breathless. 'Darling, don't worry,' he whispered. 'I've got enough love for two.' Fitting her key in the lock, he silently put his fingers to his lips and blew a kiss as she disappeared into the flat.

The flat was in darkness. Fleur frowned. Her father didn't have any official engagements this evening, usually when that happened he was pleased to spend a quiet evening at home. Then she remembered that Claudine had arrived in Paris that morning after a brief visit to London. The two of them must have gone out for dinner. She sat down on the sofa facing the terrace, deep in thought. The street lights on the Champs de Mars reflected on the Eiffel Tower rising in the moonlight. It was all so beautiful. She was happy to be back in Paris, happy to act as her father's hostess, but she did not want to spend the rest of her life doing it. Especially since he was due for an ambassadorship and could be nominated anywhere.

She remembered the conversation she had had with her godmother when they were making the inventory for Marchmount, and a sly smiled flitted across her lips. Maybe this was a prophesy coming true. Her father and Claudine had been childhood friends. Her parents had been a rock of support and comfort for Claudine when George, Claudine's Scottish husband, had tragically drowned while sailing near their house in Boulouris. And since returning with Fleur from the Riviera in early September Claudine had stayed on in Paris, and seemed happy to take over Fleur's hostessing duties. Who better than Claudine to take her place? Feeling suddenly free to live her own life, she leant back on the cushions, her hands clasped behind her head, and her mind turned to Arvind. She heard her father's key in the lock and the click of the hall light.

'Alone in the dark!' he exclaimed when he and Claudine walked into the sitting room. He flicked on the light and the room sprang to life.

Fleur slowly rose from the sofa and walked towards him. 'Papa,' she said quietly. 'I don't know what to do.'

Her father frowned, then taking her arm led her back to the sofa. 'How can I help?' he asked gently, sitting down beside her.

'I'll leave you,' Claudine murmured, slipping from the room.

'No Claudine, come back,' Fleur called. 'I want your help too, you've been a mother to me ever since the war began.' She patted the empty place beside her on the sofa and after a slight hesitation, Claudine sat down. Fleur noticed her father and Claudine exchange glances. 'It's Arvind,' she stammered.

'His promotion?' her father queried.

Fleur stared at him in surprise. 'You *know* about it?'

'I probably knew before he did,' her father remarked drily. 'You seem to forget that I work at the Quai d'Orsay.'

'He's asked me to marry him,' Fleur whispered.

Claudine turned and hugged her. 'Darling, that's wonderful news.'

'I couldn't be happier for you,' her father said quietly. 'His parents were great friends of your mother and me, and Arvind is a splendid young man with a brilliant career ahead of him. I know he will be able to help you put the past behind you, and make you happy.'

Fleur said nothing.

'You did say "yes" I hope,' Claudine queried.

Fleur shook her head.

'It was such a shock'

'But my dear girl,' her father protested, 'anyone with half an eye could see that he's been madly in love with you for months.'

'I didn't realise,' Fleur answered lamely.

Claudine frowned and took her hand. 'Darling, the war has been over for nearly two years. It's almost three years since Hugh was reported missing: I'm afraid you're going to have to accept the fact that he is not coming back. Arvind is offering you the chance to do just that.' She paused, but Fleur didn't reply. 'Is it because of Hugh you did'nt say yes?' Fleur shrugged. 'I suppose so. His memory is still very vivid, hardly a day goes by without my thinking about him.' She smiled dreamily. 'Though the memories are now more sweet than painful.'

Claudine put an arm round her and held her close. 'A woman never forgets the man who made her a woman,' she said softly, 'but one can turn the page. It' a different love, but it can be just as beautiful.' She looked across at Hubert. 'Shall we tell her?'

'I think this might be the moment,' he smiled.

Fleur looked from one to the other enquiringly.

'Claudine has taken your place as my hostess these last few months while you've been hitting the high spots with Arvind,' her father said quietly. 'So we've decided to make it official.' He took his daughter's other hand. 'Claudine and I are going to be married.'

Fleur gasped, then burst into tears.

'Darling,' her father cried, drawing her to him. 'I'm so sorry, I never dreamt it would upset you ....' He hesitated. 'Perhaps we should have mentioned it before: we've been thinking about it for some time.' He looked helplessly at his daughter.

Fleur lifted her face to his, tears streaming down her cheeks. Her father took a handkerchief from his pocket and gently wiped them away.

'No Papa,' she sobbed, 'I'm not really *crying*, these are tears of *joy*. I'm so happy for you both. The two people I love most in the world are going to be my parents.'

A week later she gave Arvind his answer.

Hugh picked up his few belongings. The cell door slammed behind him and he walked out of the prison into the crowded Nuremberg street. British uniforms were everywhere, but no-one was interested in this emaciated "German" peasant. They were too busy discussing the multiple hangings of Nazi war criminals which had taken place that morning. He sank wearily onto a bench and tried to sleep, but it was bitterly cold and he almost regretted his prison cell.

When the short winter day ended and night fell, cold, hungry and utterly dispirited, all hope gone, he dragged himself to a nearby park and curled up in a sheltered spot behind a large bush. Long before daybreak, he reasoned, his frozen body would have been released from this torture. He would have passed into a long sleep where nothing could ever hurt him again.

'When do you leave?' Hubert de Rosny enquired, opening a bottle of champagne to celebrate the occasion.

'For Copenhagen?' Arvind queried. 'At the end of next week.' He put his arm round Fleur's waist and held her tight. 'I take up my new duties in Washington at the beginning of January.'

'And you intend to marry beforehand?'

'Before Christmas I hope,' Arvind replied.

'Then since you may not be here for Christmas this might be the moment for Claudine to announce *her* news,' Hubert said enigmatically.

Fleur frowned, wondering just how many more "shocks" she could absorb. In the past few weeks so many life changing events seemed to have been aimed at her from every angle.

'I went to London earlier this month to get rid of my flat,' Claudine announced.

'Oh Claudine, *no,*' Fleur protested. Kings Court had become her refuge since the tragic events of 1940. She couldn't bear to think it would no longer be there for her.

'Wait a minute,' Claudine chided. 'Hear me out and don't interrupt. When your father and I decided to get married, we felt I no longer needed King's Court. We've got Boulouris and an official residence wherever he's posted and we'll buy a small pied-à-terrre here in Paris. Why be encumbered with a flat in London as well? So, Fleur darling, I decided to give it to you for Christmas.

Fleur gasped.

'Claudine,' she stammered. You *can't* give me your flat, it's too much.'

'Too much to give my lovely new daughter?' Claudine teased. 'Anyway, it's too late. I went to London a couple of weeks ago to see my lawyer and get everything settled, but now all the papers will have to be changed.'

'Why?' Fleur demanded.

'Because my darling I've donated the flat and its contents to Mrs. Hugh Cunningham...... and by the time the contract's signed and sealed you'll have changed your name!'

Fleur couldn't sleep. The tumultuous events of the evening both excited and frightened her. They insisted on whirling round and round in her head making sleep impossible. She got up and wrote to Hugh's father.

They had met only a few times, but there had always been a special bond between them. She received a reply almost by return of post.

"My dear Fleur," Arthur Cunningham had written. "I cannot tell you how delighted I was to receive your letter and learn that you are to marry again. Of course I don't think you have forgotten or abandoned Hugh. Life must go on. Don't let regrets or Hugh's memory spoil the many happy years which I hope lie ahead for you both. Thank you for the happiness you gave my son during the short time you were together. May God be with you as you set out on this new venture in your life. Be assured that you will be very especially in my thoughts and prayers as you prepare for the years ahead and may they bring you great happiness. My love always Arthur."

Fleur slowly folded the letter and put it back in its envelope. As she did so, she caught sight of the beautiful diamond solitaire Arvind had given her on the evening they became engaged. It winked back at her from its black velvet nest, sparkling with a thousand changing lights. He had made no comment when she did not remove her wedding ring before he placed it on her finger: but now she slowly drew off Hugh's ring and opening a drawer of her dressing table placed it in its faded blue leather box. The memories came flooding back and she knew she would never love Arvind as she had loved Hugh. Not that heart-stopping choking feeling which had imprisoned her every time she felt Hugh's touch or even knew that he was near: and a tear spilled over and slid slowly down her cheek. Brushing it away, Fleur resolutely shut the drawer and slipped Arvind's ring onto her now naked finger. 'It's better this way,' she choked. 'I couldn't go through that terrible heartbreak again.' Hugh's father's letter seemed to have closed the last chapter on her brief married life.

—ooo-O-ooo—

CHAPTER SEVEN

The early morning British patrol in Nuremberg was leaving the wooded park when one of the soldiers noticed an arm sticking out from a bush.

'Hey Fred,' he called to his companion, 'take a look at this.'

They followed the arm to where an inert body lay curled.

Fred turned it over with his boot. 'Dead as a doornail,' he announced. 'Looks as if the poor bugger froze to death.' He bent and began to feel in his clothes for some means of identification.

Hugh slowly opened his eyes and stared up at him.

Fred staggered back. 'Blimey,' he exclaimed. The bastard's come back to life!

The two soldiers stared down at him in disbelief. Hugh tried to get up but his limbs were frozen and refused to obey.

'Ere Fred give us a 'and to get 'im up,' his companion said. 'There's an all night "caffe" just outside the gates. If we can get something 'ot inside 'im, 'e might just make it.' They slowly eased Hugh to his feet.

'You all right mate?' Fred enquired. 'Ere' ang onto us.'

They put an arm round each of their shoulders and half dragged Hugh towards the café's flickering light. It was a hole in the wall affair, but it was warm and there was a rickety chair beside the steel counter.

'A large bowl of black coffee,' Fred said to the proprietor, 'and put a bloody good dose of rum in it.' He pointed to Hugh. ''E nearly froze to death.'

The proprietor nodded. Steam rising from the boiler was beginning to warm Hugh's frozen limbs.

The soldier cupped the bowl of steaming coffee round his icy fingers. 'There, y'are mate,' he encouraged. 'Get that inside you and you'll feel better. Then you'd best get off 'ome pronto. Yer missus'll 'ave a word or two to say I'll bet, stayin' out all night.' He smiled and wagged a finger at Hugh. 'Let the poor bugger" sit 'ere till he's warmed right through,' he said sternly to the proprietor, tossing a few coins and a handfull of cigarettes onto the counter. 'That should more 'n settle your bill. We're on patrol,' he explained, turning to Hugh. 'Gotta get back to barracks. But you'll be all right now.'

Hugh nodded gratefully, wary of revealing that he was English.

The proprietor had not said a word. After the soldiers left he continued to silently polish glasses. Hugh felt uncomfortable, sensing his presence was unwelcome. As soon as he was able to stand he left.

A light went on in a bakery across the road. Hugh counted the few coins in his pocket and decided to buy a chunk of bread. He was famished. The woman behind the counter looked at him curiously when he limped in. He realised that she must think him a filthy unkept tramp, but her gaze was not hostile. When she handed him the bread, he pulled from his pocket the crumpled piece of paper with the address the Mother Superior had given him when he left the hospital, and asked her for directions.

She read it and looked up in surprise. 'You want St. Hildegard's Convent?' She pulled aside a beaded curtain. 'Kurt,' she called, 'you leaving soon for the convent?'

'In a cupla minutes,' he called back. Why?'

'There's a customer here wants to go there. You could give him a lift, couldn't you? She dropped the curtain and turned to Hugh. 'My husband delivers bread to the nuns every morning at seven,' she explained.

A short middle-aged man, his face streaked with flour came through the curtain. He looked Hugh up and down suspiciously then, prompted by a look from his wife, relented. 'Yeah, all right,' he agreed. He held aside the curtain letting in a sudden rush of hot air.

Hugh held out his few coins to the woman, but she smiled and closed his hand on them.

The baker climbed into the cabin of his van. With Hugh perched beside him they left the town and bumped along unmade roads before turning into wide open iron gates and making for the back of a large building. The smell of warm freshly baked bread rising from behind the cabin was tantalising. Jumping down, the baker slung the heavy basket of bread over his shoulder as if it were full of feathers. Hugh climbed down and followed him.

'Here we are,' the baker called cheerily when they entered the large kitchen, and without further explanation, he dumped the bread on the table and left.

Hugh was left standing by the door, not knowing what to say.

'Fetch Mother,' one of the nuns whispered.

A young nun rushed off and came back with a small middle-aged woman almost dwarfed by a large wimple.

'What can I do for you, my son?' she asked kindly.

Hugh hesitated. 'I'm English,' he finally blurted out. He handed her the piece of crumpled paper with the address.

The nun looked at it, and a huge smile spread across her face. 'Mother Birgit sent you?'

Hugh had no idea who Mother Birgit was, but assumed she must be the matronly nun who had nursed him back to life.

'We have been expecting you for almost a month,' the nun went on.

But Hugh was too tired to explain.

'You look exhausted, my son.... and hungry.' She gently eased him into a wooden rocking chair beside a roaring fire. 'Give him a large bowl of hot milk with plenty of sugar in it, and some of that fresh bread with butter.'

Hugh's eyes lit up at the prospect. He could scarcely believe his luck.

'And put two hot stone bottles in his bed. There,' the Mother Superior said kindly. 'Drink up the milk and help yourself to bread and butter, then Sister Clara will take you to your room. Sleep for as long as you wish. We can talk later.'

And with a swish of her voluminous skirts, she left the kitchen.

There was a light tap on the door and a young nun entered with a plate piled high with bread and honey and a bowl of steaming milk laced with coffee. Hugh realised that he must have slept for twenty four hours and made to rise.

'No stay there this morning,' the nun smiled, puffing the pillows behind him and easing him back into them. 'Mother says you are not to get up until you are fully rested.' She smiled again. Hugh noticed that her teeth were even and dazzlingly white.

'I fed you a little soup last night,' she went on, placing the tray on his knees. 'But you hardly noticed you were so sleepy.' She looked down at him. 'You still look very tired. Have your breakfast then go back to sleep. I'll come to see how you are before lunch.' And she glided off.

Hugh stayed at the convent for over two weeks.

'Are you *sure* you are fit enough to leave?' the Mother Superior asked sternly. 'There is no hurry and you may have a hard battle ahead of you.' She sighed. 'Everyone is suspicious of everyone else in Germany to-day. And with this relentless hunt for war criminals..... I'm not sure Berlin is the best place for you to try to establish your identity'

'I can only try,' Hugh shrugged. He had no intention of trusting his luck in Nuremberg again. All he wanted was to put as much distance as possible between himself and the town which had proved so hostile. Whatever Berlin had to offer, he reasoned, it couldn't be worse.

'At *least* let me order a taxi to take you to the station,' she pleaded. 'It's a good half hour's walk.'

Hugh smiled down at her. 'A walk on this lovely fresh morning is just what I need.'

She shook her head as she accompanied him to the door.

'I don't know how to thank you,' Hugh stammered. He grasped her hand, suddenly overcome by all the kindness he had received.

'May God be with you my son,' she said. And, as Mother Birgit had done, made the sign of the cross over him.

The nuns had taken away the filthy rags in which he had arrived and he was now wearing warmer garments and a British soldier's greatcoat, salvaged from he knew not where. They had also managed to provide stout boots and a woolly cap and gloves.

'Must look an incongruous sight,' he smiled to himself as he turned at the gate and waved goodbye.

It was already November, a crisp frosty morning. Hugh relished the idea of a short walk. Before he left the Mother Superior had given him precise directions to the station, but invigorated by the thought that he would soon be in England, lost in rosy dreams of being reunited with Fleur again, he must have missed a turning. Almost an hour later, still looking for the station, he found himself on a long stretch of country road, bordered by tall leafless trees. It started to snow. Hugh looked around, but the road was empty. Shrugging, he decided to carry on.

It was not long before he realised that his legs were not as strong as he had believed. They began to give way beneath him and he felt desperately tired. He sat down by the side of the road as the snow piled up around him. It would have been bliss to snuggle into it and sleep, but he steeled himself to resist the temptation. He had come so far: freedom was almost within reach.

'A car must pass this way sooner or later,' he told himself, 'I could try to beg a lift.'

But only a farm cart piled high with logs and a few workers on bicycles manoeuvred their way gingerly through the fresh snow. The wind dropped but the snow kept falling relentlessly.

The early winter dusk was creeping up when in the distance he heard the sound of a car's engine. Struggling to his feet from behind the shelter of the trees, he brushed himself down. Through the blinding snowflakes he glimpsed the outline of a car driving slowly towards him. It was large and black and as it drew nearer he saw a small British flag on the bonnet. He hesitated, dreading being thrown into prison again. But when it drew closer he noticed a woman bundled in a fur-lined leather coat wearing a WRAAF officers' cap sitting beside the driver. Stumbling into the road, he frantically waved his arms. The car swerved to avoid him then skidded to a stop and a British sergeant wound down the window.

'What the hell do you think you're doing,' he yelled. 'You almost sent us into the bloody ditch.'

Hugh clung to the window to prevent him from winding it up. The woman continued to look steadily in front of her. 'I'm British,' he shouted, leaning in and appealing to her. 'RAF. A former pilot, escaped from a concentration camp. I'm trying to make my way home.' She turned and gave him a long hard stare. 'Let him in Bill.'* Based on an actual happening. Between 1945-47 Vera Atkins, assistant to Colonel Buckmaster Head of SOE's "F" Section toured Germany in an Army car, with a military driver attending and giving evidence at war crimes trials, visiting concentration camps and interviewing survivors and camp staff in an effort to discover the fate of many "F" Section agents who had disappeared without trace. *

The sergeant, plainly sceptical, got out and opened the back door of the car. Hugh fell in. The car carefully slithered back on to the road and manoeuvred its way slowly through the fresh snow.

'When were you captured?' the woman asked, without turning round.

'May '44. Just before D-Day.

'And what 'plane were you flying?'

'A Lizzie,' he replied, inadvertently letting slip the affectionate name the pilots used for Lysanders. 'Er, Lysander,' he correctd himself. 'I went into France to pick up a wounded agent and two others from his network who were in hiding and fell into a Gestapo trap.'

The woman continued to gaze steadily ahead, but she appeared to relax. 'What squadron you were with?' she finally enquired cagily, without turning round.

He hesitated, uncertain how much he could divulge. 'The Special Duties Squadron,' he said at last.

'138 or 624?'

Suddenly the veil which had so recently shrouded Hugh's memory lifted and everything became clear.

'138,' he said eagerly, 'based at Tempsford,' not immediately questioning why this woman should be so knowlegeable. 'We flew SOE agents from Britain in and out of German occupied territory. 624 flew from North Africa.'

The woman turned round, and leant her chin on her arm lying along the back of her seat. 'I'm very happy to meet you,' she said softly. 'During the war I was assistant to the Head of SOE's 'F' Section.'

Hugh's face lit up. 'I thought I'd seen you before,' he said warmly. 'You sometimes accompanied departing agents to the airstrip at Tempsford, didn't you?'

She smiled broadly. 'Not *sometimes. Very often.*'

Hugh lay back against the seat and closed his eyes, an immense feeling of relief flooding through him: by pure chance and when he was almost at the point of giving up he had found someone who believed him. The car was picking up speed as the roads became clearer and to his dismay, Hugh saw that they were running back into Nuremberg. The car turned and entered the courtyard of a small inn on the edge of town, pulling up in front of a heavy oak door.

'Take the luggage and reserve a room for our friend,' the woman said to her driver. She turned to Hugh.

'We'll go into the bar and have a stiff drink before dinner. You may very well be able to help me.'

Hugh didn't see how he could, but he was grateful that at least *one* of his compatriots didn't take him for a Nazi spy.

'So you were at Dachau,' his new found friend queried when they had settled into comfortable armchairs after dinner. 'Do you remember any women agents there?

'There were some,' Hugh mused. 'At least four were executed. I remember dropping a young English girl with two Frenchmen just before I was captured. She was very beautiful; she spoke with a strong cockney accent.'

'Violette,' the woman said. 'She was executed at Ravensbruck.'

Hugh sighed, suddenly overwhelmed by all the pain he had witnessed.

'And what about Flossenburg?' she probed. 'You say you were there as well'

Hugh shuddered as the memories seeped back.

'It was *terrible,*' he stammered. 'An extermination camp. We were sent there to be annihilated, disappear without trace. They once took 150 prisoners at random and shot them on a patch of grass near the crematorium.' Hugh fell silent. She waited for him to gain control of his emotions. He took a gulp of whisky to steady himself.

'Do you remember seeing any of our agents at Flossenburg, any women?' she probed gently.

'I don't remember *seeing* any, 'Hugh replied. 'There was a woman guard, Gertrud something or other, who was even more brutal than the men, so I suppose there may have been one or two women.' He frowned thoughtfully 'There were also fifteen men that I heard of. I think they were SOE. They were kept in a special cell block away from our huts so I never saw them. I got the news from my Danish friend.' His face hardened. 'Three of them were shot. But one afternoon, shortly before we left on the death march, the other twelve were flogged, then hung, three at a time.' Hugh's face was now like stone. 'Those guards weren't human beings,' he grated. He looked across at her, his blue eyes dark with pain. 'Can you believe it, they seemed to *enjoy* what they were doing!'

She reached across and held his hand. 'I can well believe it,' she murmured. 'For the past two years I've been investigating what happened to our missing agents, especially the women. Some of what I've been told doesn't even bear thinking about.' She gripped his hand tightly. 'I doubt whether people will believe the stories I've unearthed.'

In the ensuing silence, a clock in the hall struck three.

'Gracious,' she said, rising to her feet and draining the last of her whisky. 'We'd better get some sleep. I'm on my way to Hamburg to-morrow to attend a war crimes trial there; I told Bill to be ready to leave in the morning by eight o'clock.' She smiled apologetically. 'I wish I could vouch for you and hand you over to the British authorities for immediate repatriation, but I'm afraid I no longer carry any weight. Most of the SOE documents were destroyed a few months after the war ended and no-one wants to know.' She sighed. 'As far as the hierarchy are concerned, it's as if we never existed. In the light of what you have already gone through any intervention by me might be counter productive and you'd find yourself back behind bars again.' She frowned thoughtfully. 'You say you have a Danish friend from Flossenburg who could vouch for you.'

'If he ever made it back.'

'Let's assume he did. Come as far as Hamburg with me. I could put you on a train there which will get you to the Danish border.' She frowned thoughtfully and reaching for her briefcase took out a map. 'You have no papers and with this witchhunt for escaping Nazis it would be wisest to get off at Schleswig, the stop before the border. I'll give you a note to a safe house. The people there will get you over the border and onto a train for Copenhagen.' She folded the map and replaced it in her briefcase. 'Then it's up to you. The Danish police are much more relaxed and helpful: they should be able to locate your friend for you.'

'I'm afraid I haven't been of much help to you,' Hugh said apologetically.

'On the contrary,' she smiled, you've been an enormous help. There are very few survivors from Flossenburg so what you have told me is invaluable. If you can bear to talk about it again once you're back, apart from the staff at HQ, the historians will flock around you.' She paused and her face softened. 'Or perhaps you just want to forget'

Hugh gave her a strange look. 'Forget?' he said softly. '*Forget?* He took a deep breath as if to steady himself. 'I left Flossenburg vowing never to return, 'he said hoarsely. 'But.... I don't think Flossenburg will ever leave me. It's a wound that will never heal.' He smiled sadly. 'It was only the thought of Fleur, my wife, and the longing to be with her again that gave me the strength to keep going.' He thought he detected tears in her eyes. 'I-I don 't know how to thank you for making that possible' he blurted out.

She smiled, and handed him her card. 'Invite me to dinner when we're both back in London. I'd love to meet your wife.'

Hugh leant back in the compartment of the Danish train. In a few hours he would be in Copenhagen, and he remembered his fervent prayer when he went through the gates at Dachau. 'God answered it,' he breathed, 'He's allowing me to see Fleur again. Thank you, thank you Lord.' Almost without realising it he had prayed once again to the God he wasn't even sure existed. 'It's because of you I'm here my darling, 'he whispered, as if Fleur were there beside him. 'If I hadn't had you to come back to, I'd have given up long ago.'

With luck he could be home for Christmas: their first Christmas. Perhaps next Christmas he and Fleur would have the baby she had begged him for the last time they were together, and which he had denied her. His heart leapt at the thought and he almost choked with happiness. 'Fleur, he whispered.' Oh Fleur, my darling darling Fleur, I love you so much.' Hugh's head fell forward on his chest and, as the flat bleak winter countryside rumbled monotonously by, he slept. The dreamless sleep of a happy man.

'Claudine,' Fleur protested when, on the day before her wedding, her stepmother presented her with a magnificent fur coat and an elegant toque to match. 'It's *too much!*'You're *far* too generous.'

'Nonsense,' Claudine laughed. 'I always longed for a daughter. Now I've got one I intend to spoil her. Anyway you'll need it, Washington can be very cold in the Winter and Copenhagen even colder.'

Fleur held the coat against her cheek and nuzzled her face into its soft fur. Her eyes were shining, the green lights dancing, the pain in them replaced by a dazzling joy. To-morrow morning her father would lead her down the aisle of the British Embassy church to start a new life.

—ooo-O-ooo—

CHAPTER EIGHT

By the time the train arrived in Copenhagen, the short winter day had ended. Brilliant lights and scurrying Christmas shoppers greeted Hugh when he walked out of the station. Standing on the pavement wondering which direction to take a passerby smiled and addressed him in Danish.

Hugh shrugged helplessly. 'I'm English,'

'Ah,' the man replied. 'Then can I help you?'

'I'm looking for the Police Station.'

The man took his arm and zigzagging across the crowded street led him to a corner and pointed to a large building. Entering the Police Station, Hugh approached the counter. Standing behind it two uniformed policemen were drinking coffee. The pungent aroma teased Hugh's taste buds unbearably and he realised that he was famished. The two men looked at him strangely. He knew he must look a sorry sight in his collection of salvaged clothing, by now none too clean. 'I'm English, he blurted out. 'I've just arrived from Germany and I'm looking for a friend who lives in Helsingfors.'

The second policeman put down his cup. 'I suggest you telephone him.'

'I have no Danish money,' Hugh answered lamely, adding desperately as he put his hand in his pocket and spread out the few German coins he had left. 'In fact, I'm destitute. I'm trying to get back to England and I hope my friend might help me.'

'Why don't you go to your Consulate?' one of the men suggested. He glanced at his watch. 'Four o'clock. It's probably closed by now. But they'll be open on Monday morning.'

'Without money, where do I go in the meantime?' Hugh asked bitterly.

'There's a Salvation Army hostel down the road.'

Hugh felt his knees beginning to buckle beneath him. He was tired. He had come so far and now to be balked at the last hurdle. He gripped the counter in desperation. 'Please, *please,*' he pleaded. 'If you would just try to locate my friend for me....... I promise I won't bother you further.'

The two policemen looked at each other. There followed a rapid discussion in Danish.

They wavered and Hugh took the plunge. 'His name's Knud Svensen,' he said desperately. 'And he *did* live in Helsingfors.'

'Knud *Svensen,*' one them them ejaculated looking again at Hugh's weird appearance. 'Not *the* Knud Svensen.'

'Perhaps,' Hugh answered desperately, clutching at any straw, wondering who *the* Knud Svensen could be.

'Mr. Svensen is one of our most respected politicians,' the policeman went on. 'A *war* hero. He escaped from a death camp.'

'I know,' Hugh answered wearily. 'I escaped with him.'

Abruptly their attitude towards him changed. 'Mr. Svensen *senior* lives in Helsingfors,' the policeman said guardedly, 'but since he was elected Mr. *Knud* Svensen's been living in Roskilde.'

'I don't know where he lives *now,* 'Hugh said testily, 'but could you please get hold of him. Tell him Hugh Cunningham's asking for him'

Another discussion in Danish followed. One of the policemen went into a room marked "Privat". 'He may be still in the Parliament building,' he said coming back into the entrance 'We'll try there first.' He came round the counter and pulled forward a chair. 'Please take a seat sir. Would you like a cup of coffee?'

I'd *love* one,' Hugh replied, gratefully sinking into the chair.

'Mr. Svensen's secretary is trying to locate him,' his colleague said, putting his hand over the receiver. 'He has already left the office for his home. Ah, here he is.'

Hugh heard his name mentioned followed by an explosion of words.

The policeman put down the phone and beamed at Hugh. 'Mr. Svensen is on his way here sir. Would you like another cup of coffee?'

Hugh beamed back and held out his empty cup.

The door marked "Privat" opened and a man whom Hugh took to be the Police Chief came out.'Do come and wait in my office,' he invited. 'Mr. Svensen won't be long.'

'Thank you,' Hugh smiled, accepting his second cup of coffee. 'But I'm very happy here. Your officers are treating me royally.'

Hugh had hardly time to put down his empty cup before the door to the Police Station flew open, and Knud burst in. Not the Knud he remembered, the ragged scarecrow with the shaven head and sunken eyes, but a prosperous well built man, with a thatch of dark blond hair.

'*Hugh,*' he cried, throwing wide his arms. With a bound he was by his side, enveloping him in a bear-like hug. 'Hugh, you old bastard, I can't *believe* it. I'd almost given up hope of ever seeing you again.' He held him at arm's length and gazed at him. Hugh realised that his appearance must have been a shock. But Knud :ade no comment. 'When did you arrive?' he enquired.

'About an hour ago.'

'And you're not booked in anywhere?'

Hugh shook his head.

'Good. I told my secretary to ring Helga and tell her I'm bringing you home with me.' He picked up Hugh's pitiful belongings and put an arm round his shoulders. 'We've a lot of catching up to do.'

A uniformed chauffeur opened the door of a shining black limousine when they walked out of the Police Station into the frosty December evening. Knud ushered Hugh inside and sat down beside him.

'This is very grand,' Hugh remarked as the car slid away from the pavement.

Knud laughed. 'One of the perks of being a government minister.'

'You're a *minister,*' Hugh queried.

'Only a very junior one,'Knud smiled, offering Hugh a cigarette 'But it does have its advantages.' He leant comfortably back against the cushions, inhaling deeply.'I was in politics when war broke out so when I got back I had several "brownie points" in my favour.' He gave a sardonic laugh. 'The only good thing which came out of my visit to that hell-hole Flossenburg was that it shot me into the limelight when I returned. There weren't too many Danes who had escaped from that bloody "holiday camp"'.

'When did you get back?' Hugh enquired.

'Soon after the war ended,' Knud replied. 'The old priest passed me from safe house to safe house till I met up with the Americans. They repatriated me very quickly.' He stubbed out his cigarette and turned to Hugh. 'And you my friend? he asked gently. 'It doesn't look as if you had the same luck.'

'No,' Hugh said quietly. He sighed. 'If it hadn't been the thought of seeing my wife again I think I'd have given up.'

Knud put his hand over Hugh's. In the glare of the street lights, he noticed the dark shadows under Hugh's eyes: the lines of fatigue on his face. 'You're exhausted,' he said sympathetically. 'We'll talk about it to-morrow, after you've had a good night's sleep.'

They were running along the banks of a canal bordered by tall elegant houses, the lights from their uncurtained windows reflecting in the water. The dark shadow of a large church loomed into view.

'Roskilde Cathedral,' Knud explained. 'Our house is just behind.'

Almost before the car drew up a door was flung open. Silhouetted against the brightly lit interior was a young woman with shoulder length blonde hair. A plump baby blinked sleepily in her arms and a small girl peeped out from behind her skirt. Seeing Knud descend from the car, she let out a shriek of delight and ran to meet him, clasping his knees in a delighted embrace.

Knud laughed and swung her into his arms. '*This* is what I found waiting for me when I returned,' he explained. 'I had no idea Helga was pregnant when I left.'

'Well, you certainly can't deny paternity, 'Hugh remarked. 'She's the image of you.'

'That's what everyone says,' Knud answered proudly. 'Have a good weekend Bengt,' he called to the chauffeur. 'Usual time Monday morning.'

The chauffeur touched his cap and glided away.

Untwining his daughter's arms from around his neck and grasping her hand he bent to kiss the smiling woman in the doorway. Then took the sleepy baby and held him aloft. The baby gurgled with delight. 'And *this,*'Knud said proudly, 'is my son, Björn.'

Helga gave Hugh a beaming smile, and taking his arm led him into the house. 'You're very welcome,' she said warmly. 'Knud has talked so much about you. He often wondered what happened after he left you.' She opened a door leading to a cosy sitting room. 'I think he felt guilty about abandoning you,' she confided.

Hugh began to protest. But she cut him short.

'You're alive and you're here, 'she smiled. 'Now for Knud that nightmare is in the past.' She took the baby from her husband's arms and called to her daughter.'I'll leave you two together,' she smiled. She left the room cradling the baby, and Hugh's exhausted brain went into overdrive.

In Helga's place he saw Fleur. Perhaps next year...... a little voice inside him whispered.

And his heart leapt with joy.

'My parents are coming to dinner this evening to meet you,' Knud said on the Sunday morning. 'Dad was a politician and he knows everyone, I'm sure he'll be able to help us get you back to England. But in any case first thing on Monday morning we'll go to the Embassy, see the Air Attaché and go on from there.'

By Monday morning when Bengt arrived with the car, Hugh was feeling rested and stronger and much more hopeful. But his repatriation didn't prove as simple as Knud had predicted. Although not as suspicious as the British authorities in Germany, the Embassy didn't immediately accept his story. It took the combined influence of Knud and his father and endless signals between the Air Ministry in London and the British Embassy in Copenhagen before it was finally proved that Hugh had not been killed when his plane was shot down. That he was who he said he was, and his incredible story was true. Without Knud he doubted whether he would have ever got home.

It was almost Christmas before everything was finally settled. With smiles and apologies, the Air Attaché told him that his Squadron Leader's uniform had arrived. His papers were now in order, and a first class passage had been booked on the train to Esbjerg to connect with the sailing to Harwich on December 22nd. He would arrive in London on the morning of the 23rd and be met by an official from the Air Ministry.

'How can I ever thank you,' he choked, during the celebration dinner at the Ambassador's restaurant in Copenhagen which Knud organised on the eve of his departure.

'You've thanked us enough by staying alive,' Helga said softly. 'If you'd not survived I don't think Knud would ever have got over it.'

'Come back and see us with Fleur,' Knud smiled. 'And, 'he added jovially, breaking the emotional tension hovering between them. 'Have a daughter quickly and we'll marry her off to Björn.'

Liverpool Street Station was dreary, dirty and crowded when Hugh arrived in London that foggy December morning, but as he stepped off the train he thought it was the most beautiful place he had ever seen. It was so long since he had heard English voices all around him, stood on English soil, known he was home.

By the time he had been endlessly interviewed at the Air Ministry, signed innumerable documents, been whisked from government department to government department, received hearty congratulations and pats on the back accompanied by cries of "good show old boy" the day was well advanced. With his bank account richer by almost three years uncollected salary he decided to grab a sandwich, surprise Fleur at the BBC and take her out to a slap-up celebration dinner. At the thought his tiredness vanished and a feeling of exhilaration swept through him.

When he entered the lift at Bush House and pushed the button for the fourth floor his mouth was dry, his hands moist with perspiration. The frantic activity which had always greeted him when he arrived in the French Section had disappeared: everything now seemed organised and sedate. Several people he didn't recognise walked in and out of offices. The door of the News Room opened and a couple with a sheaf of papers in their hands emerged.

'Excuse me, 'he said diffidently, addressing the woman. 'But is Fleur Cunnningham on duty to-day?'

The woman stopped and frowned. 'I think you've made a mistake,' she replied kindly. 'This is the *French* Section. You must want the English News Room on the second floor.'

'No,' Hugh said desperately. 'Fleur worked in the French Section during the war.'

The man poked his head back round the News Room door. 'Anyone know Fleur Cunningham?' he enquired.

Hugh glanced over the man's shoulder into the familiar room. A sea of unknown faces looked up. 'She worked with Julian Fourcade and Jean-Pierre Lacroix......' he began.

'Oh, the *old* crowd,' a girl interrupted, rising from behind her typewriter. 'No they've nearly all gone. Jean-Pierre and several of the men left immediately after D-Day and followed the Army as war correspondents.'

'And the others?' Hugh asked desperately.

'I wouldn't know. I've only been here a year. Most of us joined after the war. The people you mention are only names to me.'

'Is Edward Adams still News Editor?'

'Edward? He left last May. Retired and went back to Ireland.'

'Why don't you come back this evening?' one of the men suggested, winding a wadge of papers into his typewriter. The Night Team might be able to help you. Pratinette's on duty and I think she was here for most of the war.'

Hugh realised that they were busy and he was in the way. 'Thank you, 'he said gratefully. 'Thank you so much. I'll do that.'

As he walked dejectedly down the steps of Bush House and into Aldwych, he realised that it wasn't going to be as easy as he had imagined to find his wife.

'How naive can you be,' he said sardonically. 'You've been missing for over two years, did you imagine she'd be lying sobbing on the sofa waiting for her hero to return?'

Hailing a taxi a terrible thought hit him, sending an icy shiver down his spine.

Officially he was "missing" But, after two and a half years could Fleur have given up hope of ever seeing him again and remade her life?

Dread paralysing his mind, he stumbled into the cab and stammered the address.

—ooo-O-ooo—

Chapter Nine

O n that frosty Christmas Eve morning when Fleur entered the old stone Victorian church she understood why Claudine had insisted on such elaborate preparations.

She had expected a quiet wedding, just the two families. But as she walked slowly down the aisle clinging to her father's arm, it seemed to her that the entire Diplomatic Corps, liberally sprinkled with old friends from her BBC days, were standing there to greet her. A ripple of amusement trickled through them when Felix, her little godson, escaped from his mother's grasp and ran to her, lifting his face for a kiss. Only to be grabbed back by a heavily pregnant Kristina and firmly anchored in Julien's arms.

Claudine had arranged for a reception after the ceremony at the Crillon, a short walk from the British Embassy church. But the Danish Ambassador insisted on the bridal couple being driven in his official car.

Fleur was in a daze. Everything seemed unreal. Her tall handsome husband was standing at her side, his ring was on her finger, her parents and his were with them, greeting the guests, smiling happily. Everyone seemed to be kissing her hand or her cheek, murmuring good wishes before wandering towards the magnificent buffet.

The happy couple cut the wedding cake, an enormous pyramid of chocolate éclairs held together with whipped cream, then amidst a shower of rice and rose petals, kisses and waving handkerchiefs Arvind led his bride to the Ambassadorial car. It snaked its way through the crowd of curious onlookers shouting 'Vive la mariée' which had gathered outside the hotel entrance and drove to the Gare St. Lazare just in time for the afternoon boat train. Climbing into their compartment, Fleur sank onto the seat and closed her eyes, happy but utterly drained. Arvind, coping with the porter pushing a trolley toppling with their mountain of luggage, jumped in just as the train began to draw away from the platform.

'Don't you want a last glimpse of Paris?' he asked. 'It may be some time before you see it again.'

Fleur shook her head without opening her eyes. She was almost asleep.

Her husband stood by the window in the corridor as the train gathered speed and the roofs of Paris flashed past. Entering the compartment and quietly closing the door, he looked tenderly down at his wife, now sleeping peacefully. Taking her in his arms he cradled her head against his shoulder. When she awoke the train was slowing down and running into the docks at le Havre where the massive bulk of the liner "Ile de France" was waiting to carry them across the Atlantic.

The quay was crammed with wellwishers, a band, and porters pushing trolleys piled high with trunks towards the liner. Their stateroom when they entered was filled with flowers, cards, good wishes and telegrams of congratulations. As she read them Fleur's eyes filled with tears. She was overwhelmed by the love these tokens showed. Some from people she had never met: members of Arvind's family in Denmark and his mother's family in Norway, all regretting not being able to attend the wedding, but welcoming her into their midst and wishing them every happiness.

A siren sounded. Raucous voices rose up from the quayside, the grinding sound of heavy chains being lifted filtered through to them, and the band began to play. Arvind held out her coat. 'We're moving off,' he announced, draping it around her shoulders. 'Let's go on deck and watch the departure. It's always exciting, no matter *how* many times one's seen it.'

When they returned to their cabin there was a note from the captain requesting they dine at his table that evening. It was to be a special Christmas Eve dinner followed by an entertainment and dancing, or a watchnight service on deck for those who wished to attend. All Fleur wished to do was crawl into the magnificent Queensize bed and sleep. The tension from the last few hectic weeks had left her drained. She sighed: this was supposed to be their honeymoon, but it seemed that her diplomatic life with Arvind had already begun.

Her husband put down the invitation and sighed in his turn. 'It says here cocktails at six thirty. We don't even have time for a ten minute snooze.' He gave a wry smile. 'Makes you wish we'd travelled steerage, doesn't it?'

The festivities wore on and on and it was impossible to slip away. When they finally returned to their cabin it was almost three o'clock. Fleur white with fatigue, flopped into an armchair and kicked off her shoes. 'I'm too tired even to have a shower,' she yawned. 'I wish I were a dog and could just curl up in my clothes.' She wearily rose from the chair and stumbled towards the bathroom.

When Arvind climbed into bed beside her, her eyes were closed. 'Darling,' she murmured. 'I'm sorry, but...... I'm exhausted.'

He turned on his side and held her close. His hands ran caressingly up and down her back then cupped her firm young breasts, but there was no answering response. No tightening of the warm flesh, no sudden pointing of her nipples. He bent and kissed them, his hands roving lovingly over her limp body.

Through clouds of sleep Fleur remembered her wedding night with Hugh. How eagerly she had waited for his touch, and she felt guilty that this time she was unable to respond. 'Arvind,' she whispered brokenly. 'Our wedding night..... 'But her words were slurred, sleep already overpowering her.

'It's all right,' he said softly. 'I have longed for this moment, wanted you so much during these past months that sometimes my whole body ached with desire' He gently kissed her lips, his hands still stroking her slim body. 'I've waited so long I can wait a few more hours. I want our wedding night to be a night we shall never forget, not a botched fumbling because we neither of us have the strength to enjoy it. You sleep, my darling, we have our whole lives before us to love each other.'

'Mrs. Scott-Forsythe, sir?' the porter said when Hugh entered the hall in King's Court, hoping to find Claudine. 'She was here a few days ago to settle the final details for the sale of the flat.'

'The *sale!*' Hugh spluttered.

'Yes sir, Mrs Scott-Forsythe remarried. A French gentleman. She's gone to live over there.'

'Do you have her address?' Hugh asked, astounded.

'I'm afraid I don't, sir. I understand her lawyer was settling all her affairs. Charlie, the Head Porter might have it, but he's off duty now till Boxing Day, you've missed him by half an hour.'

'Is Sydney around?'

'Sydney, sir? No, Sydney and Albert retired as soon as we young ones came back from the war.'

'Perhaps I could speak to the new tenant. She might be able to give me some information.'

'Mrs. Kristensen? She's not here sir. A Scandinavian lady, I believe. I've never met her myself, but Charlie told me she'll just be using the flat as a pied-à-terre as they say in France. She lives in America.'

Hugh walked dejectedly down the steps and turned into the King's Road. Bright lights and Christmas decorations glimmered through the gathering mist, and he didn't know what to do. Thrusting his hands deep into his pockets he headed into the scurrying crowd.

He had no idea how long he had been walking or even where he intended to go. He glanced at his watch. It was past eight o'clock. Hailing a taxi, he decided to book in at the Waldorf and return to the BBC that night: but at the bottom of the Strand, he suddenly leant forward and tapping at the window told the driver to stop. He would try Finch's Bar opposite the back entrance to Bush House.

The French Section staff used to retire there for drinks between bulletins, it was almost an extension of the World Service canteen. Perhaps there were some 'left-overs' from the midday shift having a final pint before going home who could help him. But the bar was almost deserted. A lone Christmas tree winked its lights forlornly at a few unknown faces lolling at the bar. Hugh walked out and crossing the Bush House courtyard entered the Waldorf.

Couples in evening dress were chatting in the foyer. The sound of an orchestra drifted from the dining room.

A young man hurried in behind him and went towards an elderly lady in evening dress and a white fur cape talking earnestly to the hall porter. He took her arm and steered her towards the door.

'I'm sorry sir,' the desk clerk said apologetically. 'I'm afraid we're fully booked for the next three nights.'

'Nothing at all?' Hugh asked wearily.

The clerk sadly shook his head.

Hugh sighed and turned away. As he did so, the head porter glanced in his direction. 'I remember you sir,' he said warmly, noting the DFC below his wings. 'You used to come in with the French group from the BBC.'

Hugh smiled, too weary to reply.

'We haven't seen you for some time.' He raised his eyebrows enquiringly.

'I was shot down, 'Hugh replied flatly. 'Taken prisoner.' Suddenly a glimmer of hope pierced the gloom; 'Do my French friends still come for breakfast?'

'Oh no sir,' the head porter replied, they all went back home as soon as the war ended.' He pursed his lips. '*Quite* a different crowd now.' He looked enquiringly across the counter. 'Were you wanting a table for dinner sir?'

Hugh shook his head. 'No, a bed. But apparently there isn't one.' He bent to pick up his bag.

'Just a minute sir,' the porter went on. 'I'm sure we can manage *something.*'

'There's not a single room available, Mr. Tomkins,' the clerk protested.

The head porter took the book and ran his finger down the pages.

'A broom cupboard will do,' Hugh put in hopefully. 'As long as there's a bed in it.'

The head porter smiled. 'I think we can do better than that sir. I'm afraid it won't be up to your usual standard. It's under the eaves, and *very* small......' He turned to the clerk. 'Have the Squadron Leader's bag taken up to his room. Will you dine downstairs sir or would you prefer room service?'

'Room service please,' Hugh said gratefully. 'And thank you. Thank you so much.'

'It's the least we can do for one who did *so much* for us,' the head porter replied.

Hugh pushed away the tray and leant back on the bed. He was dropping with fatigue, but he was determined to return to Bush House later when the Night Team would be on duty. In spite of himself he drifted off; the midnight chimes from St. Bride's church woke him. Leaping off the bed and grabbing his cap, he ran across the road and up to the Fourth Floor of Bush House. But unfortunately Pratinette on whom he had pinned a slight hope could not help him.

'I *do* remember her,' she frowned thoughtfully. 'But we never actually *worked* together. She left the Section soon after the war ended. I've no idea where she went. Perhaps back to Paris with the others?' she added hopefully.

Hugh didn't like to point out that Fleur hadn't come from Paris in the first place. He thanked her and walked slowly out of the almost deserted building and across the road back to the Waldorf. But in spite of his fatigue, sleep eluded him. He tossed and turned, wondering where he could find Fleur. The Air Ministry had confirmed that his wife's allowance was still paid regularly into her bank in Knightsbridge, so she was alive. But where?

In his misery his thoughts became maudlin. His mind drifted back to the day he had met Fleur, here in this very hotel. To their wedding.... Suddenly a bright light was switched on, and the darkness clouding his brain dissipated. Why hadn't he thought of it before? If anyone knew of Fleur's whereabouts it would be her grandmother. Leaping out of bed, he grabbed the telephone and asked for Directory Enquiries.

'I'm sorry sir,' the operator came back after a few minutes, 'but there's no-one of that name at the address you've given.'

'Are you *sure?* Hugh frowned.

'Yes sir,' she replied politely. 'There are very few telephones in Fulmer.'

'Then could you try Gerrards Cross and Windsor?' he pleaded. 'It's *very* important.'

The operator sighed. A few minutes later she got back to him. 'Nothing I'm afraid sir: I imagine your correspondent is off-listed.'

Hugh was awakened by the whirr of a vacuum cleaner. In spite of his misery, he had finally managed to fall into a restless sleep. Squinting at his watch, he saw that it was almost nine o'clock. He decided to skip breakfast and leave as quickly as possible. The night had cleared his mind: he would go to Fulmer and find out for himself. A taxi was pulling up to the entrance to Gerrards Cross Station when Hugh arrived. Hailing it he gave the address. 'Marchmount is just before you enter Fulmer village,' he explained. 'A stone's throw from the church. Lady Percy's place.'

'It *was* Lady Percy's,' the chauffeur replied. 'Been in the family for generations.'

'What do you mean *was?*' Hugh frowned, and leant forward.

The driver slowed down. 'How long since you been to Fulmer sir?'

Hugh shrugged. 'Two or three years.'

'Then perhaps you hadn't heard? Lady Percy died a few months before the war ended. January '45 I think it was.'

Hugh fell back on his seat and closed his eyes.

The driver pulled into the side of the road. 'You still want to go sir?' he enquired.

For a moment Hugh didn't reply. His last hope gone. 'What happened to the house?' he asked weakly, a feeble hope returning. Fleur was very attached to Marchmount, perhaps she was living there.

'Lady Percy left it to her granddaughter. A Mrs. Mrs....' The driver tapped his teeth with his finger nail, his brow rutted in thought.

'Cunningham?' Hugh interrupted eagerly.

'That's right sir,' the driver replied, brightening as his memory cleared. 'But she sold it soon after the war. After all why would a nice young lady like her want to live all alone in that great big house? Retired Indian Army Colonel and his wife bought it; very nice people. We live in Fulmer and my wife "does" for them. With this blasted petrol rationing still going on, they often call on me.'

'I don't suppose you have any idea where Mrs. Cunningham lives now?' Hugh asked.

'Fraid I don't sir.' They sat in silence for a few minutes. 'You still want me to take you sir?' the driver asked diffidently.

'Yes please. You never know, the new owners might be able to help me.'

When the taxi swept through the wide-open gates and up the drive Hugh leant forward eagerly waiting for the turn which would bring them round to the front of the old stone house. Nothing appeared to have changed. An elderly lady, sitting in the bay window embroidering looked up as the car stopped at the front door.

'Do you want me to wait sir?' the driver asked when Hugh leapt out.

'Yes please,' he answered. I don't think I'll be long.'

The lady herself opened the door almost before he had time to ring. He was disappointed, he had hoped to see the familiar face of either Myrtle or Ivy, explanations would have been easier. She smiled and raised here eyebrows enquiringly.

'I'm Hugh Cunningham,' he stammered. 'I'm trying to find my wife. I believe you bought the house from her.'

The lady frowned. 'You had better come in,' she said. 'I understood Mrs. Cunningham to be a widow.'

She ushered him into the drawing room. 'She never said so in so many words,' she went on hurriedly seeing the anguished expression on Hugh's face. 'Merely that her husband was a pilot who had been shot down and was missing, believed killed.'

'I wasn't killed,' Hugh said miserably, 'I was taken prisoner. I've just got back to England, and no-one seems to know where my wife is now.' He paused to gain control of his voice. 'I wondered if she left you a forwarding address,' he ended hopefully.

'How I wish I could help you,' the lady said sympathetically. 'But her bank dealt with everything. There *was* the odd letter which came here and we forwarded it to an address in Chelsea Mrs Cunningham left with us. I think I still have it.' She rose and walked towards a small desk.

'Please don't bother, 'Hugh said, rising in his turn. 'It would be King's Court.....'

'That's it, 'the lady interrrupted eagerly. Care of a Mrs.....'

'Scott-Forsythe, Fleur's godmother.' Hugh smiled sadly. 'It was the first place I went to when I arrived. But that's been sold too.' He held out his hand. 'Thank you so much,' he ended. 'You've been very kind. I'm sorry to have bothered you.'

She took his hand in both of hers, her eyes full of compassion.'I only wish I could have been of more help,' she said gently, walking with him to the door. That dreadful war, so many broken lives. I know, I lost my younger son, a pilot like you. Fortunately he wasn't married.' She stood on the step and waved until the taxi rounded the bend and disappeared.

'Where to now sir?' the driver asked as they reached the gates.

Hugh leant back wearily against the leather cushions. 'The station please.'

'Any luck sir?' the driver enquired as they bowled along the lanes between the bare hedgerows.

'Fraid not,' Hugh replied. 'But, you were right, she's a very nice lady.'

It was dark when Hugh arrived back in London. Marylebone Station was heaving with passengers scrambling to cram into the waiting trains, many carrying suitcases and gaily wrapped parcels. There was a festive air everywhere. He almost collided with a man carrying a Christmas tree under his arm. A child dressed as an angel waving three gaily coloured balloons danced from his free hand.

'Happy Christmas,' she sang as he passed.

Suddenly Hugh felt a stab of unbearable pain. It was Christmas Eve. What hopes he had had for this their first Christmas together. How he had dreamed of it, longed for it, lived it in his mind over and over again during the past few months. That Christmas when he would finally hold Fleur in his arms and give her the child she had begged him for. Blindly pushing his way through the crowd of incoming passengers, he crossed the road and entering a pub ordered a beer.

The lighting was poor, the place sordid and there were very few patrons, but Hugh hardly noticed. 'Where to now?' he sighed, taking a long draught from the frothing glass, and lighting a cigarette. He seemed to have gone down every avenue and come to a dead end.

Peter Drummond's name came into his mind; he was the one who would have broken the news that he was missing to Fleur. Hugh was sure that Peter would have kept in touch with her: perhaps his old friend would be able to help him, but where was *he* now? The Air Ministry might be able to give him an address but everything was closed for two days. And probably for the rest of the week, since few offices would open up to bleary-eyed merrymakers just for the Friday.

Hugh signalled for another beer. As he did so he caught sight of a series of pre-war posters on the wall behind the bar. The crowded beach at Scarborough. He smiled, the gaudy picture reviving memories of childhood holidays on the sands. York Cathedral. Suddenly he remembered his old home. His father. And a terrible feeling of remorse gripped him. He had been in England for two days, so preoccupied with finding Fleur, wallowing in his misery, that he hadn't even thought to telephone his father to let him know that he was alive. '*Dad,*' he whispered brokenly. 'Oh Dad, how *could* I?' Downing his beer in one gulp he leapt to his feet, and scatterig a few coins on the counter asked the bored barman for the nearest telephone booth. Without raising his eyes from polishing a glass with a non-too clean rag, the barman jerked his chin upwards. 'Opposite guv'nor,' he sniffed, a homemade cigarette dangling perilously from his upper lip 'Outside the station.'

A woman's voice answered his call.

'May I speak to Dr. Cunningham' Hugh asked, wondering who she could be. It wasn't the housekeeper, the voice was young with a hint of laughter in it.

'The doctor is out on a call. Can I take a message?'

Something in the woman's voice brought the memories flooding back 'Are you..... are you the doctor's daughter?' he asked tentatively.

'Yes,' she answered warily. May I ask who's speaking?'

He hadn't seen his sister for over four years. 'El*i*zabeth,' he choked, 'it's me..... Hugh..... your *little brother.*'

He heard his sister gasp. 'If this is some kind of joke....' she began coldly.

'Lizzie, 'he shrieked throatily, almost sobbing into the phone. 'It's *not* a joke, I *promise* you.'

For a few seconds there was a deathly silence. Hugh wondered if she had fainted. 'Lizzie, *Lizzie,*" he called urgently. 'Are you all right? Say something, *please.*'

'But,' she stammered, 'Hugh's....'

'Dead,' he interrupted. 'No not dead, only missing: I was shot down and taken prisoner. I only arrived back in England yesterday morning.'

'I'm sorry,' she said weakly, 'but I must sit down.'

Hugh heard a door open and close and his father call that he was back.

'However am I going to break the news to Dad?' his sister whispered, almost incoherently. 'The shock could kill him.'

'*I'll* tell him,' Hugh said softly.

His father took it very calmly 'Hugh, my boy I always knew I'd see you again. I never gave up hope that one day you would return, God gave me peace about that.' He sighed deeply. 'What a wonderful answer to prayer.'

Hugh thought he detected a sob in his father's voice: but the old man quickly pulled himself together.

'Where are you Hugh? In England?'

'I'm in London, Dad. Arrived yesterday morning. It's a long story.'

'And you're free to leave?'

'Well.... yes.'

'Catch the night train: it gets into York in the wee small hours. I'll meet you there and drive you home. Elizabeth's here. She leaves in January to join her husband in New Zealand, and John has come home especially for the occasion.' His father took a deep breath in an attempt to control his emotion. 'What a *wonderful* Christmas present. My three children with me to celebrate.'

Hugh realised that there was nothing more he could do in his attempt to find Fleur until the festivities were over, and the prospect of kicking around an empty London feeling sorry for himself until the New Year was not appealing. It suddenly struck him that his father might have news. 'Dad,' he said anxiously. 'I can't find Fleur. I've been to the flat and to Marchmount; they've both been sold. And nobody at the BBC has any news of her. Have *you* by any chance kept in touch?'

There was a slight pause.

'Come home, 'his father said gently. 'We'll talk about it then.'

'But Dad, 'Hugh pleaded, frantically putting more coins into the telephone slot. 'I'm going crazy not knowing what's happened to her. If you know anything, *please* tell me: whatever it is I'd rather know than go through this hell of uncertainty.'

There was another pause.

'I'd rather tell you here,' his father said quietly. 'At home with your family to help you.'

'*Please* Dad, *please*,' Hugh almost sobbed. 'Put me out of my misery if you can.'

His father paused again, then took a deep breath. 'Fleur was married in Paris this morning.'

Hugh tried to say something, but no sound came. He opened his mouth, but it was useless: he seemed to have been struck dumb. Without a word, he put down the phone and stumbled blindly out of the booth.

Fleur half opened her eyes and for a moment was disorientated. The almost imperceptible roll of the great liner brought her back to consciousness. She gazed down at the slim platinum band on her finger: she was Arvind's wife, she was on her honeymoon and they were on their way to begin a new life together. And a warm wave of happiness flowed over her. The past was gone, the loneliness over. She reached out for him, but his place was empty. Looking round she saw him standing in his dressing gown gazing through the porthole at a great expanse of grey sea.

Sensing her eyes upon him, he turned. 'It's rather late for breakfast,' he smiled, 'but I've ordered coffee, it should be here any minute.' He sighed. 'I'm afraid I promised the captain we'd attend the Christmas luncheon. A family 'do' he said, children, turkey, crackers, balloons, Santa Claus, the lot. He's asked me to present the prize for the best recitation! Apparently the "*real* celebration" is this evening.' He grimaced. 'So much for our peaceful honeymoon! You should have married a banker, darling.'

Fleur held out her arms. 'I don't want a banker,' she whispered, snuggling up to him, determined to make up for the night before, 'and I don't want coffee. Do you?'

'Not really', he whispered back, holding her close and showering kisses on her upturned face.

There was a tap on the cabin door and a waiter walked in with a silver tray in his hand.

'Leave it on the table, 'Arvind said, 'and please see that we are not disturbed. My wife is very tired.'

'Certainly sir', the waiter replied. And glided out.

Fleur thought she detected a smirk upon his face.

Arvind was an experienced lover. He was gentle with her, tenderly leading her into the enchanted garden she had known with Hugh. She clung fiercely to him, shivering with excitement as he coaxed her into the rythmn of his hard muscular body, propelling her to even greater heights until she cried out, her breath coming in short sharp gasps. She felt unable to hold him close enough as their bodies swayed in unison, her desire for him mounting as his long suppressed passion came pouring out. With a final explosion of delirious joy, she reached a pinnacle of ecstasy she had never known. As the rapture slowly ebbed away they lay panting in each other's arms, saturated with love.

Arvind turned, resting on his elbow, and smiled down at her, but her eyes were closed, her lips parted as her breathing slowly returned to normal. 'I expect the coffee's cold,' he teased.

Her eyes opened, the green lights dancing and shining more brightly than ever. 'It was worth it,' she whispered and nestled back into his arms.

They were almost late for lunch, but they managed to decline tea and Christmas cake.

Fleur threw herself on the bed as soon as they regained their cabin, and held out her arms. 'I feel a slut,' she smiled happily, trembling with excitement when her husband slowly undid the buttons on her dress.

'I like you that way,' he smiled back, turning her onto her side in order to cope with the zip. The frock slithered down her body. She felt a succession of erotic shocks catapulting up and down her spine, her heart rate increased, her breath came in staccato gasps and she shuddered with excitement, hardly able to contain her passion until their bodies united once more.

'Arvind,' she said hesitantly when they once again lay contently in each other's arms happy and replete in the afterglow of love. 'Have you made love to many women?'

He sat up and reaching for a cigarette lay thoughtfully smoking, one hand behind his head, the other absently stroking her hair lying against his chest. 'Yes,' he answered at last. 'Do you mind?'

Fleur shook her head. 'No. Not as long as it stops here.'

He stubbed out his cigarette and almost fiercely took her back into his arms. 'It will,' he whispered hoarsely, kissing her with almost cruel passion. 'It will, I promise you.' He slowly circled her mouth with his finger. 'I've known many women darling. Being a diplomat draws them like flies. But.... *I've never asked one of them to marry me!*' He held her close. 'That evening I met you I knew you were the woman I'd been waiting for, and I was prepared to wait, although I ached with passion. Since that evening I have not made love.... to *anyone*'

'Though I imagine you've had the chance?' Fleur queried.

'Oh many times,' he answered dismissively. He smiled down at her. 'But there was only you. You bewitched me the minute I set eyes on you. I don't know what it is about you darling, you're absolutely fascinating. There's an aura of mystery surrounding you which I simply can't resist.'

Without warning, the reel shot backwards and Fleur was with Hugh in a compartment of a sordid blacked-out train. He had said the very same thing. Her heart missed a beat as the memories flooded back. Their love. Their brief moments of happiness:

her utter desolation when he didn't return. And for a split second she was torn. Had she done the right thing by marrying Arvind? Should she have waited a little longer for her husband to come back? Perhaps Hugh was out there.... somewhere.... looking for her. And a cloud descended on her happiness.

Arvind sensed her change of mood and thought that his admission had upset her. Knowing how sensitive she was, he cursed himself, suddenly afraid he might lose her: afraid that those magical moments he had longed for and finally achieved might be snatched from him. He crushed her in his arms and kissed her fiercely, almost harshly, unable to stop until she was breathless and cried out for mercy.

'Forgive me darling,' he panted. 'But I love you *so much.'* He gazed longingly down at her and Fleur saw the pain and the doubt which had darkened his eyes. She smiled reassuringly up at him, pushing her own doubts out of her mind. He smiled back and gently pressed her down into the sheets. 'Do you feel like being a slut again?' he whispered.

Fleur nodded. She closed her eyes and sighed happily as his strong legs entwined with hers.

—ooo-O-ooo—

CHAPTER TEN

The 'Scotsman' jolted rythmically over the rails swaying slightly from side to side as it rattled through the night. Hugh squeezed into a corner sat wide-awake, his thoughts interrupted by the occasional snores which echoed round the dimly-lit compartment. Sighing, he got up and went into the corridor, leaning his head against the window as the lights of small stations flashed past.

'It's not possible,' he kept repeating desperately. 'It *can 't* be true. Fleur *can't* have married someone else, it's bigamy, she's married to *me*.' His father's last words drummed incessantly in his brain. 'Fleur was married in Paris this morning.' And he knew it *was* true. His lips tightened. 'So much for prayer,' he said bitterly.

He squinted at his watch and shuddered. Almost half past two. She would be on her honeymoon now; another man would be holding her in his arms; perhaps at this very moment making love to her, giving her the child he had denied her. An agonised cry shot from his lips and he glanced out at the rails. The door was not far away, it would be so easy to end this misery. He only needed to wait until another express train came in the opposite direction, one leap and it would be over. It would be considered an accident. He grasped the rail of the window and knew he couldn't do it. The coroner might class it death by misadventure, but his father would know the truth. After his revelation last evening he would guess. Hugh had suffered so much, he could not inflict his suffering on his father.

A sob dribbled from his lips, followed by another. There was no-one around to hear him, and after those terrible months in captivity he finally let go, great heaving sobs dredged themselves up from the depths of his being, wracking his body. Finally they subsided, the shaking became less violent and he found he was crying like a baby. Crying as he had not cried since his first night at Prep. School. Fishing in his pocket for a handkerchief he scrubbed it round his face. His shirt front was drenched and he realised that his eyes must be red from weeping. Stumbling to the lavatory he splashed cold water over his face again and again.

There was a knock on the door. Quickly wiping himself with the non too clean towel hanging from a hook on the wall he opened the door.

'Are you all right sir?' the ticket inspector enquired.

'Yes yes, I'm fine,' Hugh mumbled, trying to avert his face.

'Only you seem to have been in there a long time,' he said apologetically. 'I thought perhaps you might have had a bad turn.'

'No. I'm quite all right thank you: did you want my ticket?'

'If you please, sir.' He took the ticket and clipped it. 'Got a spot of leave and going home to the wife and family?' he smiled. 'Have a happy Christmas sir.'

Hugh weakly smiled back. Pulling open the door of his compartment, he discovered that the portly gentleman sitting next to him had slithered over and was now filling most of his seat. As he squeezed himself in, his neighbour grunted and shunted slightly in his sleep. The release of tension had relaxed Hugh's nerves. The rhythmic swaying of the train rocked him into a fitful dream in which Fleur was running towards him, eyes shining then slowly evaporating when he caught her in his arms. The subtle change of motion jolted him back to consciousness, and he realised that they were pulling into a large station.

'York, York' rose the throaty shouts of porters, 'all change for.....'

But he didn't wait for more. Leaving the compartment, he pushed his way along the corridor towards the door.

Hugh saw them when the train trundled past. All three of them standing on the platform anxiously scanning the compartments as they slowed down, and his frozen heart melted slightly. He realised that he had not even informed them that he was coming, so thunderstruck had he been by his father's revelation. It was 5.30 in the morning, yet they had come. Hoping. Opening the door, he jumped down and began to walk towards them.

His sister was the first to see him. Breaking free from the others, she raced along the platform and flung herself into his arms. 'Hugh,' she cried brokenly. 'Oh *Hugh*. Is it *really* you?' She burst into tears.

Hugh held her close, stroking her back. 'It's me, Lizzie,' he soothed. 'It *really* is.'

John hurried along the platform, holding his father's arm.

As brothers he and John had never been close, it had always been Hugh and Elizabeth. But at that moment when John grasped his hand their eyes met; Hugh noticed tears glistening in his elder brother's, and a new intimacy was forged.

'Hugh, my boy,' his father said hoarsely. He took both Hugh's hands in his and gripped them tightly.

Unexpectedly Hugh bent and kissed his father's cold cheek, something he hadn't done since he was eight years old. His father turned away, unable to hide his emotion.

They drove through the deserted streets of York and swung out into the country. Arthur Cunningham sitting in the back with Hugh, tentatively placed his hand on his son's knee. Hugh turned and smiled at him and the old man looked at him penetratingly as if trying to convince himself that Hugh really was the son he thought he had lost.

'Dad,' Hugh stammered. 'What you told me on the telephone shattered me.' He paused and took a deep breath. 'I *can't* believe it,' he floundered. It *can't* be true.' He looked appealingly at his father.

But his father didn't answer, and Hugh knew that his worst fears were confirmed.

'What am I going to do?' he whispered brokenly.

His father's hand on his knee tightened into a hard grip. 'I don't know my boy, 'he said sadly, staring straight ahead, not daring to meet his son's gaze. 'I only wish I had the answer.'

Hugh slumped in his seat. And they fell into an uneasy silence.

'Hugh,' his father hesitated. 'I can't pretend to know how you are feeling after all you've been through. And I want to help. But you are exhausted and in shock now, and under a great strain: you won 't be able to be rational or even think straight. Could we possibly put this conversation off until to-morrow?

Hugh looked at him blankly.

'I know very little. I promise to tell you all I know.... But not now.' His hand pressed harder into Hugh's knee. 'For two and a half years I've longed for this moment when I would know that you were alive. We all have. Your sister will be leaving for New Zealand very soon, this may be the last Christmas when I will have my three children with me for a very long time. Do you think we could try to enjoy the day?' He looked appealingly at Hugh. 'Or is it asking too much of you after the terrible news I gave you?'

Hugh gritted his teeth. The last thing he wanted to do was rejoice. Then he saw again their anxious faces at York Station, scanning the compartments as they trickled past His sister's leap into his arms. His brother's unusual warmth. His father's obvious emotion, and a little of more of the ice gripping his heart melted. He smiled sadly at his father. 'Yes Dad,' he said slowly. 'There's nothing I can do now. We'll talk on Boxing Day.'

When they entered the village and turned into their driveway Hugh was surprised to see the house ablaze with lights.

'Oh, Mrs. Blaney was up before we left,' Elizabeth laughed, 'scratching around the kitchen, clucking like an old hen. She's terribly excited. I expect she's cooked the month's bacon ration for the entire family plus all the eggs in the house by now.' She looked Hugh up and down, noticing again his emaciated frame. 'Mind you, 'she went on. 'You look as if you need fattening up.'

They sat down to the best breakfast Hugh had enjoyed in years.

'I have a few calls I must make before lunch,' his father announced when the plates were finally emptied. 'Why don't you get some sleep Hugh, you must be exhausted.'

Hugh realised that he was.

'Your old room's ready.'

'And I've turned down the bed and put in two hot water bottles,' Mrs. Blaney interrupted, poking her head round the dining room door.

'Wonderful woman,' his father beamed. 'She has even managed to get us a turkey. We'll arrange lunch for two o'clock, that'll give me time to visit my sick patients, and you a little time to recover Hugh.'

In spite of himself Hugh enjoyed Christmas. It would have been difficult not to enter into the spirit of the day, everyone was so happy to have him back. For the first time since his capture he was with his own people. Loved and cherished. And for a few hours he almost forgot the devastating news his father had given him the evening before.

That evening Fleur wore a simple black gown which Claudine's Dior "discovery" had designed for her. Her only adornment was the double strand of pearls which Claudine had taken from around her own neck and placed around Fleur's on the evening before her wedding to Hugh, and a priceless pair of emerald earrings which had belonged to Arvind's Norwegian grandmother. When they entered the dining-room Arvind almost burst with pride when all eyes appeared to be turned upon them. Fleur had never looked more beautiful. Love had given a glow to her face and put a new sparkle into her unusual eyes, so that the green lights shone with an almost dazzling brightness, dancing in the reflection from the emeralds.

Dinner over, the captain claimed the first dance, after which Fleur seemed to be whirled around the floor by one man after another. Arvind finally managed to reclaim his wife and tucking her head into his shoulder they drifted together, lost to the world.

The festivities on board fulfilled all the expectations of the season, and it was once again almost three o'clock before they regained their cabin.

'Tired?' Arvind asked solicitously, when Fleur fell wearily into bed.

'Worn out,' she replied.

He climbed in beside her and kissed her hair, but made no attempt to touch her.

She turned and tentatively put out her hand towards him. 'But still hungry,' she whispered, pressing her body close to his.

Arvind gave a low moan and caught her to him in a fierce embrace. 'Darling,' he said hoarsely. 'My darling, darling Fleur ....

The rest of the sentence was lost as they soared again into undreamed of realms of delight.

'Anyone feel like coming for a walk?' John asked, rising from the breakfast table.

'I'm cycling down to the Vicarage to help Mary wrap the prizes and sort out games for the Sunday School party on Saturday,' Elizabeth replied.

'How about you Hugh?' John enquired.

Hugh looked up from buttering a piece of toast. It was Boxing Day, and he was desperate to talk to his father. 'Do you know where Dad is?' he asked.

'He rushed out on a baby call just after six,' Elizabeth answered, as she left the dining room. 'I doubt he'll be back before lunch, if then. It was a "first"'.

Hugh sighed. He had been hoping to talk to his father immediately after breakfast to find out what he knew about Fleur. But the idea of hanging around the house all morning waiting for him to return home was unbearable, he might as well get some fresh air and corner his father as soon as he returned. 'Why not?' Hugh replied. 'I'll get my coat.' He had found his clothes in the wardrobe where he had left them when he joined up in 1940. They now hung pitifully on his skeletal frame, but it was good not to be wearing an assortment of "cast-offs. The air was crisp and frosty. Hugh nestled into his overcoat, plunging his hands deep into the pockets.

'Looks as if it might snow, 'John remarked. 'Hope it holds off till I get back to Cambridge.'

'When are you leaving?' Hugh enquired.

'New Year's Day. And you?'

Hugh shrugged. 'Around the same time I imagine.'

They walked for a few minutes in silence across the deserted moors.

'Any idea what you're going to do?' John finally enquired.

'Not really. Try to find Fleur. She *is* my wife after all, but I can't get her back until I know where she is.'

John looked at him intently. 'Has it occurred to you that she may not *want* to come back.'

Hugh stopped dead. 'What the hell do you mean?' he asked angrily. 'Of *course* she'll want to come back.'

'She's married someone else,' John said smoothly. 'Presumably she loves him.'

'She *hasn't* married,' Hugh exploded. 'She *can't* bloody well marry. She's married to *me*. As soon as I'm in London I'll get a lawyer and find her. I'll leave no damned stone unturned until we're together again.' His voice broke. 'She's not *really* married,' he said pitifully. 'It's *bigamy*.' 'Not *intentional* bigamy,' John reasoned. 'It would only be bigamy if *you,* knowing she's still alive, married again.' He turned up his collar as they reached the crest of the moor and faced the wind. 'Fleur's not British, Hugh,' John went on. 'She no longer lives here. She's married a foreigner, in another country. It could be difficult to make a case.' They began the descent, heading for home. 'It might be easier to turn the page,' he advised.

'Turn the bloody page.....' Hugh gasped. 'You must be barking *mad*.' He dug his hands deeper into his pockets, avoiding his brother's eyes. And they walked on in silence.

'If you *do* decide to consult a lawyer,' John said when they entered the village, 'a friend of mine might be able to help you.

And if he can't, he'll know of someone who can. I'll give you his card.'

Hugh was surprised and touched by his brother's concern.

'But think carefully,' John said, when the garden gate clicked behind them. 'You may be releasing a hornet's nest, and end up even more hurt than you are at the moment.' He opened the front door. 'Sometimes,' he ended, 'it's less painful to let sleeping dogs lie.'

Fleur awoke with a strange feeling in the pit of her stomach. It was pitch black outside and there was a deathly silence everywhere. She glanced at the small bedside clock. 5.30. Arvind was sleeping peacefully, one arm outstretched towards her and she wondered what had awakened her so abruptly.

A sudden nausea rose in her throat, threatening to choke her. She attempted to climb out of bed, but was thrown back onto the pillows. The motion of the ship had changed and it was heaving and rolling as if out of control. The sickness was beginning to overpower her, but staggering to her feet she was unable to stand upright. Grabbing her flimsy negligée from the bed and pressing it into her mouth she crawled on hands and knees to the bathroom, barely making it before she was horribly sick. She tried to get up, but the ship shuddered, then gave another violent roll, sending her crashing to the floor. Heaving herself to her knees, she was sick again.

Arvind zigzagged unsteadily into the bathroom, holding on to the walls for support. 'Darling,' he cried. 'whatever's happened?' He picked her up in his arms in an attempt to stagger with her back to bed, but she shook her head and pointed to the washbowl. Leaning over it, she was sick for the third time. Arvind pressed the button for the stewardess and sat down on the bathroom chair, cradling his trembling wife in his arms.

The stewardess padded in and took one look at Fleur's grey face. Helping her to her feet, she guided her back to bed. 'I've got something to settle her,' she said softly to Arvind, staggering along behind them. 'What about you? Are *you* all right sir?'

He nodded.

'You'd better have a preventive dose,' she advised. 'A sudden storm has blown up. I'm afraid we're in for some very rough weather.' She gently bathed Fleur's ashen face, wiping away the cold sweat which beaded her brow. 'I'll come back later in the morning to see your wife, but unless this storm abates I doubt she will be up to-day.' She slipped out. Arvind crept back into bed and held Fleur's shivering body against his own in an attempt to infuse some warmth into it.

She turned towards him. 'I'm sorry darling,' she said brokenly, 'our honeymoon.' Tears trickled from her eyes, wandering aimlessly down her cheeks.

Arvind kissed them away and held her close. 'Our whole life together is going to be a honeymoon,' he whispered reassuringly. 'Now try to sleep.'

They were at the pudding stage when Arthur Cunningham finally arrived. Elizabeth looked up and raised her eyebrows enquiringly.

'A fine boy,' he beamed. 'Mother and baby doing well: everybody delighted' He sat down and shook out his napkin as Mrs. Blaney fussed in with the doctor's belated lunch.

'Dad,' Hugh asked, cornering his father when they rose from the table. 'Do you have any more calls to make?'

His father took his arm. 'No Hugh. I'm sorry about this morning, I know we had promised to talk, but I brought this baby's mother into the world twenty two years ago and I promised her I'd be with her when she went into labour. Officially, my locum is on call during the Christmas period and I'm doing the New Year, when this baby was due.' His eyes twinkled. 'Unfortunately babies don't always arrive to order. But Denis has taken over now till 27th so we have all the time in the world to talk.' He steered his son towards the door. 'Let's go into my study, we won't be disturbed there.'

They sat in worn leather armchairs on either side of the fire, and for a few minutes neither of them spoke: then it all came pouring out. His father let him talk without interrupting as Hugh told him of his conversation with John: and his fears.

Arthur Cunningham leant forward and knocked the ashes from his pipe against the grate. 'John has never been married, 'he said evenly, when the flow ebbed. 'He's a scientist with an analytical mind, but he may have a point.'

'Dad......' Hugh protested. He thrust his head into his hands.

'Fleur was very attentive to me after you were reported missing,' his father said quietly. 'We kept in touch by letter and the occasional telephone call. She came here one weekend, but it was disastrous, I was called out non stop. The poor girl spent her time looking through old photograph albums, getting to know you as a child.'

Hugh looked up. A gleam of hope in his eyes.

'Did you know that her father arrived in London shortly after the war ended?'

Hugh shook his head.

'No of course you wouldn't. He wanted Fleur to return to Paris with him, but she refused to leave London in case you came back. Then about a year ago that wonderful godmother of hers persuaded her to leave the BBC and accompany her to the South of France to find out what had become of her house: she made it sound as if Fleur were doing her a favour. On the way back they stopped in Paris to see her father, and he asked her to stay and act as his hostess.'

His father leant forward and poked the fire into a roaring blaze.

'Fleur wrote to me,' he continued, 'saying that she and her father were both lonely and had nothing to keep them in England except tragic memories. It was a very sad letter, she was obviously still desperately unhappy, but I also think she was beginning to accept the idea that you might not come back. I told her she was doing the right thing.' Arthur Cunningham slowly refilled his pipe and lit it before continuing. 'She didn't write again. Then out of the blue at the beginning of December I received the most beautiful letter from her telling me that she was marrying again.' He rose from his chair and walked over to his desk. 'I have it here. I'd like you to read it.'

Hugh took it and as his eyes scanned the page tears began to roll slowly down his cheeks.

His father ignored them, leaning back in his chair, drawing deeply on his pipe. 'I wrote back telling her that I didn't think she had forgotten you or was betraying you: that she was young and life had to move on.'

'I could get hold of her father,' Hugh mused, hope blossoming. '*He'd* be able to tell me where she is.' He glanced at the letter again, and frowned. 'There's no address. Just Paris, 10th December.'

His father leant across and took the letter. 'It must have been on the envelope which I threw away once I'd replied,' he said slowly.

'Then how can I ever find her?' Hugh cried, thrusting his head back into his hands.

For a few minutes the only sound in the room was the soft thud as a log fell further into the flames.

'Fleur has suffered greatly,' his father said quietly, finally breaking the painful silence which hung between them. 'Losing her mother, and then you. Now she has found happiness it's difficult to know what to do.' He sighed deeply. 'It might be better for one person to be hurt rather than three,' he ended sadly.

Hugh looked up, an anguished expression on his face. 'Whatever do you mean Dad,' he cried. 'How *can* you say such a thing: don't you think *I've* suffered? The hell of two concentration camps, and then being rejected by my own damned people.' He clasped and unclasped his hands in his agitation. 'Fleur is the only reason I hung on during those terrible years. Without the hope that I'd see her again I'd never have survived: I'd have given in long ago and been just another frozen skeleton on a pile waiting to be incinerated. Fleur is my whole life,' he ended brokenly.

His father leant across and touched his hand. 'I know,' he said gently. 'But I'd be very surprised if you were the only serviceman who came home to face such a tragic situation, there must be others coping with the same problem.' His brow rutted in thought. 'In the New Year we'll get professional advice, *then* you can take a decision.'

Hugh looked up at him, an almost fanatical gleam in his eyes. 'I don't need to wait for the New Year to take a decision,' he muttered. 'I've already done so.' His lips tightened and he looked straight into his father's eyes.

'I'm going to Paris to find Fleur's father. He *must* know where she is.' He took a deep breath. '*Then* I'm damned well going to get my wife back!'

The storm did not abate, and Fleur was not on her feet until just before their arrival in New York. Bundling her into her furs, Arvind helped her up onto the deck as the Statue of Liberty loomed into view out of the morning mist. Still shaky on her feet Fleur clung tightly to her husband's arm.

'The New World,' Arvind mused, when the famous statue drew nearer and skyscrapers began to stand out against the New York skyline. He pressed her arm against his side. 'And a new life for us, my darling. A few days rest in New York to put some colour into your cheeks, then off to Washington where our home is waiting for us.' He smiled down at her. 'Happy?' he enquired.

She looked up at him, the frosty morning air already putting a hint of colour into her pale cheeks, and gave him a radiant smile. 'With you by my side, how could I be anything else?' she whispered.

CHAPTER ELEVEN

'Oooh, this looks exciting!' Elizabeth cooed, sliding into her place at the breakfast table and picking up an official-looking letter. Taking a knife she hurriedly slit it open. 'At last,' she beamed happily, waving a typewritten page in the air. 'I've got my marching orders. Leave from Southampton on 24nd January, arrive Wellington 27th February.' She hugged the letter, radiating happiness. 'In less than two months time I'll be with Ed,' she breathed. She suddenly caught sight of a stricken look on her father's face. 'Dad,' she cried running round the table and putting her arms round his neck. 'You'll come and see us. You'll be retiring soon, you could even emigrate. Ed. has rented a house for us on the beach at Takapuna, you could live next door and we'd swim together every day.'

'Of course my dear,' Arthur Cunningham soothed, patting her hand, angry with himself for letting his emotion at the thought of losing his only daughter momentarily surface.

'I'd like to go to Scarborough and see Aunt Dolly before I leave,' Elizabeth went on, returning to her place. 'The cousins all live around and it would be fun to revive old times.' She turned to Hugh. 'Why don't you come with me? You've got a month's leave before you have you have to go back to London to sign papers and begin the whole demob. process. We could go next week for a few days, it would be like old times.'

'I'm afraid I can't,' Hugh replied. 'I'm leaving for Paris.'

'*Paris*?' Elizabeth echoed.

'Yes, it's apparently where Fleur went when she left the BBC. To join her father. *He* must know where she is.'

'It would be much simpler and quicker to telephone,' John put in drily.

'I don't have a number,' Hugh replied.

'Do you have an address?'

Hugh shook his head.

'Then what do you propose to do when you get there,'

John enquired. 'Go from street to street knocking on all the doors asking for Fleur?'

Hugh didn't reply.

'Try the telephone,' John said quietly, his tone softening when he saw his brother's distress. 'It will probably take days, but it will be quicker and much easier than running wildly round Paris without any idea where you're going.' John folded his napkin and rose from the table. 'I'd better get moving, my train leaves at 11.30. Would you mind driving me to the station, Hugh?'

'I wish I could have been of more help to you,' John said quietly, when the two brothers stood on the country platform. Snowflakes were fluttering round them before slithering along the platform and dissolving into a soft rain. He picked up his case as the signal crashed down and smoke from the approaching train billowed in the distance. 'But if ever I can do anything, you know where to find me.'

Hugh was surprised and touched by his brother's concern.

The train slowed down and ground to a halt. Hugh held out his hand. John took it and shook it warmly, then suddenly drew Hugh to him in an enormous hug.

Hugh gasped in astonishment at his brother's unexpected show of emotion.

John pulled open the door of a compartment. 'Don't forget,' he said when the guard blew his whistle, and held up his flag, 'I *am* your brother. We must stick together.'

He leant out of the window as the train began to shunt away. 'Now that Lizzie's off,' he said sadly, 'you and I are all Dad's got.'

❧ ❧ ❧

The "bullet train" from Penn Central Station drew into Washington.

'Doesn't look as if you're going to need this,' Arvind remarked holding out her sable coat while Fleur adjusted her fur toque in the small oblong mirror. 'It's remarkably warm here for the time of year.'

Fleur smiled up at him, her eyes shining with happiness. The week in New York after the disastruous sea trip had proved to be a tonic. Once again, Arvind was overwhelmed by her beauty. Happiness and love had transformed her and, in her husband's eyes made her more beautiful than ever.

As the Embassy car manoeuvred its way through Georgetown, Fleur exclaimed with delight at every turn. Rounding a corner, it drew up in front of a row of elegant brownstones. Almost before the car stopped, a front door flew open and a plump black woman with a smile which almost split her face in two appeared on the doorstep.

'Welcome home,' she cried running down the steps to take Fleur's dressing case from her hand. 'Ah'm Ellie-Mae,' she explained as they walked back up the steps together. 'Mammy's in duh kitchen fixin' dinner for y'all.'

Fleur, unused to the dialect of the deep South frowned, wondering who the "all" could be: surely they weren't expecting guests on their first evening.

Ellie-May threw open a door leading off the hall and ushered them in. 'Now y'all sit down and I'll bring duh coffee. Mammy's just taken some blueberry muffins outa duh oven.'

Fleur looked at her appealingly. 'Tea?' she queried.

'Yes ma'am, tea it'll be. And you suh?'

'Tea will be fine, 'Arvind smiled. He picked up a silver platter with a pile of letters on it and followed Fleur into the sitting room. It was comfortably furnished and looked out onto the quiet street. There was a bright fire burning in the grate, a tea-tray already set on the low table in front of it.

Fleur sank into the deep sofa, looking around her with delight. 'Our first home,' she breathed when Arvind sat down beside her. She snuggled up to him. 'I can't wait to unpack and put all my trinkets around.'

'You're not going to have much time,' he replied absently, handing her an embossed card which he had just opened.

It was an invitation from the Danish Ambassador for dinner the following evening to meet the senior staff members and their wives.

'And this,' he went on, 'is ... well hardly an invitation. More a command from the President to attend a lunchtime cocktail party for the diplomatic Corps at the White House on Sunday, to exchange New Year greetings.' Arvind grimaced. 'It' much more civilised in Europe. There we don't officially 'greet' one another until the middle of January when we've had time to absorb the Christmas festivities.' He sighed. 'It's already Thursday. I take up my duties on Monday. Gives us one day to settle in and unpack.'

Ellie-Mae, still smiling broadly, waddled in with a tray, the steaming muffins sending out a sweet appetising smell.

Fleur bent forward to pour the tea as Ellie-Mae energetically poked the logs into a bright flame. 'There,' she announced triumphantly, replacing the poker. 'Now y'all rest till dinner. Yuh sure must be tired after duh journey.'

Fleur looked up and their eyes met. They both smiled, and she knew she had found a friend in Ellie-Mae.

Her husband was not entirely at ease the next evening when he followed the Ambassador who, with his hand on Fleur's elbow, was guiding her around the room introducing her to the couples waiting to meet this new addition to their 'family'.

Arvind had been an eligible bachelor for thirty four years. When his appointment was announced he was still a bachelor, and on both sides of the Atlantic there had been many 'hopeful' mothers. He knew that this first encounter with Fleur was vital. This dinner could make or break his wife.

She was wearing the simple black evening dress which Claudine's 'find' at Dior had designed for her. With her chestnut hair and unusual eyes she stood out amongst the blonde blue-eyed Danish women all curious to vet this latest arrival in their clan. He could see that Fleur had completely captivated the Ambassador, and by the time the evening ended her simplicity and charm had won over what he feared might have been a certain restraint on the part of the wives. And he breathed a sigh of relief.

The following Sunday at the President's reception Fleur added the final seal to her success. Wearing the oyster silk dress she had worn for her wedding, she glided around the room smiling and often greeting in their own language the people her husband introduced her to. Even the dour President smiled when, as they left, she graciously thanked him.

Arvind swelled with pride and love and could hardly wait to be back in their own home to express his feelings to her. 'I didn't know it was possible to love anyone so much,' he whispered when they lay contentedly in each other's arms, lost to the world in the afterglow of love. 'Oh Fleur, my darling Fleur, I can't believe I'm so fortunate as to have found you.' He looked tenderly down at her. 'And that you agreed to marry me. I must be the luckiest man alive.'

Fleur didn't answer. She closed her eyes, and with a deep sigh of contentment once again locked herself in his arms.

It was two days before Hugh was finally connected with International Enquiries.

'You don't have an *address*?' the astonished telephone operator spluttered.

'No I'm sorry I haven't,' Hugh said desperately. 'But it's a very uncommon name, there can't be a hundred de Rosny's in Paris.'

'I wouldn't be so sure,' the girl replied tersely. 'I'll get back to you, but it will take time.'

Hugh paced up and down all the next day, jumping anxiously every time the telephone rang. Finally the call he was waiting for came through.

'There are three persons of that name,' the girl said. 'A Comte et Comtesse de Rosny, but they live in Versailles. A Madame de Rosny in the 16th district and a Mademoiselle de Rosny in the 7th. Which one do you want?'

'Could I please have them all?' Hugh pleaded.

'All right,' she sighed. 'Got a pencil and paper?'

Hugh noted the numbers. Fleur had never said that her father had a title, but anything was possible. Except that her father was a widower, he queried. Hugh hesitated. He could have remarried of course, he reassured himself, and decided to try the Versailles number.'

When he finally got through a butler answered his call. 'Monsieur le Comte and Madame la Comtesse are at the chateau with the family. They will not be back before the end of the month. May I ask who is calling and take a message?'

Hugh's fractured French gave up at that point. That couldn't be the right number. Fleur was an only child, there wouldn't *be* a family. He tried Madame de Rosny twice, but there was no reply. For the time being, there was only Mademoiselle left. In his confusion he forgot that Fleur had remarried, and wondered whether she had reverted to her maiden name. Then lucidity returned bringing with it a flash of memory. Mademoiselle de Rosny must be Fleur's father's twin sister, the aunt Clothilde he had met at Marchmount and at their wedding. He asked for the number.

'At least four hours delay,' came the reply.

Hugh sighed and put the telephone down. It had already taken him almost two days to get through to the other numbers.

When at last the call finally came a girl's voice answered, but it was a young voice and Hugh 's heart sank. It couldn't be the aunt.

'I'm looking for a Monsieur de Rosny,' he began.

'Would you prefer to speak English?' the girl cut in.

'Oh yes please,' he gasped in relief.

'Is it my father you want?' the girl enquired.

'I-I don't *think* so,' Hugh answered evasively. 'Unless,' he went on hoping against hope. 'Unless you're Fleur.'

'No,' the girl answered. 'Fleur 's my second cousin. She and I share a great-grandmother.' She laughed. 'But she's not Fleur de Rosny any more, she married again just before Christmas. Are you in Paris? Were you hoping to see her?'

'I'm in England,' Hugh said miserably. 'I was hoping to have news of her.'

'I imagine you're a friend from her wartime days,' the girl went on. 'Poor Fleur had a terrible time. Lost her mother, then her husband was killed.'

'I know,' Hugh cut in. 'I-I was at her wedding.'

'Oh *really*,' the girl exclaimed, 'so you knew her first husband?'

'Very well,' Hugh replied.

'I'm sure Uncle Hubert would love to meet you. But he and Aunt Claudine are in the Midi at the moment.'

'Claudine?' Hugh queried. 'Not Fleur's godmother?'

'Yes,' the girl replied. 'Do you know her as well?'

'I've met her,' Hugh said guardedly.

'She and Uncle Hubert married recently.' She paused and her voice became confidential. 'Fleur was in a terrible state when her father finally persuaded her to join him in Paris last April. She couldn't accept her husband's death, then she met Arvind at some Embassy 'do' in May and her life completely changed. I've never seen her so happy as on her wedding day.' She paused. 'As a matter of interest, who am I speaking to? I'd like to tell Uncle Hubert about our conversation when he comes back. I'm Ghislaine de Rosny by the way.'

Hugh hesitated.'I'm an old friend of Fleur's from her BBC days,' he said at last. 'I may be coming to Paris and I was hoping to see her.'

'Oh what a pity you didn't telephone earlier, there were a number of her BBC friends at the wedding. But I'm afraid you're too late, the happy couple left for Washington immediately after the reception. Her husband should be taking up his duties as First Secretary at the Danish Embassy there about now. Fleur'll be in her element. The diplomatic life is really all she's ever known.'

'Her husband's Danish?' Hugh questioned, the pieces of the jig-saw puzzle beginning to fall into place. His mind went back to his conversation with the porter at King's Court.

"Mrs. Scott-Forsythe recently remarried. A French gentleman." "The flat now belongs to a Scandinavian lady who lives in Washington." So it wasn't the lady who was Scandinavian, but her husband. Claudine must have given the flat to Fleur.

'Yes,' the girl replied. 'If you want to write to her send a letter to Mrs. Arvind Kristensen c/o Danish Embassy, Washington D.C. I'm sure she'd be delighted to hear from you.'

I'm sure she would, 'Hugh thought bitterly.

"Kristensen." That was the name the porter had mentioned.

'I won't take up any more of your time,' he said hurriedly, now longing only to end the conversation. 'I've enjoyed talking to you.'

'If you do come to Paris,' the girl went on......'

'I'll let you know,' Hugh interrupted.

And put down the receiver.

As he did so the front door opened and Arthur Cunningham walked in, stamping his feet against the cold. Hugh glanced up and smiled wearily.

'Come into the study,' his father said. 'You look as if you could do with a glass of whisky.'

Hugh followed his father into his study, and slumped into an armchair by the fire. Arthur Cunningham handed his son a glass and settled opposite him, but Hugh made no attempt to drink. He merely gazed into space. His father didn't interrupt his thoughts. At last Hugh gave a huge sigh and looked up.

'I think perhaps you were right Dad when you said it might be better for one life to be ruined rather than three.'

Arthur Cunningham raised his eyebrows enquiringly, and Hugh told him of his conversation with Ghislaine de Rosny.

For a moment his father said nothing. Then he reached across and patted his son's hand. 'I wish I could say something to ease the pain,' he sympathised. 'Or at least give you a pill. But there's nothing I can say..... or do which can make the news any easier to bear.' He leant back in his chair and reached for his pipe. 'I don't know what the legal position is, but perhaps John is right. Fleur was French, not British, when she married you. Now she has married a Dane in Paris and gone to live in America, the chances of your bumping into her or of the bigamous marriage ever coming to light are very remote. And if it did, it would probably ruin her husband's career. Which would hardly endear you to her. It might well do just the opposite. On the other hand, knowing she's remarried does condemn *you* to a life of bachelordom.' He looked intently at Hugh. 'Does that sound terrible?'

Hugh gazed into the leaping flames. 'I think I'm a one woman man,' he said quietly. 'After Fleur, I can't imagine myself ever wanting any other woman. She's the only reason I'm still alive.' He gave a tight smile. 'I suppose that's the one positive thing which came out of those years of hell.' He went back to staring into the fire. 'Dad,' he pleaded earnestly, looking up at last. 'You with your religious beliefs, do you think that since I *did* survive, for her, there's a chance that one day in the impossible future we might be together again?'

His father thoughtfully patted down the tobacco in his pipe before putting a match to the bowl. 'Anything is possible Hugh,' he replied quietly. 'The Bible tells us that all things work for good for those who love the Lord, even the worst tragedies in life: I've seen it happen. As a doctor one meets many scientifically inexplicable occurences.' Taking his pipe from his mouth, he leant towards his son. 'Why don't you stay here for the time being and get your strength back. *Then* think about your future, unless you've decided to stay on in the RAF and make flying your career.'

Hugh shook his head. 'I was a wartime pilot Dad, there was never any question of my staying on once it was all over.'

'There's not only the RAF,' his father replied. 'Have you thought about a commercial airline? They'd probably jump at a pilot with your experience.'

Hugh shook his head. The idea of becoming a commercial pilot with the newly formed BOAC did not appeal to him, not after his time in the RAF.

His father frowned thoughtfully. 'You were going into your third year of medicine in 1940,' his father continued, 'it's a pity to waste that training. You could go back to medical school in September, and in the meantime help me out in in the surgery. It would ease my work load and be good practical experience for you.' He pulled deeply on his pipe 'Whether Fleur comes back or not, you're going to need a profession.' His face broke into a smile.

'Medicine isn't such a bad career, Hugh. It's given me a great deal of satisfaction, and.... it leaves one little time to think.'

Mrs. Blaney put her head round the study door.

'Dinner will be on the table in five minutes,' she said briefly, then withdrew.

Arthur Cunningham got up. 'Go to Scarborough next week with your sister,' he cajoled. 'It would please her *and* your aunt, and the sea air would do you good. Then we can both go down to Southampton to see Elizabeth off to New Zealand. On the way back I'll arrange for you to have a thorough check up at Tommy's where there are still consultants I trained with. How does that sound?'

Hugh dragged himself up from the depths of the sagging arm-chair, 'It sounds,' he replied, an edge of bitterness to his voice, 'as if my future has been decided for me.'

Arthur Cunningham turned in the doorway, and looked intently at his son. 'Your future is in your own hands,' he said quietly, 'and always will be.'

CHAPTER TWELVE

The letter arrived towards the end of January.

Fleur carefully slid a knife across the top of the envelope. 'I can't believe it,' she breathed, looking across the breakfast table at Arvind, skimming through the morning's newspapers.

Her husband glanced up and raised his eyebrows enquiringly.

'Listen to this,' Fleur went on. 'It's from Claudine. "As you know from the diplomatic grapevine, your father has been appointed Ambassador to Iran, to take up his duties early in April. Probably his swan song before retiring. So we are leaving the flat to-morrow in order that his successor at the Quai d'Orsay can move in, and going down to Boulouris to rest and shut up the house. *Then*,' she's underlined the word several times Fleur smiled, 'we're sailing mid-February on the Ile de France (your ship!) to spend a month in the States before returning to Paris for the final round of goodbyes. Can you two join us in New York where we intend to stay? Or could you bear it if we descended on you for a few days?" 'Arvind,' Fleur exclaimed excitedly. 'Isn't this wonderful news? You *will* be able to get time off to go to New York, won't you?'

Her husband shook his head. 'I'm afraid not darling. I've only just taken up my duties, I can't decently go on leave after only a month on the job.'

Her face fell, and his heart lurched. He couldn't bear to disappoint her, to refuse her anything.

'But you go, darling. Be there when they arrive and stay as long as you wish. Then bring them back here. It will be lovely to see them again.'

'It won't be the same without you,' Fleur murmured plaintively.

'I'll try to come back with you when they leave to see them off,' he consoled.

Fleur glanced at the envelope. 'It was posted on 2nd January,' she frowned. 'Taken nearly three weeks to get here. I must write back immediately or they'll never receive it before they sail.'

'Telephone,' Arvind put in, rising from the table. 'It's quicker and safer.'

Fleur's face fell. 'I don't have the Boulouris number.'

Arvind smiled, affectionately ruffling her hair as he passed. 'My secretary will find it and let you know.' Shrugging himself into the overcoat Ellie-Mae held out for him, he grabbed his hat and ran through the open front door and down the steps.

Fleur poured herself another cup of coffee. Sitting at the cluttered breakfast table in a hazy glow of love, she let her thoughts drift on the warm surging tide of her husband's devotion. It seemed that their passion for each other increased daily. Arvind's love and pride in her thrilled her, sending shivers rippling up and down her spine whenever she recalled his touch, and his surge of passion when she responded. She felt happy and fulfilled, safe and secure, her doubts about remarriage having vanished once they were installed in their own home.

The telephone rang. It was Arvind's secretary with the Boulouris number.

'At least two hours wait,' the operator announced. Could be as much as five.'

The call came through just before lunch.

'Don't bother to come to New York to meet us,' Claudine exclaimed, when Fleur revealed her plans. 'The ship arrives at some ungodly hour of the morning. We'll take a taxi to the St. Regis where we're staying, get some rest after our early start and settle in. Why don't you come on the morning train the next day and join us for lunch. I'll book you into the hotel for as long as you can stay.' She gave her infectious laugh. 'We'll stroll down Fifth Avenue and shop 'till we drop as the Americans say. Then in the evening your father can take us to see all the shows on Broadway. How does that sound for a programme?'

'Wonderful,' Fleur breathed. 'Oh it *will* be good to see you both again.'

Standing with Arvind on the platform waiting for the New York train that bright February morning, Fleur suddenly realised that this was the first time they had been parted for more than a few hours since they married. She thought of the empty room waiting for her at the St. Regis, where they had spent the latter part of their honeymoon, and the large empty bed where she would sleep without him.

'Arvind,' she cried, clinging to his coat lapels. 'I can't go. I can't leave you.'

He smiled and gently released her clinging fingers. 'Come on,' he soothed, 'you're a big girl now, and you're going to have a wonderful time in New York. Just think of that.'

Fleur was on the verge of tears. 'Not without you,' she whispered hoarsely.

The train was approaching the platform. Opening a door when it slithered to a halt, Arvind ushered her in and put her suitcase on the rack. 'I've bought you some magazines with the latest revues of films and shows in New York. You can sort out what you want to see on the journey.' Doors were banging. A whistle sounded. 'I'll call you this evening before dinner,' he smiled, bending to kiss her before jumping back down onto the platform. 'And..... I'll be here waiting for you when you come back.'

Fleur's reunion with her father and Claudine was ecstatic: they were so pleased to see one another. Although barely two months had passed since she and Arvind had left Paris, there seemed to be so much news to exchange.

The following morning Claudine decided to attack Fifth Avenue. 'You look positively blooming,' she confided when they stopped for lunch in a secluded restaurant Claudine had discovered. 'I can't help wondering whether we might expect to become grandparents in the near future.'

Fleur stiffened. Her mood abruptly changed, and she didn't know why.

'Oh forgive me, darling if I've opened my mouth too wide, 'Claudine said contritely. 'You don't have to answer. It's just that your father and I were saying last night that we had never seen you looking so beautiful: your eyes are more luminous than ever.' She smiled. 'The effect of love perhaps'

Fleur relaxed. 'Perhaps,' she agreed. 'But I don't want a child yet. Not for a long time.' She smiled reassuringly at Claudine. 'I love Arvind so much,' she said dreamily, 'I want him all to myself. I couldn't bear to share him, even with our baby.'

'So the heartache's over?' Claudine queried. 'You've finally managed to put the past behind you?'

Fleur nodded. Then she suddenly remembered her last night with Hugh in that small hotel in Scotland. She had wanted a baby then. She had begged him to give her one. What had changed? But Claudine had signed the bill and risen from the table. 'Back to work,' she smiled. 'We haven't sampled half the shops yet.'

Bewildered by her own attitude, Fleur rose from her chair and followed her into the street.

Claudine had organised a hectic programme and they whirled from shopping expeditions to theatres and smart restaurants. Fleur, half her age, could barely keep up with her. After ten days of festivities Fleur suddenly had an overwhelming longing to see Arvind again: to feel his arms around her, the warmth of his body, the passion of his kisses. 'I think I'll take the afternoon train back to Washington to-morrow,' she announced at breakfast.

'So soon?' Claudine exclaimed. 'We haven't done half the things we'd planned to do with you.'

Fleur was embarrassed. Claudine had been so good to her, so generous, she felt an ungrateful wretch to be walking out on her and her father like this. But this ache in her very bones for her husband was so overpowering she felt she couldn't spend another day without the comfort of his love.

Claudine looked at her, and immediately understood. 'Of course you must go back to Arvind,' she said. 'We'll come to Washington next week for a few days and see your little nest.'

'And we'll come back to New York before you leave,' Fleur cut in eagerly. I'm sure Arvind will be able to manage that.'

When the waving figures of her father and Claudine vanished as the Washington bound train rounded the bend and disappeared from view, Fleur left the window and sank back in her seat. Ignoring the numerous glossy magazines they had piled on her when she boarded the train, she closed her eyes and gave herself over to the thought of her reunion with her husband. And a thrill of excitement leapt from her loins and zig-zagged through her body.

Arvind,' she murmured dreamily. 'Oh, *Arvind.'*

'I can't believe it,' Arvind said throwing his hat onto a chair in the hall and handing his coat to Ellie-Mae. He bent to kiss Fleur who had come to the drawing room door to greet him. 'We've actually got an evening at home to ourselves..... It's been a wonderful month, but my goodness those golden oldies have more energy than I have. I'm exhausted!'

Arvind had rushed straight back to the Embassy when he and Fleur returned to Washington that morning after waving Hubert and Claudine goodbye as the Ile de France sailed majestically out of New York harbour on it's way back to Le Havre.

Ellie-Mae, smiling broadly came in with a tray of cocktails. 'Mammy's fixin' y'all a special dinner,' she announced.

'Could we have it in here by the fire?' Fleur asked wistfully.

'Yes ma'am, yuh sure can,' Ellie-Mae announced cheerfully, and her smile wider than ever, she waddled back to the kitchen.

'Claudine will make a wonderful ambassador's wife,' Arvind went on, sitting down on the sofa beside Fleur, and taking the cocktail she handed him.

Fleur smiled. 'I'm so pleased my father's found happiness. It was a hard blow for him to return to London after learning that his wife had been killed.'

Arvind put his arm round her and drew her towards him protectively. 'Going on to more cheerful subjects,' he said, 'how do you feel about spending Easter by the sea? It's early in April this year, the first week I believe, so Spring should be on its way.'

Fleur looked up in surprise.

'Nils Magnusson has asked us to join he and Lauren on Martha's Vineyard for the four days. Lauren's family have a holiday home there. We could fly up on the Thursday evening and return on Tuesday morning. What do you say?'

Fleur snuggled up to him. 'As long as you're there,' she whispered, 'I don't mind where we spend Easter.'

It was on their last night on Martha's Vineyard that the question came up.

The weather had been warm and blustery, wonderful for sailing. The four of them had spent the day on Lauren's father's small yacht, picnicking in a sheltered sandy inlet, returning home in the evening, suntanned and relaxed.

Nils and Arvind were leaving the following morning on a very early ferry and taking the first flight from Boston to Washington. Lauren and Fleur were to follow at their leisure later in the day.

'There,' Fleur announced, snapping a suitcase shut as Arvind walked in from the bathroom. 'I'v e packed your things, all you have to do in the morning is pick up your case and go. I'll bring anything you leave later in the day.' She turned to smile at her husband.

He walked across the room and took her in his arms. 'You smell of sea and sand and sun,' he murmured into her hair, 'and you look more beautiful than ever.' He held her at arms length and gazed at her tenderly. 'Will our honeymoon never end?' he teased, gently slipping her negligée from her shoulders. It fell with a whisper of satin onto the floor. Picking her up in his arms Arvind carried her to the bed. Climbing in beside her he drew her close, his hand gently smoothing her body until it fell caressingly onto her thighs. 'Darling,' he said hoarsely, 'wouldn't this be a wonderful moment to conceive our baby? If it were a girl we could name her Martha.'

Fleur abruptly stiffened. He felt the muscles in her soft thighs tighten, and she half turned away.

'What's the matter?' he puzzled, leaning on one elbow and gazing at her in the moonlight filtering through the window.

'I don't know,' she stammered.

He drew her to him and began to kiss her breasts.

'Arvind, no,' she cried, panic in her voice.

He let his hand drop, bewildered. 'I don't understand......'

'I'm very tired,' Fleur said desperately. 'All that sun......' Her voice trailed away. 'I just want to sleep.' She turned on her side and closed her eyes.

It was the first time she had refused him. The first time she had not been eager for his touch. All day she had admired his magnificent body: his muscles rippling as he helped Nils hoist the sails, and had longed for him. She was bewildered by her reaction to his approach. How could she explain it to Arvind, she didn't understand it herself.

Arvind turned on his back, and fumbling on the bedside table for his cigarettes, lit one and lay staring into the darkness.

When Fleur awoke the next morning, he had left.

Lauren was sitting in her dressing gown at the cluttered breakfast table in the sun porch when Fleur went downstairs. She looked up and smiled. 'I'm a dreadful slut,' she grinned. 'But life is so hectic in Washington, I like to relax when we're here.' She picked up the coffee pot and raised her eyebrows enquiringly. 'Just reading a letter from the boys,' Lauren went on. 'They seem to be having a wonderful time: falling off rocks and leaping about on craggy ledges.'

Fleur put a piece of bread in the toaster.

'These school trips during the holidays are great,' Lauren continued. 'But I'll never know how they come back in one piece.' She smiled: a flash of perfectly matched white teeth. 'Wait till you have children,' she warned. 'You'll suffer the tortures of hell worrying about their safety, especially if they're boys. The antics they get up to!'

Fleur had a sudden urge to talk to Lauren about her refusal to give Arvind the child he desired. She liked her American friend and felt she was someone she could confide in, someone who would understand and give her sensible advice. Perhaps she had had the same problem at the beginning of her marriage. She opened her mouth, but at that moment Lauren intervened.

'We don't have to be back in Washington until this evening,' she announced. 'Would you like to go into Boston? Or would you prefer to poke around here? It's a quaint old place. We just need to keep an eye on the ferry times.'

'I think I'd prefer to explore Martha's Vineyard,' Fleur replied. And the moment passed.

Arvind was already home when Fleur returned. He greeted her with his usual warmth, making no reference to the night before. It was at Whitsun that the first crack appeared in their marriage.

'I've got to go to Charleston to represent the Ambassador at some military ceremony at the Citadel on Friday,' Arvind announced. 'Would you like to come with me? We can stay on for the weekend and sightsee. You'll love Charleston, darling, it's old and full of history, and with any luck it won't be too hot.'

On their last day in Charleston they had wandered round a street market. Fleur picked up a beautiful bronze music box in the shape of a heart, its top encrusted with small precious stones.

'That's old Russian,' Arvind said.

'You're right sir,' the dealer replied.

'How did you get hold of it?' Arvind queried.

'Oh, after the Revolution in order to live the émigrés sold their jewels and any precious possessions they had managed to take with them when they fled the country.'

'But they settled mostly in Europe,' Arvind pursued. 'I don 't think any came to the States.'

'Probably not,' the dealer agreed. 'But many of their children decided to try their luck in the New World. This little music box must have belonged to one of them. I bought it at an auction but I'm afraid I don't have its history. Would you like to hear the tune?'

Fleur nodded, and handed it to him. He carefully wound it up, then lifted the lid to reveal a red velvet interior. Brahms cradle song filled the air.

'I imagine it came from an aristocratic nursery,' the dealer went on. 'The nanny would play it to soothe the baby to sleep.'

'Would you like to have it?' Arvind asked.

'Oh please,' Fleur breathed, her eyes shining.

That night as Fleur sat brushing her hair in front of the large oval mirror in their old-fashioned bedroom, Arvind came up behind her and put his arms round her neck. She looked up at him and smiled. He leant forward and picking up the music box from the dressing table, carefully wound it up. Brahms Lullaby filled the quiet room.

'Does that give you any ideas?' he enquired softly. 'We've plenty of room for a nursery.'

Fleur hurriedly put down her hairbrush and attempted to get up, but Arvind caught her by the shoulders and drew her to him as the music wafted sweetly round them.

'Arvind, I......' she began, pulling away from him.

But he held her firmly, forcing her to look at him. 'Fleur,' he pleaded, 'I don't understand. What *is* the problem. Don't you *want* children?' He shrugged helplessly. 'Perhaps it's something we should have discussed before we married, but it never occurred to me that you would feel this way. Can't you tell me what's wrong?'

Fleur sat on the bed, avoiding his eyes. He sat down beside her and put his arm round her. 'You say you love me....' he faltered.

'Oh Arvind I do, I do. But......'

'But what?'

Fleur had a sudden longing for Claudine: *she* would be able to explain what was the matter with her. But Claudine was in Teheran. She looked up at Arvind and saw the bewilderment in his eyes. Leaning closer into the shelter of his arms, she told him of her conversation with Claudine during their lunch together in New York, when her godmother had discreetly enquired whether she was pregnant. Her fears that a child would come between them and spoil the magic of their love.

'But darling,' Arvind smiled in relief, 'that's *ridiculous*. How could our baby ever come between us? A child would draw us even closer.'

'It's not only that,' Fleur said desperately, attempting to explain something she didn't understand herself. 'I'd be out of action for some time.'

'You needn't be,' Arvind replied. 'You'd look even more enchanting in flowing maternity gowns. Tell you what, you could get Claudine's discovery at Dior to make you a whole new wardrobe to wear while you're pregnant. How does that sound?'

Fleur smiled weakly. 'Our life in Washington is *so* exciting Arvind, I'm enjoying every minute of it. I don't want it to change,' she answered feebly.

Arvind shook his head, at a loss for words.

'But it's also very hectic,' Fleur went on hurriedly. 'We're either invited out non-stop or giving dinner or lunch parties ourselves. How could I ever find time to look after a baby?'

'Sweetheart, you wouldn't have to. There are countless black Mammys in Washington who adore children. We could easily engage one.'

'If I have a baby I want to look after it myself,' Fleur said stubbornly, clutching at straws.

Arvind clucked in exasperation.

'When you're posted back to Copenhagen,' she pleaded, 'it will be easier. For the time being let's just enjoy being together...... and the wonderful life we have while we're here. A baby would be a drag.' she ended lamely.

'A baby would *not* be a drag,' he said firmly. 'And, may I remind you my posting here is for three years. Maybe four.' He rose wearily from the bed and released the cord of his dressing gown. 'But if you've made up your mind, there's not a great deal I can do about it.' Removing the chocolate which the maid had placed on his pillow, he climbed inbetween the sheets.

Miserably Fleur slid in beside him, but he made no attempt to touch her, or even to draw close. He merely turned on his side and switched off the light.

PART TWO
LONDON 1950

———

CHAPTER THIRTEEN

Hugh rose with the other newly qualified doctors to recite the Hippocratic oath, and abruptly, the past resurged. He gave a twisted smile, remembering the SS doctors at Dachau who once had repeated the same challenging words, swearing "to preserve life". And he wondered what had happened: what circumstances had caused them to go back on their oath and commit such dastardly crimes.

Memories of Fleur invaded his thoughts. He had been so immersed in his studies he had had little time for nostalgia during the past three years. Now another phase of his life was beginning, and he wondered had he not been shot down whether he would be standing here to-day, what he and Fleur would have made of their lives. And regret tugged at his heart when these thoughts floated to the surface. Yet as the memories surfaced, he realised that the agony he had felt, the excruciating pain which had haunted him night and day when he returned and found that she had gone, had softened to a dull ache. His wife had become a beautiful dream, and he could scarcely believe their love had ever existed. There was a rustle as his fellow doctors sat down again. Names were called and the first row walked forward.

Stepping down from the platform after receiving handshakes, congratulations and his certificate, he saw his father on the other side of the great hall beaming with pride. John, sitting beside him, caught Hugh's eye and gave him a discreet 'thumbs up".

'I'm proud of you my boy,' his father said, warmly shaking his hand when Hugh disentangled himself from the crowd of guests and doctors streaming towards the door.

'*Really* proud. You've done it. Now after you've completed your housemanship, I can retire and leave my thriving practise to you.'

John shaking his brother's hand in his turn, raised his eyebrows enquiringly, Hugh gave a discreet shrug. He had no desire to become a country doctor. But the last thing he wanted to do was upset his father, especially to-day when he was brimming over with happiness.

'I've booked a table for our celebration lunch at Simpsons,' his father went on. 'We can walk across Westminster Bridge and along the Embankment. The fresh air will do us all good after the emotion of the morning.' He beamed again at Hugh and patted his back.

'I'll just get rid of this fancy dress,' Hugh explained, taking off his mortar board and wriggling out of his gown. 'See you in the main hall, next to Flo's statue in ten minutes. You might like to look around and revive old memories, Dad.'

'You still call the venerable lady Flo?' his father laughed. He glanced around him. 'Nothing much has changed since my day, except for that great empty space where the bombs dropped. My goodness the old place did take a pounding.'

'You'd better tell him now,' John hissed when they handed in their coats at the restaurant. 'No point in letting him go on making plans.'

Hugh grimaced. 'He seems so happy....' he replied lamely.

'He'll probably take it better than you think,' John advised.

The two brothers had drawn very close since Hugh's return, and John seemed to sense that a country doctor's life was not what Hugh had in mind.

After they had given their orders, Hugh fished in his pocket and pulled out a telegram. 'This was waiting for me when I went back to my room. It's from Lizzie. "Heartiest congratulations," he read out, "Ed. Lizzie, Angus and Moppet three quarters of the way there."'

They all three laughed.

'If she hadn't been so heavily pregnant I think she'd have come over for the ceremony,' his father put in. 'Ed suggested it.'

He beamed again. 'Now that you're launched Hugh, I can think about going to New Zealand to meet my grandchildren, knowing that you'll soon be taking over.'

John kicked his brother under the table.

'Dad,' Hugh said hesitantly, as the waiter arrived with a trolley laden with dishes. 'I had thought about specialising after I've done my two years as a houseman. In fact,' he went on hurriedly, 'I've enquired about the possibility of doing it at Tommy's or the Westminster. And they both look hopeful.'

His father put down his fork. 'Really Hugh, how interesting,' he said quietly. 'In what branch?'

'Obstetrics,' Hugh replied.

His father frowned. 'Is Bill Williams still Head of that department? I remember him as a houseman.'

'No,' Hugh said eagerly, grateful that his father had shown no signs of disappointment. 'He retired a couple of years ago and his son took over. I-I've talked to him about it.'

'Splendid,' his father replied, wiping his mouth with his napkin and raising his glass. 'Here's to you my boy.'

'So..... you don't mind?' Hugh ventured.

'Not in the least. I have a very good assistant. He married a local girl and is longing to take over the practice, but I wanted to give you the offer. Denis will be delighted with your decision.' He patted Hugh's hand. 'And so am I,' he said softly. 'I always wanted to specialise, but I fell in love with your mother.' He smiled to himself. 'She was enchanting in her nurse's uniform with that lacy butterfly cap perched on her curls. Elizabeth is very like her. Once I qualified, we couldn't wait to get married. I never regretted it, but I'm pleased you've got the chance.'

Hugh relaxed and the rest of the lunch was truly a celebration.

'Will you be coming back with me this evening?' his father asked, when they left the table.

'I'd love to Dad,' Hugh replied. 'I've a week free before I start my time as a houseman.' They walked out into the Strand and strolled back across Westminster Bridge in a companionable silence.

'I'll pop into the hospital and see if I can find any of my former colleagues still on the beat while you pack your bag,' his father smiled.

Hugh crossed the road and ran up the stairs to his room. Throwing a suitcase onto the bed, he began to toss clothes into it. 'Better take a couple of thick jumpers,' he murmured as he was about to click the case shut. 'Never know what the weather will be like up there.' He pulled open a drawer and began rummaging through a pile of assorted woollies. Suddenly his fingers closed on something hard, and he drew out the studio portrait of Fleur which had always stood on his bedside table before he was shot down.

Sitting down on the bed, he gazed at her perfect oval face smiling up at him, lips slightly parted, her unusual eyes sparkling. He had put it at the bottom of the drawer when he embarked on his new life but now, suddenly, the memories of their time together came cascading back with incredible intensity, piling in one upon the other; blocking out everything but her face. For a few minutes as the late afternoon sunshine flitted across the walls, he sat there, oblivious of everything but Fleur. Through the open window the boom of Big Ben chiming the hour rang out across the river. He stood up, and placing the photograph face downwards at the bottom of the open drawer he firmly pushed it shut. Picking up his suitcase and slinging his mac. over his arm, he turned towards the door. 'The past is dead,' he muttered through clenched teeth. 'It can no longer hurt me.' Yet even as the words reverberated in his brain, he knew that the past had never been so alive as at that moment.

Fleur looked up from adjusting her earrings in front of the dressing table mirror when her husband walked into the bedroom.

He came up behind her and dropped a kiss on her hair. 'You've won as usual,' he smiled. 'We're staying in Washington for another year.' He sat down on the stool beside her and put an arm round her shoulders. 'Happy?' he asked.

She leant her head against his shoulder. 'You know I am,' she whispered. She looked up at him, the green lights dancing in her tawny eyes. 'And you?'

Arvind got up. Shrugging himself out of his jacket, he began pulling at his tie. 'If you're happy, I'm happy,' he said quietly, and headed for the bathroom.

Arvind seemed to be more in love with his wife every day. Three years of marriage had not dimmed his ardour and he was prepared to sacrifice anything for her sake, even his own happiness. He sighed as he turned on the taps. He had hoped to return home before Christmas to work for a few years, until his next foreign posting, at his base the Foreign Office in Copenhagen. But he knew Fleur was longing to stay in Washington, so when the offer to prolong his appointment was given him he had accepted. He was aware that his success in his career was due to a great extent to Fleur. She was a dazzling light in their diplomatic circle, thriving on the endless social merry-go-round.

The question of a child had not been raised again since that evening in Charleston. Arvind knew it was pointless to do so and clung to the assurance Fleur had given him then that once they returned to Denmark, having a baby would be easier. With that promise in mind, they had gradually slipped back into their old habits, the passion between them undimmed by time.

'I spoke to my father on the 'phone this afternoon,' Arvind remarked on the way to their dinner party. 'I think he was disappointed we wouldn't be returning: he rang back and asked whether we could go to Copenhagen for Christmas. I have home leave coming up, what do you think? Apart from that short visit my parents made to us when they were on holiday in Florida last year, we have hardly seen them. They don't really know you, and I'm sure my mother is longing to get acquainted with her new daughter.'

'Of course Arvind,' Fleur replied, wanting only to please him now that her wish for an extension of their stay had been granted. She had been hoping to go south for Christmas, to the Everglades or Atlanta, but suppressed the disappointment she felt at the thought of celebrating in what she considered to be the frozen North. Apart from her early years in Russia, and wartime winters in England she had always lived in warm climates.

'My father's retiring next Summer,' Arvind went on. 'He's taking mother back to Norway, to Arendal where she was brought up and has a brother and two sisters still living there. He suggested we might go over for a few days: they want to show us the retirement house they've bought. You'll love Arendal darling,' he went on enthusiastically, 'it's in the South of Norway, by the sea. A wonderful place in summer for sailing..... with safe beaches for children.'

He looked at Fleur out of the corner of his eye. But she didn't react. 'Most of my family have never met you,' he remarked, drawing up in front of another brownstone. 'It will be an opportunity for me to show off my beautiful wife.'

Fleur gave him a radiant smile, already anticipating the evening ahead with pleasure.

'And,' he added, putting on the brake and turning off the lights, 'my parents are leaving us the house in Hellerup so that we have somewhere to live when we return.'

Fleur smiled weakly, not wishing to think about their return. It would come soon enough.

'And then.... what?' she silently asked herself.

Hugh, dozing under the crab-apple tree stirred, then blinked, shielding his eyes against the bright sunlight streaming through the leaves.

'The wonderful Mrs. Blaney is bringing us tea out here,' his father announced sitting down beside him. 'A beautiful day like this is rare in these parts, so we have to take advantage of it when it happens.' He leant towards his son. 'Mrs. B's made hot scones especially for you.'

Once again Hugh's mind unaccountably went back to Fleur. To the day they had become engaged. It was the promise of hot scones for tea at Marchmount which had almost caused him to be late back at his base. He shook his head in bewilderment, not understanding. It was strange the way that now he had convinced himself he was on the brink of a new life, the past safely tucked away behind him, seemingly insignificant details suddenly brought back a vivid memory of Fleur.

'That's the last of the Dundee cake,' Mrs. Blaney announced, setting down the tray.

'Don't worry,' his father confided, 'she's made one for you to take back to-morrow.' He put his finger to his lips. 'But it's top secret!'

Hugh smiled and leant back in his chair while his father poured the tea. He felt excited at the prospect of returning to the hospital as a fully fledged doctor.

'I doubt whether you'll have much time for sitting in the sun once you're a houseman,' his father remarked. 'It's round the clock on call, unless things have changed drastically since my day.'

'They haven't,' Hugh grimaced. 'But it's good experience.'

'What made you choose obstetrics?' his father enquired, pouring them both a second cup of tea.

Hugh's brow rutted in thought. 'I think it was Fleur.'

His father frowned in bewilderment.

'On our last night together she begged me for a child,' he reminisced 'I refused, saying it wasn't reasonable as long as the war lasted. Fleur was hurt and very upset. I've regretted it ever since.'

'So you haven't entirely got over your hurt?' his father asked gently.

Hugh turned and smiled at him. 'Yes Dad, I have. Now Fleur is just a beautiful memory......One I shall never forget.'

'But what has this to do with your choice?' Arthur Cunningham puzzled.

'A great deal. "Tommy's" is in the middle of the "Cut", one of the poorest areas of London. While I was in training I came across women having children in appalling conditions, often living in a sixth floor tenement without any mod. cons.' He popped the last piece of cake into his mouth. 'I also met many who longed to have children yet were unable to,' he went on, clasping his hands behind his head. 'I decided then, perhaps in memory of Fleur, to do all I could to help them. Obstetrics seemed to be the solution.' He paused and gazed up at the sky now beginning to cloud over. 'I may go into research later on. Who knows?' He picked up the tray as the first drops of rain began to fall. 'One advantage to being "single" is that one can do as one likes,' he grinned.

CHAPTER FOURTEEN

Fleur turned before entering the Embassy car and hugged Ellie-Mae and Mamy. They were both standing on the pavement in floods of tears.

'There won't never be another lady like you,' Ellie-Mae wailed, putting her apron over her face and sobbing loudly.

Fleur glanced back at the brownstone where she and Arvind had been so happy for four years. It looked empty and forlorn, the curtainless windows bleakly reflecting the pale winter sunshine. And a lump rose in her throat.

Arvind took her arm gently coaxing her towards the car where the last pieces of luggage were being stacked into the boot. 'Come on darling,' he urged, 'no point in prolonging the agony. They'll get over it once we've left.'

On the verge of tears herself, Fleur swiftly embraced the two sobbing women and climbed into the limousine. It purred away leaving two waving figures weeping loudly on the pavement. Fleur leant back and closed her eyes. She didn't want to see her familiar haunts as they cruised by, and she was exhausted. So popular had she become in the diplomatic circle that the past two months had been a frantic round of festivities. Everyone wanted to have them for lunch or dinner or to give a cocktail party for them before they left, with the result that they sometimes had three engagements in one day; all very emotional.

And on top of it the packing of their treasures, plus all those Fleur had accumulated during their stay, deciding what they could take on the plane with them, what could go into the containers and what would have to be sent by sea had left them both drained.

Fleur was surprised on entering the VIP's lounge at Dulles airport to find it crowded with well-wishers, gathered to say a final goodbye. There were more hugs and kisses and glasses of champagne, so that by the time she boarded the 'plane her emotions were in shreds: and she burst into tears. The short journey to La Guardia before boarding the internatioinal flight to Copenhagen gave her time to compose herself and redo her face.

Taking Arvind's arm, she stepped off the 'plane determined once again to put the past behind her and step confidently out into the unknown future.

By the time they finally touched down at Kastrup after the long flight, she was more weary than she ever remembered being: the fatigue and tensions of the past two action packed months had finally caught up with her. The spring on the tight coil which had wound itself around her emotions finally sprang and zipped her down to zero, leaving her weak and lifeless.

It was a grey November Sunday with a depressing drizzle. Walking across the tarmac Fleur shivered and turned up her collar against the rain, which had begun to trickle down her neck. Arvind hardly noticed it: he seemed exhilarated and became excited when he saw his parents frantically waving at them from the other side of the barrier. All around them Danish voices shouted greetings to alighting passengers and Fleur realised that she had made very little effort to learn her husband's language: in Washington there had been no need. She began to wonder how she would manage now that they were back on his native soil, and her tired spirits sank even lower. Her mother-in-law rushed forward and warmly embraced her son, talking excitedly in her sing-song Norwegian accent. Chattering back Arvind hugged her: and Fleur felt isolated.

Solveig Kristensen turned to her and held out her arms. 'Fleur,' she purred, 'how wonderful to have you so near us at last.' She held her daughter-in-law at arm's length. 'And even more beautiful than I remember.' She smiled, and her whole face lit up.

In spite of herself Fleur blushed, bringing a touch of colour to her wan cheeks. She saw that Arvind's mother had herself once been a very beautiful woman. Her blond hair was now almost white, piled high upon her head: her eyes deep blue like Arvind's, and her perfect bone stucture revealing high cheekbones and a small slightly tilted nose.

Her mother-in-law tucked her arm in hers and guided Fleur towards the entrance where Arvind and his father were coping with their mountain of luggage.

'Now don't you worry that Jorgen and I are going to be on your backs,' she confided. 'We came over to be sure everything is in order for you at the house, but we'll be off in a day or two. Kamma, my former maid, is there. When you're settled, she'll go back into retirement and her niece Sigrid will take her place. Once your luggage arrives, get rid of any of the furniture we've left behind: I want it to be *your* home.'

She smiled fondly at Fleur, and Fleur's jaded spirits rose, her mother-in-law's warmth dispelling her earlier misgivings. Perhaps living in the frozen North wouldn't be so bad after all she told herself: she had Arvind and they could move to the centre of Copenhagen later on. But as she looked at the leaden sky, the rain falling in an incessant drip, and the short winter day already darkening although it was only three o'clock, her spirits began to droop once again.

The telephone was ringing as Hugh fitted his key into the lock of the small flat he had rented near the hospital, but it had stopped before he had time to pick up the receiver.

'If it's an emergency, they'll call back.' He walked into the bathroom and turned on the taps. He was dog-tired. He seemed to have been on call for ever. All he wanted to do was soak in a hot bath then tumble into bed. But before he had time to climb into the suds the 'phone rang again. Wearily pulling his dressing gown round his naked body, he strode down the hall and picked it up. 'Dr. Cunningham,' he announced.

'Good evening Dr. Cunningham, so you are at home sometimes: I've been ringing all day.'

'John,' Hugh replied happily, hearing his brother's voice. 'What's the hassle? Are you coming to London?'

'No,' John replied. 'But I'm calling to ask *you* to come to Cambridge.'

'Out of the question, I'm afraid. I seem to be on call night and day at the moment. There's nothing but damned emergencies.'

'This *is* an emergency.'

Hugh frowned. 'Is it Dad?' he enquired.

'No,' John laughed. 'It's *me.*'

John,' Hugh answered wearily. 'I'm deadbeat. Stop talking in bloody riddles and tell me what this is all about.'

'I'm getting married a week on Thursday, and I'd like you to be my witness.' He paused. 'I did it for you, remember?'

Suddenly the reel in his head shot backwards again and he was standing beside John when the organ burst into the wedding march, and Fleur, breathtakingly beautiful, drifted down the aisle towards him lost in a mist of tulle and old lace.

'Hugh,' John called anxiously. 'Hugh, are you still there.'

Stunned, Hugh dragged his thoughts back to the present and sat down heavily on the chair by the telephone table. 'John,' he answered weakly. I can't believe.....'

'That your crusty old bachelor brother has finally made it?' John laughed. 'Well, it's happened, and I'd like you to be there. Dad's coming. Ruth has no family so it'll be a very quiet affair: midday at Cambridge Registry Office.' He paused. 'You will come, won't you?' he pleaded.

'Of *course* I'll come. I'll manage it somehow.'

'Dad is taking us out to dinner on Wednesday evening and my colleagues are giving us a small reception after the ceremony. Very informal, nothing spectacular.'

'But who is she?' Hugh queried. 'You've kept it very quiet.'

'She's a colleague. And yes I suppose it is rather sudden, but it just grew..... like Topsy. I never thought I'd marry....'

'I thought you were married to your blasted codes,' Hugh teased.

'Well, I suppose I still will be,' John laughed. 'Ruth's a brilliant cryptologist.'

'You're being very cagey. Do we know her?

John paused. 'No. She's an Austrian Jewess. She lost her mother to the holocaust and she's no idea where her father is. He was sent somewhere else and is almost certainly dead. Ruth is one of the few survivors from Maunthausen concentration camp.' He paused again. 'Her number is tatooed on her wrist.'

For a moment Hugh was speechless, the horrors of Dachau and Flossenburg flooding back, and he felt an immediate empathy with John's bride 'She'll have a family now,' he said gently. 'She'll have us.... and Lizzie. And perhaps you'll have a family of your own,' he went on brightly when John didn't reply, 'forty-nine isn't too old to become a father.'

'I'm afraid that won't be possible,' John said quietly. 'Ruth was experimented on while in the camp. There's no hope of her ever having children.'

Hugh's heart went out to his brother. 'Oh, John,' he said brokenly, and he didn't know how to go on. His brother came to his rescue.

'But we'll have our codes.'

And the tension broken, they both laughed.

—ooo-O-ooo—

Chapter Fifteen

'I hope you're willing to take charge of the white elephant stall again this year.' Helena Davidson raised her eyebrows enquiringly, and smiled across the room at Fleur. 'Last Christmas your charm enabled us to get rid of all the unsellable items we'd been storing for years.' Taking Fleur's acceptance for granted, she ran a finger down her list. 'There, I think we've more or less covered everything: shall we meet here again at the same time next month to finalise the details?'

There was a murmur of assent from the ladies gathered in Fleur's sitting room as they rose to leave. Helena was the wife of the British Consul in Copenhagen. She was older than most of the other diplomatic ladies now streaming through the door, and as such had been asked to organise the annual Embassy Christmas Fayre.

'Could I beg another cup of tea from you Fleur?' she enquired, shuffling her papers together. 'There are one or two matters I'd like to discuss.'

'Of course,' Fleur replied, ringing the bell for Sigrid. She was surprised by Helena's request.

Since her arrival in her husband's country Fleur had thrown herself into charitable works in an attempt to keep herself occupied. Copenhagen's social life was tame in comparison with Washington and she found it difficult to make friends outside the restricted diplomatic circle. The Danes were friendly but reserved and she had turned to Embassy charities run by Embassy wives in an attempt to fill her days and also be useful. But it didn't really satisfy her. She felt like a square peg in a round hole and often found herself sinking into an apathy which was foreign to her nature.

'There's nothing like a real English cup of tea, is there?' Helena said, leaning back in her chair. 'I don't know what it is, I've been all over Europe with Henry, but no-one seems to be able to make tea properly anywhere else.'

'I think I've managed to tame Sigrid,' Fleur laughed.

'Lucky you,' Helena smiled, 'I wish I could say the same for my Anitra.' She put her cup down on the low table at her side. 'Forgive me if I'm interfering my dear,' she began, 'but is everything all right?'

Fleur looked up, a puzzled frown on her face. 'In what way?'

'You seem to have lost your sparkle recently. And..... you've also lost weight.' She paused. 'I was wondering whether there is something wrong, something worrying you with which I could perhaps help.'

There was a great deal wrong, but Fleur was not sure that anyone could help. She looked across at Helena, who had reached for her cup and was now thoughtfully sipping her tea. She had been married for thirty years and had four strapping grown up sons: she and Henry must have experienced some of the traumas she now felt she and Arvind were going through. Traumas of which Arvind didn't seem to be aware.

'Helena,' she began hesitantly, 'there's nothing really wrong. It's me, I'm afraid: I can't seem to adapt to living over here. I dread the long winter with its dark dreary days: the cold seems to eat into my bones so that I feel unable to function between October and April.'

'I know what you mean.' Helena sympathised, 'there's nothing in this flat country to stop the wind from coming straight in from Siberia. Do you remember last year? After Christmas the temperature fell to well below zero... and stayed there.'

Fleur nodded.

'You'd better get Arvind to buy you an ankle-length mink coat,' Helena smiled. She waited, realising that the weather wasn't the only reason for Fleur's apparent unhappiness.

'And the language defeats me,' Fleur burst out at last.

'I think it defeats everyone except the Danes,' Helena said drily. I've been here for nearly four years and I still can't get my tongue round anything more than "good morning" and "pass the salt". Henry's first posting after we were married was Oslo and I picked up the basics of Norwegian very easily. But Danish....' she rolled her eyes expressively.

'It's Arvind's language,' Fleur protested, 'his country, I *should* be able to communicate. What if we have children? That's the language they'll be brought up to speak.'

'Fleur, I wish I could help you,' Helena said sympathetically. 'Why don't you talk to Arvind about it?

'I can't,' Fleur stammered. She paused and carefully studied her nails. 'We don't seem to have anything to talk about any more. The.... the flame seems to have gone out of our marriage.'

'Then I suggest you work at putting it back,' Helena said firmly. 'Starting a family might be a good way to begin. I was very unsettled and unhappy when we lived in Oslo, but once I had David it made all the difference.' She smiled at Fleur. 'I suggest you try it.'

Fleur froze and didn't return her smile. Sensing from Fleur's attitude that the subject was closed and she did not wish to continue the conversation, Helena gathered her papers together and rose from her seat. 'Diplomatic life is not always easy, Fleur,' she said taking her arm as they walked towards the door, 'moving around from place to place, no real home.' She squeezed Fleur's elbow affectionately, and planted a swift kiss on her cheek. 'Don't let it break your marriage, my dear.'

Fleur waved through the window as Helena walked sedately down the steps to where her car was waiting, and watched till its lights disappeared round the corner of the road. Helena's words had stung, and she remained staring disconsolately at the drizzle pattering against the panes. It was late September, but winter seemed to have come early, sneaking in with gusts of wind and sudden outbursts of rain. The smell of burning leaves rising from the garden brought with it the dank scent of Autumn. She remembered nostalgically the golden September days in Washington and Paris: the pavement cafés alive with people, carefree crowds strolling along the Champs-Elysées, and her spirits spiralled down once again. Night was already falling and she sighed at the thought of the long Danish winter stretching ahead of her. Hearing her husband's key turn in the lock, Fleur drew the heavy curtains to shut out the approaching darkness.

He bent to kiss her, but he seemed tense and preoccupied. 'Fleur,' he said hesitantly when Sigrid brought in a tray of cocktails.'We have to talk.'

Fleur looked at him in surprise. 'What about?' she queried.

Arvind took a cocktail, removed the cherry, popped it into his mouth then quickly swallowed the drink. Carefully replacing the glass on the tray, he turned to face her. 'Us,' he said briefly.

'*Us*' Fleur puzzled. What do you mean?'

'What I say,' he replied tensely. '*Us.*'

'Oh, Arvind,' she snapped irritably, 'tell me what you're talking about: endlessly repeating "*us*"doesn't make sense.'

Arvind took another cocktail and gulped it down. 'Doesn't it?' he said tersely, 'it seems clear enough to me. I mean *us. Our marriage.*'

'But what about it?' Fleur asked bewilderedly. 'What's wrong with our marriage?'

Arvind stared intently into the fire then thrust his head into his hands. 'Everything,' he replied hoarsely.

Fleur gasped, her glass trembling in her hands.

Arvind sat up and taking it from her, placed it on the tray. 'Don't you see darling,' he said gently. 'It isn't working any more.'

Fleur closed her eyes, but didn't reply.

'Fleur,' he pleaded. 'We've been married for almost six years.....'

'And we've been very happy,' she cut in.

'As long as we were in Washington, in an international circle with a frenetic social life. But...... since we came back to Denmark everything's changed. You've lost weight, you've lost interest in most things and..... the sparkle has gone out of you.'

Helena's words came back to Fleur. 'The sparkle has gone out of you... and you've lost weight.' Was everyone aware of her unhappiness, she asked herself.

Arvind took her hands. 'I'm at a loss to know what to do to make you happy. You promised me that once we were back in Copenhagen we could start a family...... but..... you hardly ever want to make love these days. And when you do....... I sense it's a duty.'

'I've been very tired,' she cut in lamely.

'For almost two years?' he queried wearily. 'No darling, it's more than that.'

Fleur removed her hands and turned away from him, staring into the fire. She knew that what her husband said was true, and she didn't know what to reply.

'I engaged a good teacher so that you could learn Danish,' Arvind went on. 'You have an amazing gift for languages, but apart from the basic phrases you've gone no further.'

'It's a difficult language,' Fleur protested.

'I agree. But be honest Fleur, you've made very little effort.'

'I *have* tried Arvind,' she pleaded, 'believe me I have. I don't understand why I'm having such difficulty. Helena Davidson was here this afternoon to discuss arrangements for the Christmas Fayre and we happened to be talking about how difficult Danish is.' Fleur took a deep breath. 'She said it was an impossible language, and after almost four years she still couldn't say more than good morning and pass the salt.'

'The British are not renowned for their language skills,' Arvind replied caustically.

'Perhaps not,' Fleur shot back defensively. 'but it doesn't help that wherever I go everyone is dying to practise their English or their French on me. I learnt German and French as a child and had no problem.' She gave a feeble laugh. 'Perhaps after thirty the brain cells controlling languages slough off.'

'Perhaps,' Arvind said tightly, 'but I doubt it. No Fleur I think it goes deeper than that. You didn't want to come back to Copenhagen, and now you're here you're inwardly rebelling by refusing to learn the language.

'Arvind,' she burst out, 'that's not true!'

'Oh, I don't mean *intentionally.*' His lips tightened. 'It's like your refusal to have a child. Something you say you don't understand.' He sighed. 'And I certainly don't.'

They seemed to have reached a stalemate, each anchored in his own opinion, unable to see the other's point of view. Fleur was almost in tears. This was as near as they had ever been to a serious quarrel. But, she reflected, in Washington their life had been so hectic they had scarcely had time to talk, let alone quarrel, and since their arrival in Denmark they had never seemed to want to talk. Were they drifting apart she wondered? Was Arvind regretting their marriage? He had been a much sought after bachelor for many years, perhaps he was yearning to return to those carefree days. As these thoughts catapulted backwards and forwards in her brain her heart seemed to wrench itself from it moorings and race crazily around her chest, crashing against her ribcage, seeking an escape. And the past suddenly kalaidescoped before her eyes in sudden knife sharp bursts as the faces of her mother and Hugh slowly passed in review. She had loved them, yet they had abandoned her. Her reason told her it was not true, but her heart refused to listen. And now Arvind, the rock she had clung to: the man she believed had been able to erase those painful memories: the man she thought would never reject her, now he, like the others, was slipping away leaving her raw and unprotected. And she couldn't bear it. She could not bear to be hurt again.

As if from a long way off she heard Arvind's voice. 'Copenhagen is my base. I'll have foreign postings, but it's here to the *Danish* Foreign Office that I'll inevitably return. It's my country, Fleur, it's where I belong...... and I had hoped it could become your country too.' He sighed and ran his fingers through his hair.

Fleur sat up and looked straight ahead of her, willing herself to be strong: not to let him see how much his words had hurt her; 'So what do you suggest? she asked tightly.

For a few minutes Arvind didn't reply: he sat with his head in his hands. Then the bomb fell. 'I suggest we part,' he said flatly.

'*Part?*' Fleur gasped. Her heart stopped thundering against her ribs. It seemed to miss a beat then plummet, falling heavily before crashing in a thousand pieces: and something broke in Fleur. It was as if the last strand of hope to which she had clung in the midst of her tortured emotions suddenly snapped. She knew she was on the verge of tears, and she didn't want her husband to see how much his words had wounded her. She held her breath willing the tears to recede, furious with herself for her weakness, now convinced that she would never make any man happy, that she was destined to bring only suffering and heartache to those she loved. She felt incapable of thinking clearly, and pressed her lips tightly together to prevent the bubble of hysteria which she felt simmering within her from rising to the surface and exploding. For a brief shocked second a wave of despair followed by a sudden surge of anger overwhelmed her, and she understood that her only escape route was to attack.

'Why don't you be honest and say you want a divorce 'she cried, hardly aware of what she was saying.

'I *don't* want a divorce,' he cried. 'You've misunderstood me. I mean part...... *temporarily.* Perhaps a change is what you need.' He shrugged helplessly. 'Then if you feel you can't come back to the life I have to offer you, I'll give you your freedom. Anything is better than watching you day after day wilt before my eyes.'

Fleur turned to him, her eyes hard, her face set in granite, her breath spurting forth in sharp gasps as the pain now clutching her, constricting her chest became almost unbearable. 'I see,' she muttered, 'you could at least have the courage to say you've found someone else. A Danish woman perhaps who's dying to give you six children.... and sit here all day watching the rain.' She rose abruptly, hating herself for her spiteful outburst. Walking over to the window, she savagely pulled aside the curtains and stared out at the rain and the sodden grey clouds drifting aimlessly across the sky. Night had finally fallen, and the short Northern day had ended.

Arvind realised that he had failed to put across his argument as he had intended, and Fleur had misunderstood him. Now that the damage was done, he was at a loss to know how to put things right. 'Fleur darling,' he pleaded, coming quickly behind her and taking her in his arms. 'I haven't looked at another woman since the day I met you.' He held her desperately to him. Her breathing eased and she half collapsed into his arms, soft and yielding. Then abruptly she stiffened and tore herself away, not daring to submit to the feelings stirring within her; afraid of yielding and being hurt again, convinced that Arvind was trying to tell her, without hurting her, that he wanted his freedom. 'I love you as much as ever Fleur,' he whispered, 'but I can't bear to see you so unhappy. Try to understand....'

'There's nothing to understand,' Fleur cut in. Nothing that she could understand. Arvind had sent her world crashing around her ears. She turned away from him, but he caught her and held her tightly, almost fiercely to him. 'We have *everything* to be happy,' he whispered. 'We *were* happy,'

But Fleur remained unresponsive. Hurt and bewildered, he released her. 'I know you hate the long winters here,' he acquiesed. 'Your father's retired now and he and Claudine are living in Paris. It might do you good to go and stay with them for a while: after a few months perhaps you'd settle better. If not........' He shrugged helplessly. 'I think the only solution would be for me to give you your freedom.'

Fleur felt frozen. 'He'll be saying "let's remain friends next", she thought bitterly. *Friends!* Arvind, her lover, her life.... a friend! No, she almost shrieked. And she knew she had to get away before they reached that point. Before her final humiliation. Gathering together what few shreds of dignity she felt she still had left she set her lips in a hard line. 'I'll go and pack...... and leave in the morning.'

Arvind turned, an agonised expression on his face. 'Fleur,' he cried. 'That's not what I meant.'

But she had already left the room. That night she slept in the spare bedroom. Arvind came to her, but she turned away, feigning sleep.

The following morning when Arvind awoke Fleur had gone. Throwing on a few clothes, he leapt into the car and raced to the airport. The Paris flight was about to take off. The plane was taxiing along the runway before slowly rising into the air when, breathless he arrived on the terrace. He saw his wife's face at a small porthole: she was staring bleakly in front of her, her expression lifeless. Cupping his hands round his mouth he called, but the roar of the plane's engines drowned his voice, and if she saw him she did not acknowledge his wave, just remained staring woodenly ahead: And he agonised over what he had done.

Claudine noticed the change in Fleur as soon as she stepped off the plane, but neither she nor Hubert remarked on it, nor her abrupt departure from Copenhagen. It wasn't until Fleur had pleaded a headache and retired to her room immediately after dinner that the subject was raised.

'Something's gone very wrong' Hubert sighed. 'I wonder when she's going to tell us what it is.'

Claudine put down her coffee cup and smiled at her husband. 'Give her time,' she advised.

But the days went by and Fleur remained tight-lipped. Her eyes held a hunted, bewildered look and Claudine longed to comfort her, but she felt at a loss how to begin.

Arvind telephoned regularly and was as warm as ever with his parents-in-law, but when Fleur was called to the 'phone the conversation was always brief. She appeared to answer more out of duty than pleasure, and never commented on their conversation: always going to her room immediately afterwards.

Claudine and Hubert felt helpless.

'Perhaps if I invited her out to lunch, just the two of us, she might open up,' Claudine suggested.

Hubert shrugged. 'You can always try.'

Claudine was about to suggest it the following morning when Fleur announced that she would be out for most of the day.

'I've rented a flat,' she announced at dinner that evening. 'Near Notre Dame. It's furnished and I'll be moving in next week.'

Claudine gasped. 'But darling, *why?*'

'I need a place to live: I can't stay here forever.'

Her father shook his head sadly. 'Fleur,' he said gently. 'Could you explain what this is all about?

'Arvind and I have parted,' she said briefly, and rose from the table.'Now if you'll excuse me, I'm very tired. To-morrow is going to be busy. I need to find a job.'

Claudine and Hubert looked at each other. He shook his head. 'I thought they were so happy.'

'They were,' Claudine replied grimly, 'but something's happened to bring this about. Do you think we should telephone Arvind and ask *him* what's gone wrong, since Fleur doesn't seem inclined to tell us.'

At that moment the telephone rang. It was Arvind. But when called, Fleur replied that she was in bed.

'Did you ask him?' Hubert enquired, when his wife joined him in the drawing-room.

Claudine shook her head. 'I hadn't the courage.'

'This nonsense about getting a job,' Hubert said grimly. 'She's not really qualified to do anything.'

Claudine didn't reply, just sat staring into the fire. Suddenly she got up and walked towards the telephone. 'I have an idea,' she called over her shoulder to her husband. 'I'll tell you about it if it works.' When she returned she curled up on the sofa and flicked on the television. 'I think I've fixed it,' she said enigmatically. But didn't elaborate.

Claudine looked up from reading her mail when Fleur walked into the dining room the following morning. 'Feeling better?' she smiled.

Fleur smiled back, but only with her lips. Her eyes remained blank and hard.

'I'm having lunch at the Cercle Interallié with an old friend who's longing to meet you,' Claudine went on brightly. She gathered up her letters and left the table. 'I have an appointment this morning, so I'll see you there at a quarter to one.'

Fleur opened her mouth to protest, but Claudine was already at the door. 'And wear your best bib and tucker,' she said sternly, before closing it firmly behind her.

Fleur looked angrily at her father.

'When Claudine gets a bee in her bonnet,' he smiled. 'It's best not to argue.'

Claudine was sitting in a deep armchair leaning forward in animated conversation with someone sitting opposite her when Fleur walked into the sumptuous salons of the exclusive Paris club. She looked up and waved. A tall slim man with aristocratic features and thick silvery hair rose to greet her.

'Come and meet my old friend Prince Postovsky,' Claudine smiled.

The man bowed. As his lips brushed her outstretched hand, Fleur had the distinct impression that she had seen him before. He raised his head and their eyes met. Fleur's heart sank: they were cornflower blue. Was she never to escape that fateful colour?

—ooo-O-ooo—

Chapter Sixteen

Hugh and his father settled into comfortable chairs in the lounge of the old fashioned hotel where Arthur Cunningham was staying the night.

'We'll have an early dinner, then you can catch the last train back to London,' his father said when their drinks arrived. 'Life at the hospital is still as hectic I gather.'

'More so than ever. But I enjoy it.'

His father swirled the golden liquid round in his glass thoughtfully.

'What a very special day,' he mused. 'I never thought I'd live to see John taking marriage vows. I'm so happy for him.' He sighed. 'I only wish the same thing could happen for you.'

'I'm fine, Hugh smiled. 'I've finally turned the page. Fleur is just a beautiful dream. I'm married to the job now.'

'That's what I thought about John,' his father laughed. 'They both seem to be very well thought of at the University. That was a wonderful reception their colleagues gave them.'

Both Hugh and his father had been captivated by John's bride. She wasn't beautiful, or even pretty, but there was something about her eyes which was arresting. Very dark and luminous, with a depth of sadness which time would never erase. She reminded Hugh of the pictures of Old Testament Jewesses in his Childrens' Bible.

'I'm sure they will be very happy,' Hugh murmured thoughtfully.

And they sat in silence for a while, each lost in his own thoughts.

'Tell me about your trip to New Zealand,' Hugh remarked, while scrutinising the menu in the small dining room. 'You were away a long time. I thought you'd emigrated. '

'It's strange you should say that,' his father replied. 'Because that's what I'm thinking of doing.'

Hugh looked up in surprise.

'My former assistant who took over the practice when I retired now has two children and is anxious for me to sell them the house. I've resisted up till now: it holds so many memories.' He smiled. 'It's where the three of you were born...... and where your mother and I were so happy.'

Hugh said nothing. His father 's eyes were far away, and Hugh knew that the step he was considering would not be an easy one.

'But it does seem silly to rattle around in that barn of a place on my own. Mrs. Blaney is well past retirement age, she's only waiting for me to move on so that she can go and live with her sister in Whitby. And.... I've now got *three* grandchildren in New Zealand who are growing up far too quickly.'

'When were you thinking of going?' Hugh enquired.

'In the Spring: that will give me the winter to sort things out at the house. More than fifty years of memories will take time to sift through.' Arthur Cunningham sighed. 'Once I leave I doubt I shall ever return. It's a long journey, and I'm not getting any younger.' He wiped his mouth with his napkin and lifted his wine glass, gazing thoughtfully at the contents. 'I was wondering Hugh, whether you might like to join me over there.'

Hugh laughed. 'At the moment I'm not thinking of going anywhere. But once I'm through with all these b lasted studies I'll certainly have deserved a holiday. So why not?'

'I meant *permanently.* ' his father stressed. 'There's a wonderfully modern hospital in Wellington. English nurses especially those trained at the big London hospitals are going over to Australia and New Zealand by the boat load, and are welcomed with open arms. It appears that the working conditions and certainly the salaries are very much better. You'd probably find it's the same for doctors.'

'How do you know all this?' Hugh probed.

Arthur Cunningham looked embarrassed. 'Elizabeth told me. She very much wants me to emigrate, but I hesitated.' He gave a mischievous smile making him look almost boyish. 'I didn't want to leave you two bachelors with nowhere to go for Christmas, so she made enquiries, and organised us all. Knowing my daughter, she's probably already arranged a job for John at the University.' He laughed. 'But now that he's got Ruth to watch over him, that won't be necessary.'

'Lizzie always did boss us around,' Hugh smiled. He glanced at his watch. 'Dad, I'll have to go if I'm to catch that last train. No, don't get up, sit there and enjoy your liqueur. I'll come up to Yorkshire as soon as I have a few days off.'

'Do that my boy, and..... think about what I said.'

'Let's have coffee in the lounge,' Claudine said rising from the table. 'You're not in a hurry are you, Seigei?'

Prince Postovsky glanced at his watch. 'I have to be back at the Quai d'Orsay by four.'

'Quai d'Orsay?', Fleur queried, as they settled into the comfortable armchairs. 'You work at the Quai d'Orsay?'

'For my sins,' Sergei Postovsky smiled.

'Then perhaps you know my father?'

'Very well.'

'Is that how you two met?' she enquired.

'No,' Claudine laughed. 'I knew Sergei long before his Quai d'Orsay days. There used to be a large White Russian Colony in Nice. George and I spent a lot of time at Boulouris and we got to know them all.'

'Are you a diplomat?' Fleur pursued.

Prince Postovsky laughed.

'Sergei is chief interpreter at the Quai d'Orsay,' Claudine explained. He always interprets for the President when there are important conferences. You've perhaps seen him on the television standing behind the President's chair, whispering in his ear.'

'I *thought* I'd seen you before,' Fleur exclaimed. 'But I couldn't think where.'

'Now you know,' Claudine exclaimed. She glanced across at him, and raised her eyebrows. He gave a slight nod. 'Sergei speaks several languages,' Claudine went on. 'You may have noticed that he darted back and forth from one to the other when we were having lunch.'

Fleur had noticed.

'It was a test,' Claudine went on enigmatically.

Fleur frowned wondering what on earth Claudine was talking about.

'I went to see Sergei this morning,' Claudine explained. 'When you mentioned you wanted to find a job I thought he might be able to help you.'

'And I think I can,' he put in. 'Would you be interested in interpreting?'

'Interpreting what?' Fleur puzzled.

'Paris is going to be the centre for many of the international agencies which are being set up. The Marshall Plan is here and has already developed into the OCD, and UNESCO's also on the way to becoming something big. Simultaneous interpretation which began at the Nuremberg Trials......

'Were you interpreting there?' Fleur interrupted.

He nodded. 'I think you might do very well at it.'

'But I've no training,' Fleur protested.

'I had no training. Most of the interpreters at Nuremberg had no training, we learnt on the job. Schools for interpreters now have been set up, but I've found that the best interpreters are intelligent, cultured multi-lingual people who dive in at the deep end.'

'I'm hardly multi-lingual.'

'Your French and English are perfect, and your accent in German is almost imperceptible. I'm sure with a little help your Russian would come back.'

'But I left Russia when I was *four*,' Fleur protested.

'One never really forgets languages one learned when very young. And mostly interpreters interpret into their own language. But you'd be valuable because you are equally at ease in either French or English, and you could interpret *out* of German.' He smiled. 'If you're interested, I can put you in touch with a colleague of mine who has opened an interpreters' school: but I don't think you'd need that. He could give you a test and I'm sure you would be accepted immediately at OCD. It's conveniently near, in Passy, at the Chateau de la Muette, one of the former Rothschild homes.'

'I'd be terrified,' Fleur exclaimed. 'I wouldn't have a clue what to do.'

'You wouldn't be put into the box alone,' Sergei smiled, 'there are always two interpreters. But at first you'd listen and learn. You'd soon get the hang of it.' He glanced at his watch and hurriedly rose. 'I'm sorry Claudine, but I have to go.' He turned to the bewildered Fleur and handed her a visiting card. 'Telephone my friend Paul Chatto, his number is on the back. I'll tell him you'll be contacting him. Then you can meet and talk it over. Now would be a good time.' He smiled at her as he bent over her hand 'Don't be apprehensive. It's exciting work: you'd enjoy it. And.... I think you'd do very well.'

Fleur felt punch drunk.

'What do you think?' Claudine enquired. 'You said you wanted a job, and conference interpreting would certainly be more interesting that selling underwear at the Galeries Lafayette.' She rose from her chair. 'Come on, let's go and telephone this Mr. Chatto. Sergei said this would be a good time.'

Fleur got slowly to her feet. 'Claudine,' she said suspiciously, 'you organised this didn't you?'

'Of course I did,' Claudine laughed.

Fleur returned from making the telephone call more bewildered than ever. 'He knew all about me, he was expecting my call.' She shook her head. 'Prince Postovsky has only just left, he couldn't possibly have had time to contact him.'

'He didn't. Claudine remarked smugly. 'He rang him this morning.'

Fleur frowned. 'Claudine what on earth are you talking about? I hadn't even heard of him much less met him this morning.'

'But *I* had. I rang Sergei last night and went to see him this morning. I told him all about you. He said you sounded interesting and rang his friend before we came to lunch. So, when does he want to see you?'

'He said *now*,' Fleur answered lamely. 'At the Chateau de la Muette.'

'Good,' Claudine replied collecting her handbag and gloves. 'We'll grab a taxi and I'll drop you off on my way home.' She tucked her arm in Fleur's as they walked across the courtyard and out into the rue du Faubourg St. Honoré. '*Now* you don't need to rent that flat on the other side of Paris, you can stay with your father and me. La Muette is just round the corner.'

'I've signed a lease for six months,' Fleur said stubbornly. 'I'll stick to my original plan.'

It was eight o'clock before Fleur returned to the Square Lamartine. When she entered the drawing room a sudden silence fell, and two pairs of eyes swivelled towards her.

'I start to-morrow,' she said wearily, sinking into a chair and accepting the drink her father poured out for her.

'Wonderful,' Claudine exclaimed. She bounced off the sofa and hugged Fleur. 'I'm *so* pleased darling,' she enthused. 'Tell us all about it.'

'Well,' Fleur said hesitantly. 'He asked me a lot of questions, jumping backwards and forwards in several languages like Prince Postovsky did and expecting me to keep up. Then he gave me a test.' Fleur dimpled. It was the first time she had smiled since her arrival. 'Those interpreters cabins are really cute. There are two places: one interpreter works for twenty minutes and then they swop over: the concentration needed is so intense it's difficult to keep it up indefinitely. You can see the audience, but I don't think they can see you. Paul Chatto is working to-morrow morning. He's taking me into the cabin with him so that I can see what it's all about. "Get the feel of it," he said. 'Then I'll be with seasoned interpreters for a while before I'm actually launched.' She gave a delightful giggle. Apparently the cardinal sin is to say "um". So I mustn't forget. He took me around to show me the ropes and introduced me to some of the interpreters who work with him. They seem awfully nice, I think I'm going to enjoy it.' She yawned. 'Now I'm going to have a bath and flop into bed. I don't want any dinner, I'm too exhausted.'

'I'll bring you up a tray,' Claudine insisted. She turned to her husband when Fleur left the room. '*What* a transformation.'

He nodded. 'Yes,' he answered thoughtfully. But is it a good thing? She *is* Arvind's wife. And whatever went wrong I wouldn't be surprised if it wasn't eighty percent Fleur's fault.'

'Whatever do you mean?' Claudine puzzled. 'We've no idea what went wrong.'

'I wonder if Fleur didn't marry a ghost.'

Claudine frowned in bewilderment.

'Hugh was never officially declared dead. I don't think she's ever accepted the fact that he's not coming back. I always had the feeling even when she married, though I'm sure *she* wasn't conscious of it, that she was still waiting for Hugh. Expecting to find him around every corner.'

'Hubert, that's preposterous. She and Arvind were madly in love.'

'I agree. But deep in her subconscious was she using Arvind as a stop gap? Hoping to find in him a replacement for her lost husband?'

'Darling, you're looking for problems where none exist. Of course she wasn't. Don't get into all this Freudian stuff. She and

Arvind have had a problem like all young married couples, that's all'

'They've been married for six years, and still no children.'

'They've hardly had time! Their life in Washington was one mad whirl.'

'But they've been back in Copenhagen for almost two years.'

Claudine sighed and got to her feet. 'It'll work itself out you'll see.' She dropped a kiss on her husband's hair.

He smiled up at her. 'I sincerely hope so.'

In spite of Claudine's protests, Fleur moved into the flat near Notre Dame that weekend. She seemed to be completely transformed. The taught expression had gone from her face, and her eyes had lost their hard, haunted expression.

'Your little ruse seems to have worked,' Hubert remarked that evening when he and Claudine sat down to dinner.

As they rose from the table, the telephone rang. It was Arvind.

'I'm afraid Fleur isn't here, 'Claudine replied hesitantly.

'Shall I call back later..... or to-morrow morning?' he enquired.

Claudine took a deep breath, at a loss for words. 'She's no longer living with us,' she stammered. 'She's rented a flat for a few months near the Latin Quarter: I can give you her telephone number.'

She heard Arvind take a quick intake of breath. 'If Fleur wanted me to have her telephone number she would have given it to me herself,' he said tightly.

'I'm sure she will,' Claudine assured him. 'She only moved in yesterday.'

'Then we'll wait and see, shall we?' Arvind replied.

The pain in his voice devastated Claudine. '*Arvind*,' she cried, 'Hubert and I are dreadfully worried about you and Fleur. Why is she here? You seemed so happy.....'

'We *were* happy.'

He paused, and Claudine had the feeling that Arvind was battling with himself, trying to decide whether to end the conversation or confide in her. Then suddenly it all came pouring out.

'Do you think it would help if I came over to Paris?' he ended hopefully.

'Perhaps not at the moment,' she replied. 'But I'm sure Fleur will soon come to her senses and come back to you...... If by then you still *want* her.'

'I will,' Arvind said softly.' 'Fleur is my whole life.'

'I hope she's worthy of you,' Claudine said grimly.

Arvind gave a slight laugh.

'Worthy or not. She's the only woman I want.'

Claudine walked slowly back into the drawing room. 'That was Arvind on the telephone. He told me what happened between him Fleur and it's all a dreadful misunderstanding.' She down on the sofa and leant unhappily against her husband. 'I've messed up everything Hubert. Helping Fleur to become an interpreter was a terrible mistake. It would have been better to let her find a job on her own: there wouldn't have been much choice and she'd soon have tired of being a shop assistant, and realised how lucky she was to have Arvind. *Now*, thanks to my interference she seems to have blossomed and embarked on a career.'

'Is that such a bad thing?'

Claudine looked at him in surprise. 'Of *course* it is. She'll *never* want to go back to Denmark.'

Her husband smiled reassuringly. 'I've been thinking a lot about what has happened, and I've come to the conclusion that this is an outcome of the tragedy Fleur lived through during the war finally surfacing.' He reached for his pipe and carefully patted the tobacco into the bowl. 'My disappearance, followed by the death of her mother, then her husband in quick succession destroyed her security, and her confidence in herself. They've got to be built up again.' He carefully lit his pipe and threw the match into the empty grate. 'For some strange reason she's convinced herself that she's responsible for all these dramas, and until she works through that one, she'll never be happy with any man.' He put his arm round his wife. 'Don't worry darling, this may be the best thing that has happened to her. Given time, she'll come round.'

Ten days later Sergei Postovsky telephoned. 'Paul Chatto is *delighted* with Fleur,' he announced enthusiastically. 'Says she's a "natural". In fact, he's thinking of letting her fly on her own next week.'

'How splendid,' Claudine answered, with as much enthusiasm as she could muster. Since her conversation with Arvind she had hoped that Fleur would fail hopelessly in her new venture and be obliged to face reality.

'Could the three of you come down to Montfort l'Amaury for lunch next Sunday?' Sergei went on. 'Larissa has been marooned there with a cluster of grandchildren since the end of June and would love to see you all. I'll invite Paul Chatto as well, then he can tell you himself how well Fleur is doing.'

Her husband looked up questioningly when she returned to the breakfast table. 'That's splendid,' he said, when she told him the news.

Claudine frowned in surprise. 'Do you mean the lunch or the news of Fleur's success?

'Both,' he replied enigmatically. He put down his newspaper. 'It's a good thing Fleur has found her feet and discovered something she can do well. It's what she needed. To prove to herself that she's worth something.' His eyes twinkled at her. 'By interfering darling you may even have *solved* the problem.'

Lunch at Montfort l'Amaury the following Sunday was a huge success. The weather held and Fleur was in sparkling form.

'I can't believe the change in Fleur,' Sergei Postovsky remarked to Hubert as they sat together under the trees watching Fleur play croquet with a handful of grandchildren. 'When I first met her I recognised her linguistic talent and quick mind but.....'

'She appeared tight-lipped and reserved and... rather unpleasant,' Claudine interrupted.

'Well.... yes,' he admitted. 'But she's a different woman to-day.'

'Thanks to you,' Claudine smiled.

'And you darling,' Hubert teased. 'Your meddling did the trick.'

Claudine gave her husband a playful kick.

Even Paul Chatto, known not only for his brilliant mind, but also his preference for male colleagues, seemed to have fallen beneath her spell. She was back to being the fascinating hostess who had captivated Washington.

Arvind had not telephoned again, and Fleur had not contacted him.

'I've been so busy,' she explained when Claudine tentatively asked whether she had given her husband her new address. 'I will do it, I promise.' But the promise remained unfulfilled.

In the end Arvind cracked and called Claudine.

'He sounded *so* unhappy,' Claudine lamented, when she rejoined her husband. 'What *are* we going to do?'

'Nothing,' he replied. 'These young people must work out their own problems.'

Finally, after constant bullying from Claudine, Fleur telephoned her husband. She chattered away happily, as if nothing had happened, giving him all her news, yet making no mention of her return: and Arvind was left in limbo. But, contact re-established, he telephoned Fleur regularly. She was always charming, though evasive, and after every call he felt more frustrated and unhappy than ever.

'You'll be coming home for Christmas, won't you?' he pleaded at the beginning of December. 'I thought we might go to Norway and ski.'

'Oh Arvind,' she replied. 'That would have been lovely, but I'm afraid I'll only have a very short break. I'm going to free-lance in the New Year and I'm booked for a conference in Madrid on the 28th.'

'Then I'll come to you,' he said grimly.

'I-I don't want to ruin your Christmas,' she began.

But he cut her short. 'You already have,' he said tightly, and put down the receiver.

'That man's a saint,' Claudine sighed, when Fleur mentioned that Arvind would be with them for the festivities. 'I wonder how much longer he's going to put up with her.'

'Anyone's guess,' Hubert replied. 'Perhaps Christmas will be a reconciliation.'

'Claudine and Hubert would be happy for you to stay with them,' Fleur announced, when Arvind telephoned to tell her his time of arrival.

'Can't I stay with you?' he gasped.

'My flat is very small, little more than a studio. There simply isn't room for two.'

'Then I'll book a room at an hotel,' he replied curtly. And rang off.

The conference on Christmas Eve at which Fleur was interpreting was followed by a reception. Arvind had already arrived at the flat in the Square Lamartine when she rushed in.

'I'm *so* sorry', she said to the room in general. Arvind stepped forward, his arms outstretched, but Fleur avoided them.

'How lovely to see you,' she smiled, kissing him briefly on both cheeks.

Claudine glanced at her husband in amazement. He gave a slight shrug and turned to pour Fleur a drink. Arvind looked as if he had received a sharp slap in the face.

'Happy *Christmas*,' Claudine sighed, flopping into an armchair when Fleur and Arvind left. 'However are we going to get through the next two days?'

Fleur had been as sparkling as ever. But apart from the usual polite niceties Arvind had hardly said a word: he seemed punch drunk.

'Whatever's the matter with that girl,' Claudine rattled on irritably. 'She's got a wonderful husband, and look at the way she treats him.'

'Fleur is very sensitive and highly strung. She's obviously been badly hurt,' Hubert replied, sitting down beside her.

'What about?' his wife snapped.

'Arvind suggesting they part.'

'Oh for heaven's sake, 'Claudine replied sharply, 'it's time she got over that. He doesn't *act* like a man who wants a separation.' Claudine sighed. 'I'm thankful we've got friends coming to lunch to-morrow, I couldn't stand another meal like the one we've just endured. Everyone being polite and no-one enjoying themselves.' She got up and began angrily puffing the cushions. 'This is supposed to be *Christmas*,' she exploded. 'A time when families get together and *enjoy* themselves.'

'I'll go to the corner and hail a cab,' Arvind said as he and Fleur walked into the square 'there are bound to be plenty passing in the Avenue Victor Hugo.'

Fleur dimpled and held up a bunch of keys. 'No need. I've got my little beetle just here.' She opened the door of a small bright green car.

'You've got a *car*?' Arvind frowned in amazement.

'Only a tiny one,' she smiled, climbing in and leaning across to open the passenger door, 'it'so handy for going to work. This just whizzes round Paris.' She smiled sweetly up at him as they drove away. 'Much pleasanter than the metro where one needs to eat a diet of garlic in self-defense.' She laughed happily, weaving expertly in and out of small streets. 'Where exactly is your hotel Arvind? I can drop you at the door.'

He looked at her in amazement. 'I had thought I might come and see your apartment,' he replied. 'It's not late, and..... Fleur, we *do* have things to discuss.'

'Not to-night, Arvind,' she replied. 'I've had a very busy day and I'm whacked. I'll pick you up at midday to-morrow for lunch.'

'Then drop me here,' Arvind said coldly, as they passed Notre Dame. The bells had begun to chime for midnight Mass making further conversation impossible. 'And don't bother to pick me up in the morning, a walk will do me good.'

'It's a long way,' Fleur demurred.

'There *are* taxis,' he replied icily, 'and.... thank you for the tie. It's beautiful.'

Fleur had given Hermes ties to both her father and her husband.

'Thank *you* for the earrings,' she smiled. Arvind had offered her beautiful butterfly ear-rings in beaten Danish silver. 'I'll wear them to-morrow.'

'Please don't feel obliged,' he replied stiffly. 'They're not exactly emeralds. But,' he added tightly, 'it's not exactly the same situation.'

Fleur sighed. She slowly started up the car watching Arvind walk across the square in front of the great cathedral. To her surprise he walked through the massive oak doors and into the dim interior. The following day the atmosphere was more relaxed. Fleur mingled happily with the guests Claudine had invited to lunch, Arvind remained quiet, but impeccably polite. Claudine's heart went out to him when she saw the misery in his eyes, but her husband gave her warning glances, daring her to interfere.

'What time are we expected at the Postovsky's to-morrow?' Fleur enquired, when she and Arvind were leaving.

'For lunch,' Claudine replied. 'Be here around eleven thirty and we'll drive out to Montfort l'Amaury together.' She smiled across at Arvind. 'The Postovsky's are really looking forward to meeting Fleur's husband.'

Hubert noticed the stress she put on "husband".

Arvind was silent as Fleur drove through the quiet streets. Light escaping through the shutters of the apartments they passed glowed, spattering strange patterns onto the pavements, and occasionally bursts of laughter seeped through. Arvind sighed, imagining the families rejoicing together inside. He wondered whether it wouldn't have been better for him to have gone to Arendal to join his parents for the festivities, and face the polite enquiries as to Fleur's absence. He had hoped that this meeting in Paris would solve their problems, but Fleur seemed to be avoiding him. And the days he had hoped to spend quietly with her had become action packed, leaving them no time together.

'Do you still not want me to drop you at your hotel?' Fleur enquired, when Notre Dame once again loomed into view.

'Fleur,' he said quietly, 'you say you're leaving for a conference in Spain the day after to-morrow.'

She smiled happily. 'My first leap into the world of free-lancing. It's scary... but exciting.'

Arvind sighed. 'I had hoped we might have had some time to be alone together to talk and sort out our problem. Can't I come and see your apartment now?'

Fleur hesitated. 'Yes Arvind,' she said at last. 'If that is what you want.'

'It *is* what I want,' he replied. 'More than anything.'

She slowed down and drew up in front of a large old building. 'Fourth floor,' she said quietly, when they entered the lift. 'It's furnished,' she explained, flicking on the light when they walked into the flat, 'not at all in the way *I* would have chosen. It's very basic, but it does. And I'm hardly ever here. The flat is really only a dormitory. Drink?' she smiled holding up a decanter as he gazed round the small sitting room.

He nodded absently, walking towards a door in the corner. 'May I?' he enquired, his hand on the knob.

She nodded, and Arvind entered the tiny bedroom. 'Fleur,' he queried, returning to the sitting room and accepting the glass she held out.'I don't understand. You said the apartment was too small for us both. But..... there's a double bed.'

'All French furnished apartments have a double bed,' she replied offhandly, 'but they're very small, nothing like the Danish or American ones. Not *really* enough room for two.'

'I could have slept on the sofa.'

'Your legs are too long, they'd have hung over the edge.'

He put down his glass. Walking towards her he pulled her to her feet and held her close. 'Fleur,' he murmured into her hair. Fleur *darling,* let me stay the night. Let me prove to you how much I love you: how much I want you back. I don't care if the bed's too small, we'll manage.'

But she pushed him gently away, and slipped out of his arms. 'Arvind,' she said quietly. 'You suggested we separate.......'

'And I've regretted it ever since,' he cut in desperately. 'It was a ghastly mistake.'

'But there must have been a reason,' Fleur went on levelly. 'I left believing that you had found someone else.

'I *told* you there was no-one else. There never has been.'

'We made a pact that day to separate, to give each other time to reconsider our feelings, and decide whether we wanted to stay together or not.' She paused. 'You reproached me for not giving you children. I don't know why I'm reticent, and I *still* don't know. I wish I did. It's unreasonable and...... unfair to you.'

'Fleur... I'

'Let's stick to our pact. Give ourselves a year to decide.'

'A *year!*'

'Well at least until the Spring: we can review our situation in May. I don't want it to be a spur of the moment decision. I want you to have time to find someone more suitable. Someone who is willing to give you children.'

'But.....'

'Arvind, it's pointless to go on. Let's leave things the way they are for the moment. I'll pick you up at eleven in the morning. Sleep well.' Fleur walked to the front door and held it open.

Arvind gave her an agonised glance. As he entered the lift he saw Fleur close the door of her apartment, and a sudden rage gripped him. He was the suave diplomat who had everything under control, who only had to snap his fingers and a host of pretty girls would come running, eager for the chance to share his life: to fit in with his wishes. Why couldn't he close the door on this chapter. Why did he have to live in misery, enslaved by a capricious woman who didn't appear to want him. He walked angrily back to his hotel. Entering his room, on a sudden impulse he picked up the telephone and asked to be put through to the airport at le Bourget.

The next morning he telephoned Hubert, thanked him and Claudine for their kindness and hospitality and said how sorry he was, but he would not to be joining them for the luncheon party at Montfort l'Amaury. 'I have to return to Copenhagen,' he explained, without giving any further details.

When Fleur arrived at the hotel later that morning to collect Arvind she found a letter addressed to her waiting at the reception.

CHAPTER SEVENTEEN

By the time Arvind's 'plane landed at Kastrup his anger had subsided, to be replaced by a feeling of hopelessness and desolation. Sigrid had gone to spend the holiday period with her family, and the house when he entered seemed bleak and unwelcoming.

Throwing his suitcase on the bed he picked up the telephone in search of company, but everyone was either away or otherwise engaged, and he wondered whether he had been wise to rush off as he did. Perhaps had he stayed he could have persuaded Fleur to see reason. He had hoped to bring her back with him, but now the possibility of her returning seemed even more remote.

Winding his scarf round his neck and shrugging back into his coat, he picked up his hat and left the house. He had no idea where he was going, but he felt he had to get away and think. Dusk was already falling and Copenhagen was deserted. Driving blindly he found himself on the coast road winding North.

It was dark when he ran into Klampenborg. Parking the car he headed for the beach. A full moon lit up the long stretch of silver sand. Thrusting his hands into his pockets, he walked blindly, oblivious of the angry waves crashing in from the Baltic and curling menacingly around his feet. Stopping to stub out a cigarette, he noticed lights from the Hotel Belle Vue spilling out onto the beach and, heading in their direction, entered it's warm foyer. A tea dance was in progress. Leaving his coat in the cloakroom, he crossed over to the bar.

Sitting alone in a corner with a large whisky in his hands, music from the ballroom drifted in, and a wave of misery engulfed him.

He remembered dancing with Fleur in that ballroom not long after they returned from Washington. Looking back, he realised that she had already begun to distance herself from him, and for the hundredth time he wondered what had gone wrong. Draining his glass he got up and walked back to the car.

It was still early when he drove into Copenhagen. Arvind couldn't face an evening alone in his silent house, which now appeared more like a tomb. He wondered whether that was how Fleur had felt, and a momentary wave of sympathy trickled through him. But it was quickly replaced by anger.

He parked the car and walked towards the Hotel d'Angleterre. Glancing into the dining room, he hoped he would find friends with whom he could share the long evening ahead, but there was no-one he knew. Heading for the bar, he ordered another large whisky, and sought a secluded corner where he could be alone with his misery. Arvind was not used to downing hard liquor on an empty stomach. Apart from social drinking he hardly ever touched whisky. After the third whisky he was beginning to feel extremely unsteady and knew he was incapable of driving himself back to Hellerup. Stumbling into the street he hailed a taxi. He would pick up his car in the morning. By the time he arrived home he no longer knew or cared that the house was bleak and empty. He had only one desire: to sleep. Tearing off his clothes and leaving them in an untidy heap, he fell into bed.

Opening one eye, he glanced at the bedside clock: A quarter past ten. Arvind sat up but immediately fell back onto the pillows, his head throbbing abominably. He called for Sigrid to bring him some strong black coffee, but his voice echoed hollowly around the empty house. With a groan he remembered that since he had planned to be in Paris until this evening he had told Sigrid he would not need her before the following morning. Turning on to his side, he tried to sleep, but the pain would not let him. Staggering out of bed, he searched blindly in the bathroom cupboard for something to relieve it. Grabbing a handful of pills, he swallowed them and limped back to bed.

It was three o'clock before he woke again. The pain in his head had almost gone, but he felt like a limp rag. Unreasonably, he blamed Fleur for his sorry condition, and once again anger overtook him. But it also energised him. Crawling out of bed, he headed for the shower.

'Right, 'he said grimly as the warm water cascaded down his body. 'She doesn't want me to contact her before May, so I won't. She suggested I find someone else, so I will. I *won't* be enslaved by her any longer.' Wrapping a towel around him, he went back into the bedroom and picked up the telephone.

'Alfhild?' he queried, when a woman's voice answered. 'You're back!'

'Arrived ten minutes ago. How was Paris?'

'Hectic.'

There was a pause, and he knew she was waiting for news of Fleur.

'Would you like to have dinner with me to-night? Sigrid's not here and I'm hungry.'

Alfhild gave a brief laugh. 'Not very flattering for me.'

Arvind laughed in his turn. It was the first time he had laughed since his arrival in Paris. 'I'm sorry,' he apologised 'but you know what I mean.'

'I'll forgive you. Yes, I'd love to have dinner with you, as long as you don't expect me to go to bed with you afterwards. I have to work in the morning, and I'm whacked.'

Arvind was taken back. Alfhild was the Norwegian ambassador's private secretary. Is that what the diplomatic corps thought of him since Fleur had left? That he was sleeping around? Perhaps they all believed that was *why* Fleur had left. His lips tightened. 'There are absolutely no strings attached,' he said quietly. 'I'll pick you up at seven.'

⚜ ⚜ ⚜

Arvind stuck to his resolve, and did not contact his wife.

Fleur had half expected him to call early in the New Year when she returned from her first free-lance venture in Spain. But as the days stretched into weeks she realised that she missed their friendly telephone chats. At the beginning of February she concluded that he had taken her at her word and found someone else: and she didn't know whether she was relieved or shattered.

Dropping into the flat in the Square Lamartine one afternoon in March, Fleur found her father alone.

'You've lost weight,' he remarked. 'Are you sure you're not working too hard? Or....' he went on. 'Is it something else?'

Fleur looked at him and suddenly her resolve melted. 'Oh Papa,' she cried, and burst into tears.

Hubert walked across to where she was sitting and put his arms round her. She leant her head dejectectedly against his shoulder. 'Arvind?' he queried.

She sniffed and took the handerchief he offered. 'I suppose so,' she said, wiping it around her face.

'I've stopped Claudine enquiring every five minutes whether you'd heard from him. But..... have you?'

'No,' Fleur whispered. She sat up. 'Papa,' she cried desperately, 'what's the matter with me? I bring disaster and pain on everyone I love. Arvind and I were so happy.'

Hubert said nothing for a few minutes. Reaching for his pipe, he thoughtfully patted down the tobacco, then lit it. 'Do you *really* want my opinion?' he asked throwing the match into the fire.

Fleur looked at him.

'I think you're living with a ghost.'

His daughter frowned in astonishment. 'Whatever do you mean?'

'You've never really accepted Hugh's death. Until you've laid that ghost to rest you'll not find happiness.... *with anybody.*'

'But.... that's *ridiculous,*' Fleur exploded.

'You asked for my opinion: I gave it to you,' her father replied placidly, drawing contentedly on his pipe. 'You're not obliged to accept it.' He looked straight at her. 'Why don't you telephone Arvind and try to sort things out between you.'

'I-I can't,' she stammered. 'I suggested he find someone else: someone who would give him children. He probably has by now.'

'And you don't *want* to give him children?'

Fleur shook her head miserably. 'I don't know why,' she whispered. But every time Arvind mentions it, I-I..... freeze.'

Her father sighed. 'Probably something to do with Hugh.'

The front door opened and Claudine walked into the drawing room. Seeing Fleur's red eyes she looked from one to the other in surprise, but Fleur had no desire for further confidences. She got up.

'Don't go,' Claudine pleaded. 'Stay and have a cup of tea.'

'I can't I'm afraid. I've got to be back in the box in half an hour. I just popped in to find out how Papa was recuperating after his "flu."'

'Well, come and have dinner with us very soon,' Claudine called, as Fleur clicked open the front door.

'Will do,' she replied. And without waiting for the lift ran hurriedly down the stairs.

Claudine raised her eyebrows enquiringly at her husband.

He picked up the evening paper his wife had brought him. 'I suppose this sorry situation will work itself out one day,' he sighed. 'But when?'

All visitors ashore,' the tannoy blared.

Hugh, Ruth and John were crammed into their father's small cabin on the great ocean liner bound for New Zealand. They rose awkwardly, almost relieved that the moment they all three dreaded had arrived.

John took his father's hand in both of his.

'Goodbye Dad,' he said warmly. 'I think you'll have a smooth passage. They tell me April's a good time to be sailing through the Suez Canal.'

'It'll be May by the time you arrive there,' Hugh laughed, thankful to have found something to say. The last few moments had been awkward with the tension of imminent parting.

Ruth threw her arms round her father-in-law's neck, kissed him lovingly on both cheeks, then held him at arms length, tears streaming down her face, before throwing herself into his arms and hugging him again.

He held her close.

John prized her away.

'It is not goodbye,' she said emotionally. 'John and I will come to see you very soon. I promise.'

'Yes, my dear,' he comforted.

Hugh took his father's outstretched hand and shook it warmly.

'I'll come and see you next Spring,' he smiled 'as soon as my exams are over. But *I'll* have to come by air, I won't have time for a luxury cruise like you. You'll have a wonderful trip Dad, this ship is crammed with young nurses going to the New World, you'll be able to talk shop all the way over.'

His father nodded and gave a brave smile. 'How do you know?' he enquired.

'Didn't you see them coming aboard, chattering like a lot of magpies. You can tell them a mile off.' Impulsively, as he had done on York station all those years ago, Hugh drew his father to him in an enormous hug.

'All visitors ashore,' came over the tannoy again. 'Last call. All visitors ashore, we are about to sail.'

'You three go on up,' Arthur Cunningham said urgently, turning away to hide his emotion. 'I'll follow at my own pace and wave to you from the deck.'

They scrambled ashore minutes before the gangplank was raised.

'Where on earth is he?' Hugh queried, anxiously scanning the sea of faces crammed at the rail as a sinister grating and grinding announced that the enormous anchors were being lifted. 'I can't see him, can you John?'

His brother shaded his eyes against the late afternoon sun. 'No, I can't either.'

The great ship began to slowly move away from the dock, turning slightly as she headed out to the open sea.

'There he is,' Ruth squealed against the noise and clamour all around them. 'There.... look. Papa, Papa,' she shouted, waving frantically at the stooped figure who had appeared at the rail. But the wind carried her voice away.

Arthur Cunningham's eyes were searching for them among the gesticulating crowd on the quayside. Hugh cupped his hands round his mouth. 'Dad,' he screamed, '*Daaad.*'

His father turned and his wrinkled face lit up.

John and Hugh took off their hats. Arthur Cunningham removed his own and smiling broadly waved back.

Ruth jumping up and down agitating a brightly coloured scarf, began to cry again.

'Let's push our way through this crowd and get back on the train before Ruth goes to pieces altogether,' John said tightly when their father's face disappeared from view. 'She became very attached to Dad, especially when we were helping him clear out the house. I think these goodbyes remind her of the way she lost her family during the war.'

He put his arm round his wife and began to forge a passage through the crowd.

'We'll go straight to the restaurant car, I could do with a cup of tea, couldn't you?'

Hugh nodded.

Ruth turned and slipped her arm through Hugh's, pressing it warmly against her side. 'You still have John and me,' she whispered.

Hugh squeezed her arm in response. Her gesture had touched him, and he understood why John had waited so long for this exceptional bride.

⚜ ⚜ ⚜

Fleur threw herself into her work. As she became more widely known for her interpreting skills, she realised that her fears about taking Sergei Postovsky's advice and going freelance had been groundless. She had more requests than she could cope with and became very selective in her choice of assignments, only accepting those held in places she knew she would enjoy visiting.

In April, she was asked to interpret at an international conference in Copenhagen. Fleur hesitated, but finally refused. There was no fear of meeting Arvind at the conference. But it was early Spring: the Danes would be out on the streets in droves rejoicing that the long winter was almost over, and she had no desire to bump into Arvind with another woman on his arm. She wasn't unhappy, but she wasn't happy either; endlessly torturing herself over her inability to love without causing pain and disaster. She had dismissed her father's theory out of hand, and the subject was never raised again.

Hubert and Claudine watched helplessly. Claudine longed to try to bring about a reconciliation between Fleur and her husband, but Hubert held her back. Apart from a polite "thank you" letter for her hospitality no-one had had any news of Arvind since his abrupt departure on Boxing Day.

Arvind had also thrown himself into his work. He had decided to follow Fleur's advice and find someone to replace her, and as soon as the New Year festivities were over he began to wine and dine the cream of Danish society It would have been easy to have taken most of them home for the night, but something always held him back. Often after a lingering kiss when he left them at their door, they clung to him, craving more. Yet instead of excitement he felt only iriritation and quickly left returning to the large double bed he and Fleur had once shared, angry and frustrated, cursing himself for his stupidity: and his inability to forget her.

Several times during a lonely Sunday afternoon he lifted the receiver to telephone Fleur. But when he heard the ringing tone the memory of her offhand treatment of him in Paris and her ultimatum to wait till May before coming to a decision rose and blinded him, and tight-lipped, he had replaced the receiver.

By the end of April, Arvind was wearying of his endless social round in an attempt to dull his despair. The lengthening days and the sight of colourful Spring flowers appearing in the public parks tugged at his heart, and sent his spirits spiralling down. Fleur had always filled the house with large bowls of fresh sweet smelling flowers.

'What's the point of it all?' he sighed one balmy evening at the beginning of May. He was walking along the canal. Young couples were strolling, their arms round each other, often stopping to gaze dreamily at the water before entwining in a lingering embrace. And he envied them. Arvind sighed and headed back to his car.

He had hoped Fleur would contact him now that May had arrived. The long winter she dreaded was over and the magical Nordic summer was beginning. But it was already the third of the month, and he had received no news. What little hope he had that she would change her mind and come back to him was trickling away. 'Why can't I just forget her and find someone else?' he asked himself. He laughed, but without joy. 'Heaven knows,' he added bitterly, 'there's no lack of opportunity.'

The following day, he was informed that he was to be appointed Chargé d'Affaires in Rome, the last stage before an ambassadorship. It was a huge promotion, and his immediate thought was that Fleur would have been so happy. Arvind knew his parents would be thrilled, so he decided to go to Arendal on the 17th to celebrate Norway's National Day with them and announce his good news. He would also tell them that he and Fleur had separated. The decision now seemed inevitable and he knew he could no longer keep up the pretence.

On 8th May Europe was celebrating the victory over Naziism, the eighth anniversary of the end of World War 2. After the parade, Arvind wandered alone through the Tivoli gardens, mingling with the crowds. He had wearied of being the handsome eligible diplomat escorting hopeful young beauties. Suddenly the band on the podium broke into the theme song from "Gone with the wind" and vivid memories of taking an excited Fleur to see the film not long after they arrived in Washington invaded his mind. They had held hands in the darkened cinema, and he had put his arm round her and held her close when she cried after each poignant scene. Fleur had identified with the dying Melanie, and the stricken Scarlett when, beautiful but dishevelled she sat among the ruins of Tara, her burnt out home, after Rhett Butler had abandoned her.

'It's only a film, darling,' he had consoled, when the lights finally went up and Fleur attempted to repair the damage to her swollen eyes.

She had sniffed and blown her nose for the 'nth time on his handkerchief. 'I know,' she had stammered. 'But it's so *sad.'*

As the memories resurfaced, an overwhelming love for his wife imprisoned him, and he knew that no matter what happened he wanted her back. He'd forget his dream of having children. She could carry on with her interpreting, if only she would come back to him. In desperation, he decided that he would even abandon his own career; his dreams of becoming an ambassor to which this new posting was pointing. They could live in France or anywhere else in the world if it would make her happy.

For one crazy moment, he even considered going to Kastrup and taking the next 'plane to Paris. Then a semblance of sanity returned to his tortured mind. Quickly returning to his car, he decided to telephone her. They had agreed to take a decision in May. It was now the second week of the month and Fleur had not contacted him. Perhaps she was waiting for him to contact her. Buoyed by this faint hope, he drove back to Hellerup.

Hugh smiled when he read his sister's letter.

'We're all looking forward to Dad's arrival in a few days time,' she wrote. 'I've just had a card from him, posted in Port Said. He seems to be enjoying his trip now that they are out of the Bay of Biscay; apparently the weather there was pretty rough. Angus can't wait to see him and Moppet - her daughter's in-the-womb name, though not official, had not changed - asks hourly whether this is the day Grandpa is coming. He's wonderful with them. Spends hours helping Angus with his bow and arrow practise, painting pyschedelic pictures with Moppett and endlessly reading stories to Fuzz.'

Hugh shook his head. 'Fuzz! What a name for a boy, especially when he's been given a civilised name like Ian.' He wondered what name number four would inherit: so far he or she had only been referred to as 'it'. 'She'd better make this one her last,' he murmured. 'She's getting a bit old for this caper.'

'I've made enquiries at the hospital in Wellington' the letter ended. It's a wonderful place, all the latest equipment. I had the three children there and I'll be going back in August. They'd very much like to see you when when you come. A new ultra modern maternity section will be opened next year and specialists (especially highly-qualified ones like you!) would be most welcome. Do you want me to get them to write to you, or will you make your own enquiries?'

The letter ended with a series of drawings and scrawls from the children.

'Lizzie's enthusiasm for life *and* for organising everybody else's hasn't changed,' he smiled, folding the flimsy closely written pages, and dropping them in his pocket. But the idea of starting a new life on the other side of the world was not displeasing. 'We'll see,' he murmured to himself.

Fleur picked up the telephone almost as soon as it rang.

Arvind took a deep breath, a sudden fear gripping him, not sure whether he wanted to know Fleur's decision. Perhaps the agony of indecision was preferable to what he feared might be the death blow to their marriage.

'Arvind!' she exclaimed.

He relaxed: she appeared to be pleased to hear him.

'What a long time it's been since I heard from you.'

'I could say the same thing about you,' he replied. There was an edge to his voice.

'I'm sorry Arvind,' Fleur began. But........ '

'You've been so busy,' he cut in.

'Well, yes.'

Arvind realised that his confrontational comments were counter-productive. 'I understand,' he acquiesed. So have I'

They appeared to have reached a stalemate. Neither of them saying anything.

Arvind took the plunge. 'Fleur.... we did agree to come to a decision in May. It's now the second week......' He paused, waiting for some reaction. But for a few seconds, there was silence and he held his breath.

'Have you finally come to a decision?' she asked quietly.

'Have *you*?'

'*You* were the one who suggested we part.'

'*Fleur,*' he said wearily. 'We've been all through this. I've *told* you it was a terrible mistake. I regretted having suggested it almost immediately.'

'But you *did* suggest it.'

'Because I couldn't bear to see you unhappy. It was for *you* Fleur, not for me.'

She didn't reply.

'Fleur,' he said desperately. I've had a big promotion. Been appointed Chargé d'Affaires in Rome and will be leaving in August to take up my new post.' He paused, waiting for some reaction from her. But none came. 'Darling,' he went on brokenly. 'I *love* you and I want you to go with me... but I can't force you.'

Still Fleur didn't reply. Abruptly his recent resolution to abandon everything if only she would come back to him vanished, and a wave of anger gripped him at her apparent indifference. 'I'm tired of living a bachelor life,' he exploded. 'I'm forty years of age. I want a home.... and a family. If *you're* not prepared to give me one then...... I'll find someone who will.'

A tense silence fell between them.

'And *have* you found someone?' Fleur enquired at last. Her voice seemed to come from far away.

'You *know* I haven't' he answered tensely. 'There never *has* been anyone else. Not since I met you.' He paused again. 'But I'd only have to snap my fingers and they'd come running,' he ended bitterly. He sat down abruptly, suddenly tired of this conversation which seemed to be going nowhere.

'Arvind,' Fleur said slowly, 'you've caught me unawares.'

'*Unawares*,' he burst out. 'Heavens above Fleur I've waited almost nine months for you to make a move. You *promised* in December that we'd come to a decision one way or the other in May. It *is* May. The 8th to be precise. How much longer do you expect me to wait?' His anger seemed to jolt Fleur.

'A week,' she answered quietly.

'A *week?*' he said angrily. 'Why a week? Why not a month.... a year....' He was now beside himself. All the frustration and misery he had felt since she left coming to boiling point and spilling over.

'Not a month or a year Arvind,' Fleur broke in, 'a week. At the moment I'm in the midst of packing. I leave early to-morrow for a conference in London. It starts on Monday so I should be back by next weekend.' She paused and took a deep breath. 'I *promise* I'll telephone you then.'

He did not reply.

'Arvind,' she said brokenly. 'I'm still not sure I can give you the family you want. I don't know why: I only wish I did. But I want you to be happy. All I seem to bring to people I love is pain and disaster.'

Arvind's anger collapsed. 'So.... you *do* love me?'

Fleur paused. 'I don't want to cause you pain.'

'Fleur....' he began.

'I'll call you next weekend,' she cut in, abruptly putting down the receiver.

And Arvind knew she was crying.

CHAPTER EIGHTEEN

Fleur arrived in London armed with a large folder, brimming with documents. The conference at which she was to interpret was a medical one, a subject she had not dealt with before and she needed the weekend to study the technical terms she would encounter. On Monday morning she entered the box feeling slightly apprehensive.

'Norman,' she cried, sitting down beside her co-interpreter who was already in place. Like her he was totally bilingual, switching effortlessly from French to English. 'I'm *so* pleased it's you. This is my first medical congress and it was such a relief when François told me that we'd be working together.'

He looked up and smiled. 'And *I'm* pleased to be working with the glamorous Mrs. Kristensen.'

Fleur grinned back, immediately reassured. Norman would help her out if she stumbled. He leant towards the window. 'Quite a crowd down below,' he remarked, nodding at the delegates streaming into the hall. Seems to be a popular conference.'

The team leader popped his head round the door of the booth. 'I did tell you, didn't I, that you'll be helping out in the English booth on Thursday?'

They nodded.

'There's an eminent French professor speaking in the morning, and another one in the afternoon, Odile and Martin will need reinforcements. But the other four days it'll be into French.'

He disappeared. Norman tapped the microphone and put on his headphones.

'You begin,' Fleur whispered, 'I'll jot down the figures for you.'

'Lily-livered,' he hissed, as silence fell on the assembled crowd and the conference was officially opened. Turning on his microphone, Norman plunged in.

When she left the box later that morning Fleur felt more confident. It was comforting to be with Norman, a seasoned interpreter who had learned the ropes at the Nuremberg trials, and with whom she had often worked before. When, after twenty minutes listening, she took over from him, like an actor who has trembled in the wings is transformed once on the stage, all fear left her. The concentration needed was so intense that there was no room in her mind for anything but the subject in hand.

Charlie Williams, head of the Obstetrics Department at St. Thomas's Hospital, glanced round the almost deserted dining-room. It was late and Hugh was sitting alone in a corner. He looked exhausted. Crossing the room Charlie sat down at his table.

Hugh looked up and smiled. 'Good meeting?' he enquired.

'Very good,' Charlie replied enthusiastically, 'even better than yesterday.' He scrutinised Hugh's face and frowned. 'Don't imagine you've had such a wonderful time. You look all in.'

'I am,' Hugh sighed. 'Called out three times in the night, then a bloody heavy workload to-day.' He pushed aside his unfinished meal and made to rise, but Charlie restrained him. 'You're not on call to-night?' he queried.

Hugh shook his head. 'Mercifully no. If I were I don't think I could make it,' he smiled wearily. 'I've got a break till to-morrow, then after that, bliss. Two nights off.'

'All the more reason to listen to what I have to say. To-morrow you're going to this conference.'

Hugh started to protest, but Charlie interrupted him. 'No arguments. As your boss I *order* you to go. You have three very good housemen who are longing to get you off their backs, so give them a break. To-morrow there are two eminent French professors who will be speaking on the latest developements in obstetrics. Just up your street. Especially,' he added menacingly, 'if you insist on abandoning us and taking up this post in New Zealand. They're sure to have all the latest technology there, you'll damn well need to be on the ball.' He paused. 'Have you taken a decision?'

Hugh grimaced. 'Not yet.'

'I don't want to lose you. If I didn't have a wife and family I'd jump at the opportunity, but now that the children are settled in schools I don't think Heather would take kindly to having to upsticks and move to the other end of the world.' His eyes twinkled. 'Otherwise...... you wouldn't have stood a bloody chance.'

Hugh settled back in his seat as a hushed silence fell over the conference hall. He decided to listen to the professor in his own language to test whether after so many years he could still understand French. The speaker rose and walked to the microphone. Hugh was surprised, he didn't appear to be very much older than himself. Given his international reputation, he had imagined he would be nearing his dotage.

The professor spoke fluently, but rapidly and after a few minutes Hugh realised that he was missing vital information. Hurriedly putting on the headphones he twisted the knobs until he came to the English interpretation: a man's voice came over the waves keeping in rhythm with the professor's words. Hugh had never experienced simultaneous interpretation before, and he was amazed at how the man could speak so calmly, accurately interpreting what the professor said almost before the words had been spoken. Charlie had been right, the conference was well worth attending.

Suddenly the voice changed, and a woman began to speak.

Hugh frowned. The voice sounded familiar, and he wondered where he had heard it before. Probably a radio announcer he concluded. But the voice kept puzzling him. He pulled himself together realising that by trying to solve the mystery he was missing what the professor had to say: the problem though puzzling was not that important. Focusing his mind back on the presentation, he concentrated on the content rather than the interpreter. The man's voice returned to the waves, making concentration easier. Then the woman took over, and again Hugh was distracted.

Suddenly he went cold. His flesh began to prickle, and he trembled. It couldn't be: and yet it was; that voice was unmistakable. Only Fleur had spoken like that. Only she had that intonation, those distinctive tones, that very slight French inflexion which had always fascinated him. He turned in his seat and looked upwards to where the interpreters' booths were lined in a row. But only shapes were visible behind the large glass panels. Hugh's mind was in a turmoil. He could no longer concentrate on the talk which he had found so interesting, and which would certainly have been of great help to him in his work. He was distracted, confused, wanting only to leave the room and discover for himself whether his suspicions were founded.

'Immediately the session's over I'll leave the hall and watch the interpreters come down from their booths,' he muttered to himself. 'Then I'll know.' 'But,' his reason teased, 'what will you do if it *is* Fleur?' And he didn't know. All he knew was that he had to have the question settled, the riddle solved in his own mind. He would consider what to do if his suspicions were confirmed.

Hugh was one of the first to leave his seat when the morning session ended. But he was sitting near the front of the podium, and by the time he reached the middle of the aisle it was crammed. The delegates moved forwards slowly, meeting and greeting one another on the way out, and by the time he reached the door, the staircase leading to the interpreters' booths was empty. They had all left.

He wandered into the restaurant glancing around, hoping to see them there. But if they were there, Fleur was not with them. He decided that he had been mistaken. He was tired, and his imagination was playing him tricks. Yet something told him that he was wrong.

Finding a pillar near the staircase leading to the booths, he stood in its shadow when, after lunch, the delegates began to pour back into the auditorioum. He glanced at his watch. Three minutes left before the afternoon session began, yet still no-one mounted the staircase. Once again he had missed them: they must all have arrived before him.

Finding a seat in the back row he fitted on his headphones and turned the switch to French when the second professor was introduced. Hugh smiled: this was more like what he had expected. The professor was a tall, elderly man with a scholastic stoop.

The woman's voice came down the line. Hugh's heart leapt into his throat almost choking him, then fluttered crazily like a terrified bird caught in a cage, before settling and dropping slowly into position. It *was* Fleur. He was sure of it. He'd never heard a voice like hers before. But the lilt of laughter he remembered was missing.

He tried to concentrate on what she was saying, but his mind refused to obey him. It kept rocketing the reel into backward drive in his brain: running over and over again and again the few precious hours he had shared with Fleur.

The afternoon conference was wasted on him. Every time Fleur went off the air and the man's voice took over he was in anguish, imagining that she had disappeared and he would never be able to establish the truth of what his brain told him was real.

The minute the day's session ended, Hugh was out of his seat and through the door. He took his place behind the pillar, his eyes glued to the staircase. Within minutes the booths emptied and a group of interpreters came streaming down the stairs. He recognised Fleur immediately: she had hardly changed. She was slimmer than he remembered and instead of framing her face her chestnut hair was now drawn back, accentuating her high cheekbones and perfect bone structure, giving her an air of sophistication she had lacked when they were together. He caught his breath: he had always thought his wife was the most beautiful woman he had ever known, but this was no longer the girl he had married. This was a mature elegant woman, dressed in the latest Paris fashions.

When she reached the bottom she turned round, laughing at something the man he took to be her co-interpreter had said. He jumped the last two steps, and coming swiftly to her side threw his arm around her shoulders. And they disappeared into the crowd.

Hugh stood where he was, unable to move. His feet seemed to have become rooted in concrete, and his mouth felt dry. Had he wanted to call after her, he knew he would not have been able to. No words would have come. Turning back into the corridor he saw a man with a sheaf of papers walking down the stairs. All the interpreters had now left and he wondered who he might be. 'I beg your pardon,' Hugh said tentatively, not knowing why he had approached the man, and now that he had done so what he intended to say: his feet seemed to have moved towards him of their own accord.

The man looked up from his papers and smiled.

'I was wondering,' Hugh stammered, 'whether you could tell me who the lady interpreting into French was?'

'There were two,' the man said. 'Odile and Fleur.'

Hugh hadn't realised that the voices had changed. His mind had been in such confusion he had hardly taken in what was happening during the conference.

'Er... Fleur,' he stammered.

'Ah, Fleur.' The man's face broke into a wide smile. He showed no surprise that Hugh knew her name. 'The beautiful Fleur,' he grinned. 'You're not the only delegate who wants an introduction. But I'm afraid she's very aloof.'

'It's not that,' Hugh stumbled over his words. 'I recognised her voice and now you've told me her name I'm sure she's the same person.'

The man smiled, obviously wondering what other stories people could concoct in order to have an introduction to Fleur.

'I.... I knew her during the war, when she was working for the BBC. She was Fleur Cunningham then.'

The man frowned thoughtfully, satisfied that Hugh was not just another delegate wanting a night out. 'That must have been her first husband's name,' he murmured. 'He was a pilot shot down over France unfortunately. She remarried after the war. She's Fleur Kristensen now.'

'Was that her husband who was with her in the booth?' Hugh enquired.

'Norman?' the man replied. 'No, he's a colleague: they often work together. Fleur's husband's a diplomat, based in Copenhagen as far as I know.'

Hugh raised his eyebrows in surprise. 'So they're not together?'

'No. I've never met him, but I don't *think* they're divorced. Fleur's a very private person; she doesn't tell one much about herself. But they're certainly separated at the moment. Why don't you get hold of her? I'm sure she'd like to see you if you're an old friend from her wartime days.' He looked around him. The hall was rapidly emptying. 'I don't know where she is now, probably having a cup of tea. But all the interpreters are staying here at the hotel, you could easily contact her.'

'Perhaps I will,' Hugh said slowly.

The man shuffled his papers together. 'I'm the team leader by the way. My job's to organise them all. Would you like me to tell Fleur you've been asking after her?'

'No, I'd rather you didn't,' Hugh cut in hurriedly. 'I have to rush now. I'll get in touch with her to-morrow.' He realised that he had committed himself to returning, after having sworn to Charlie that he couldn't possibly be away from the hospital for more than one day.

'Yes, do that,' the man smiled. 'It'll be a nice surprise for her. She'll be here till she leaves for Paris on Saturday morning.'

Hugh collected his coat and walked slowly back to his flat. Feeling more exhausted than he had done after three night calls and a heavy day's duty at the hospital, he flopped into a chair by the window and sat idly watching the Thames flow by, his mind in a turmoil. His thoughts drifted to Fiona, the English nurse he had met when he had visited the hospital in New Zealand. There had been an instant 'rapport' between them, but Hugh had held back, knowing he was not free. Yet since his return there had been an emptiness in his life, and his thoughts constantly returned to the evenings he had spent with Fiona, when without anything having been said he had known that her feelings towards him, like his own, were far from neutral. And in spite of everything, believing that his marriage to Fleur was at last behind him, he had begun to hope. Now Fleur had come back into his life, apparently free: and he didn't know what to do. 'What a mess' he muttered, 'what a bloody awful mess.'

The daylight faded, and evening shadows began to chase each other round the walls, darting in zig-zags backwards and forwards as if following the movement of the river below. Darkness fell. And still he remained at the window. Too mentally and physically exhausted to move. The telephone rang. But he ignored it. It rang again. On and on. But he hadn't the strength to stretch out his hand and pick up the receiver. It rang for a third time. Wearily he reached across and unhooked it, more to stop the incessant ringing than from any desire to discover who it was.

'Hugh?' It was Charlie. 'Where where you?'

'Here.'

'Then why didn't you answer the bloody phone? This is the third time I've called.'

Hugh sighed. 'I don't know why,' he replied listlessly.

There was a pause.

'Hugh,' Charlie's voice was anxious. 'Are you all right? You sound very odd.'

'I'm fine,' Hugh replied. But there was a hint of sarcasm in his tone. 'Just *fine.*'

'What's the matter?' Charlie said slowly.

Hugh took a deep breath. 'I met my wife.'

'You *what,*' Charlie gasped.

'*I met my wife,*' Hugh enunciated, pronouncing every word very clearly.

'Fleur? But where? I thought she'd married a Dane and was living in Washington.'

'So did I,' Hugh said miserably. 'But apparently he's back in Copenhagen and she's living in Paris.'

'Funny sort of marriage,' Charlie said drily. 'Or are they divorced?'

'I've no idea,' Hugh said wearily. 'The fellow who told me didn't know either.'

'But where did you meet her?' Charlie probed.

'At that blasted conference you forced me to attend. She's an interpreter.'

'Holy smoke,' Charlie spluttered.

'Look Charlie,' Hugh interrupted. 'I'm exhausted. Let's continue this conversation some other time, shall we?'

There was a slight pause. Hugh was about to hang up.

'I'm still at the hospital,' Charlie said quietly. 'I'll be with you in five minutes.'

Hugh groaned and put down the receiver.

'Hugh, you've *got* to meet her and get this sorted out.,' Charlie reasoned, when Hugh told him about the day's events.

Hugh didn't reply. He was already regretting having approached the team leader, and he had now no intention of returning the following day. The wound had healed. Or so he thought. And he saw no point in prizing it open.

'But,' a small voice inside him whispered. 'What if she *is* divorced or separated from her husband? You always wanted her back, now's your chance. After all, legally you're still married, she could be in your arms to-morrow night.' But Hugh was afraid. Even if Fleur were no longer with her diplomat, would she want to come back to him? Or would he even want her back? He was not sure. After ten years would they still have anything in common, apart from a desperate wartime love? He shuddered. Perhaps it would be better to remain in ignorance. He had tried to remake his life, and it hadn't been easy. He *couldn't* go through that heartache all over again. As these thoughts crossed his mind Fiona's tranquil face floated in front of his eyes.

'You're to go back to the conference to-morrow,' Charlie said firmly. 'Get in touch with her, and damn well thrash this out.'

Hugh began to protest, but Charlie held up his hand to stop him. 'Don't you realise you'd never have a moment's peace if you didn't? I know it's a risk, but it's one you've bloody well got to take. You *must* find out and either get back together or divorce.'

Hugh knew Charlie was right, but he was afraid. He glanced at his watch and rose wearily from his chair. 'I have to get over to the hospital,' he said heavily. 'I'm on call to-night.'

Charlie pushed him back into his chair. 'You *were* on call' he announced firmly. 'But you're not any more. You're not in a fit state.' He got up and went to the kitchen returning with a glass of water. Here,' he said, fishing in his pocket. 'I've brought something to make you sleep.' He handed Hugh the glass of water and shook some pills into the palm of his hand. 'Take these and go straight to bed. I'll call in to-morrow evening to see how the day went.' He glanced slyly at Hugh. 'Perhaps then you'll be able to tell me that you'll soon be free to propose to that nurse you've been pining for ever since you returned from New Zealand.

Hugh swallowed the pills in one go and put down the glass. A slow smile spread across his face as, for the first time, he dared allow himself to dream of a future with Fiona by his side.

—o–O–o—

CHAPTER NINETEEN

Hugh took in very little of the day's papers. He sat in a stupified silence, listening, but not hearing: not even understanding some of the speakers, so apprehensive was he of turning the knobs and hearing Fleur's voice. During the afternoon he finally tuned into the English interpretation. A man's voice he didn't recognise came over the waves. He waited, then another unfamiliar male voice took over. Hugh frowned. Perhaps Fleur had already left and he had lost the opportunity he was not sure he wanted to contact her. Switching to the French interpretation he heard the familiar voice of Fleur's colleague, then she came over the waves. Tears pricked his eyes, remembering the voice he had not heard for so long, the voice he had thought he would never hear again. Bewildered by the events of the past twenty four hours, during which his ordered life appeared to have been turned upside down, he returned to the English interpretation, not sure whether he was relieved or afraid, knowing she was still there. The minute the afternoon session ended and the conference was finally declared over, Hugh didn't join in the tumultous applause, he slipped from his seat and waited outside in the shadows.

Fleur came dancing down the stairs. She seemed very happy, or perhaps he told himself it was relief that the strenuous week was over. She was holding the handrail and Hugh noticed an enormous solitaire diamond winking on her wedding finger, but he was unable to see whether she was wearing a wedding ring as well. 'She could still be married,' he mused, 'or she could be engaged: perhaps to the colleague she appeared to be so friendly with'. At that moment he came up behind her and, arm in arm they joined the crowd making for the exit. Hugh concluded that his supposition had been correct. That was *his* ring she was wearing. Not her husband's. Slipping in among the thinning group of delegates leaving the hall, he bumped into the team leader.

'Oh, hallo again,' he smiled. 'Did you get in touch with Fleur?'

'No-o,' Hugh mumbled, adding hastily. 'Not yet.'

'Don't leave it too late, we're all off in the morning. Perhaps you're coming to the closing dinner to-night? You'll see her then.'

'Yes, that's what I'll do,' Hugh said hurriedly.

'Must go,' the man ended. 'Got to get into my 'penguin suit' for the grand occasion. Without my wife it takes me hours to fix that blasted bow tie.' And with a wave, he was gone.

The previous evening Charlie had given Hugh a ticket for the gala dinner. 'At the Dorch., old chap, should be a good show. It'll take you out of yourself.'

The ticket was on the table in Hugh's flat. But he now had no intention of using it. Thrusting his hands deep into his pockets, he decided to walk back to the hospital: the fresh air would clear his head after the whirlwind of emotions which had buffeted it during the past twenty four hours. Crossing Westminster Bridge, he stopped and leant over the parapet. The day had clouded over and reflections from the lights in the Houses of Parliament rippled and danced in the dark expanse of water below. Hugh remembered that long ago Christmas Eve when he had stood in the corridor of the night train rattling it's way to York, and contemplated suicide. He had been held back by the thought of his father's pain. But his father was far away now in New Zealand. Everyone would think it was a tragic accident. He could see the headlines:

"Young consultant on the brink of a brilliant career tragically drowned in the Thames."

He smiled. Yet as these thoughts penetrated his mind, he discovered that he had no desire to end his life. He no longer felt the desperation he had experienced in the train. With the passing years the pain of losing Fleur had become a sweet nostalgic memory, and with a shock he realised that he had been so absorbed in his work that he rarely thought of Fleur these days. Until yesterday, when the memories had come hurtling back with tremendous force.

Without warning Fiona's face once again rose before his eyes. She was the opposite of Fleur. Tall and blonde, radiating a quiet serenity. He smiled, remembering his sister's remark on the evening of his arrival in New Zealand:

'There's an English girl, Fiona Craig, trained at the Westminster, in charge of a new premature baby unit at the hospital in Auckland. If you're interested, she'd be pleased to show you round'.

But as the weeks went by Hugh had discovered that his emotions which he had thought dead, were coming back to life: and he was almost pleased, though at the same time torn, when his month's holiday ended. Yet as he boarded the plane the pleasure he had anticipated at the thought of returning to England and the work he loved was absent. Opening the door to his empty flat he too had felt empty, and he knew that his relationship with Fiona had changed. It was no longer a friendship between two colleagues. He had come very near to falling in love with her.

Gazing into the murky waters he thoughtfully stroked his chin, and his father's words at the height of his pain, which had meant nothing at the time, slowly began to have a meaning.

'All things work for good for those who love the Lord, Hugh. I'm sure that in the end God will bring something good out of all your suffering.'

Hugh had smiled sceptically at the time. He admired his father's strong Christian faith, but it was a faith Hugh had long since discarded. 'How could anything good possibly come out of my present agony?' he had asked himself bitterly. 'Anyway, I don't love the Lord so it hardly applies.' He pursed his lips as he thought back to that time, and he realised how far he had travelled along this road of pain to reach almost complete healing. Almost.... until yesterday.

Could meeting Fleur again be the "something good" his father had spoken of? The catalyst which would change his life? If so, where did Fiona fit in?

'I haven't really lived since I fell into that bloody Gestapo trap.' he murmured absently. 'I'm almost forty. I'd like to think I have some kind of future outside of medicine. But would Fleur, used to the glittering diplomatic life, be content to settle down as the wife of a hard-working doctor?' Hugh grimaced. There wouldn't be very much glittering social activity, if any, were she to come back to him, and especially if he emigrated to New Zealand as his father had suggested. Could Fleur, essentially European, settle in the outback, light years removed from the sophisticated culture into which she had been born? Or even to life in London as the wife of a, hopefully, successful obstetrician.

Unbidden Fiona's face once again rose before him. And Hugh knew that Charlie was right. He had to meet Fleur. Had to know one way or the other what the future held for him: for them both. Straightening up, he hailed a taxi and gave directions back to the hotel. 'Could you put me through to Mrs. Kristensen's room?' he asked the clerk behind the counter.

'Certainly sir,' he replied. 'Room 305. Third floor.'

'I don't want to go up,' Hugh explained. 'I'd like to speak to her on the telephone.'

The clerk picked up the phone, putting his hand over the receiver when Fleur answered. 'Who shall I announce sir?' he enquired.

'I'll announce myself.' Hugh held out his hand for the receiver. 'We met during the war,' he said, surprised that his voice was so steady when Fleur came on the line. 'I was at your wedding in '43.'

Fleur gasped. 'You were at my *wedding*? Were you in the RAF?'

'Yes.'

'So you must have known Hugh, my first husband.'

'Yes, yes, I did,' he stammered. 'I knew him very well. I'm a doctor now. I was at the conference, and I was wondering whether we could meet for a drink.'

'I'd *love* to,' Fleur answered.

'I'm down in the hall. I'll wait for you there.'

'But how shall I know you?' Fleur queried.

'There aren't many people here at the moment,' Hugh replied. 'I imagine they're all changing for the dinner. Don't worry, I'll recognise you.'

'I'm just dressing for the dinner myself,' Fleur replied. 'I'll be down in a few minutes. What is your name by the way?'

'I'm afraid *I'm* in my working clothes,' Hugh said, hurriedly changing the subject. 'I hadn't planned to attend the dinner. I'll see you in a few minutes.' And he hung up, avoiding any further questions as to his identity.

Hugh sat in a deep armchair facing the lift. He watched it rise, and then descend. The doors slowly opened, and his heart began to thunder against his ribs. But it was Fleur's colleague wearing a dinner jacket accompanied by two women interpreters dressed to the hilt who stepped out. Chattering animatedly they headed for the bar. Hugh settled back into his chair, breathing deeply until his heartbeat slowly returned to normal. Twice more he felt his adrenalin rise when the lift doors opened, but it was always unknown people in evening dress who stepped out. Hugh gathered that the closing dinner at the Dorchester must be some occasion.

Finally the lift doors opened and Fleur walked into the foyer. Hugh gasped. Could this really be his wife: that exquisite young girl he had married all those years ago? And who was still legally married to him? She was more breathtakingly beautiful than ever. Remembering the other women who had crossed the foyer in evening dress Fleur's frock was simplicity itself, but it moulded her slim figure to perfection. Her only adornments were emerald ear-rings, and the beautiful double strand of pearls he remembered Claudine placing round her neck on the evening before their wedding, and which he had unfastened at their honeymoon hotel, watching as they snaked sensuously into her palm before he had slipped her negligée from her shoulders and gazed at her perfect untouched body for the first time. Overwhelmed, he staggered to his feet.

Fleur stood and looked around the foyer. Then she saw him. For a moment, he thought she was going to faint. She grasped the back of a large wing chair, staring unbelievingly at him, her eyes wide with shock. Regaining her poise, she walked unsteadily towards him, her eyes never leaving his face.

He held out his arms, and she stumbled into them, burying her face in his shoulder.

'Hugh,' she floundered, her voice muffled in his coat. 'Hugh, I can't believe it. Is it really you? I-I thought you were......'

'Dead,' he said tightly, releasing her from his arms and easing her onto a sofa. 'So did everyone else.'

She looked at him, her expressive eyes dark and bewildered. 'What - what happened?' she stammered.

'I fell into a German trap and was taken prisoner.'

'You were taken prisoner,' she gasped. 'But why wasn't I told? All the telegram said was that you were missing believed killed. If I'd known you were a prisoner I could have written to you, sent you food parcels, done everything possible to keep up your spirits.' Her voice broke, and Hugh thought she was going to cry. 'Whatever must you have thought of me,' she cried brokenly. She bit her lip to hold back the tears. 'Peter Drummond kept in touch with me, but there was never any further news. If you were a prisoner of war, surely the authorities were informed.' She looked up at him, her eyelashes glistening with unshed tears. 'I waited for you for over two years, hoping against hope. Thinking you might have been taken prisoner or were in hiding somewhere. But everyone, even Claudine who had been so positive ever since you were reported missing, said there was no chance of your returning.' Fleur shook her head distractedly, her eyes anguished. 'All the prisoners of war had been repatriated. I was lonely and miserable in London where there were so many memories of you, so I gave up and joined my father in Paris. She twisted her hands together in despair. 'Why, oh why did the authorities not inform me?'

Hugh crossed over and sat down beside her on the sofa. 'The authorities didn't know,' he said slowly. 'I wasn't an ordinary prisoner. The Gestapo insisted I was a spy. They sent me to a concentration camp.'

She stared at him wildly. 'You were in a *concentration* camp?' she gasped, her voice little more than a whisper.

He nodded. 'I was in two. Then on a death march.'

She leant back and closed her eyes.

'I think we need a drink,' he said gently, signalling to a passing waiter.

Fleur remained with her eyes closed, her breast heaving as she tried to control her breathing. Hugh wondered if his revelation had not proved to be too much for her.

The drinks arrived. And for a while they sat in silence.

'Why didn't somebody tell me you were alive,' she blurted out at last. 'When the war ended *then* the authorities *must* have known.'

'They didn't,' Hugh replied shortly. 'Once you were in one of those camps you were lost to the world. 'Nacht und Nebel', disappear into the night without trace, they called Flossenburg, the last one I was sent to. Once there, *no-one* knew what had happened to you. He shook his head. 'It's a long story Fleur. And...... not a pretty one. I don't know whether you are in a fit state to hear it, or even whether I should tell you.'

She put down her glass and sat up straight, looking directly at him, her eyes blazing with an intense fire. 'I want to know,' she said fiercely. 'I have a *right* to know. I want to try to share some of the terrible anguish and pain you suffered.' She took a deep breath in an effort to control her emotion. You were,' she stopped, confused. 'I mean you *are* my husband.'

Hugh looked at her steadily. 'You said "were", he put in softly.

Fleur picked up her glass and gazed into its contents, then nervously drained it. 'I married again,' she answered almost inaudibly, without looking up.

'I know,' he said tightly, 'on the day after I returned to England. I looked for you everywhere, then my father told me that you had married in Paris that morning.'

Fleur said nothing. Just sat staring blankly into her empty glass.

Hugh signalled to a waiter.

Without looking up, Fleur took a glass from the tray the waiter offered her, and took a series of short, rapid sips. Putting it down, she looked steadily at Hugh, her face creased with sorrow.

'Hugh,' she whispered. 'I want to know everything. If you could stand it, then I can.'

Hugh took a deep breath, and drained his glass. 'All right,' he said tightly. 'But stop me if it becomes too much.'

A burst of laughter came from the bar. Fleur's colleague with a group of other interpreters surged into the foyer. 'Fleur,' he called, and waved.

She looked up Almost without recognition.

'We've ordered a series of cabs to take us to the Dorch. Do you want to come with us?'

Fleur gave a weak smile, and shook her head. 'No, you go ahead. I'll make my own way.'

'Don't be late,' one of the women called. 'Or you might miss a wonderful dins.'

Hugh half rose. 'Don't let me make you late for your party.'

But she pulled him back down beside her. 'It doesn't matter. Anyway I don't feel like a party.'

'But you're dressed and ready,' Hugh protested.

'Go on with what you were saying Hugh,' she said firmly.

The clock in the foyer tinkled and struck the hour.

'Nine o'clock,' Hugh frowned. 'Fleur, you *must* go. I'll call a cab.'

But she shook her head. 'No Hugh, carry on. P*lease* just go on.'

Midnight struck. Hugh had come to the end of his story. They were sitting close together on the sofa, and a deep silence had fallen between them.

'The others should be coming back very soon,' Fleur remarked at last.

'I'll leave you,' Hugh put in quickly, athough they had come to no conclusion.

Fleur put a restraining hand on his arm. 'No, I don't want you to go. Not yet.' She looked around the foyer, as if seeking an avenue of escape. 'I was going to the flat to-morrow morning to sort out a few things before returning to Paris.' She fumbled with her small evening bag. 'We could go there,' she said slowly, without looking up.

Hugh caught his breath. Her suggestion had taken him by surprise, and he wasn't sure he wanted to go back to the flat which held so many memories. But the appeal in Fleur's eyes was irresistible. He stood up and held out his hand. Without a word they crossed the foyer and walked through the door into the street.

CHAPTER TWENTY

Hugh looked around him in amazement when Fleur flicked on the lights. 'It's all exactly as I remember it,' he said. 'You haven't changed a thing.'

'There was no need,' Fleur replied. 'Claudine gave me the flat *and* the contents when she married my father.'

Hugh hovered in the drawing room doorway feeling ill at ease. Uncertain what to do.

'Shall I make us an omelette?' Fleur asked tentatively, as she drew the curtains.

Hugh smiled. 'This is where we came in.'

'A long time ago,' she replied sadly. She sat down in an armchair. He sat opposite her.

'Except that then we sat side by side on the sofa,' he ventured.

Fleur smiled again, but made no attempt to move.

'Perhaps it was *too* long ago,' Hugh probed.

She gazed at her hands. 'I don't know Hugh. I only wish I did.'

And they sat in an uncomfortable silence. Hugh hesitated. He wondered whether it might not be better to leave. But they had come this far, he knew they either had to go forward, or say goodbye. He couldn't leave before they came to some final solution. 'Fleur,' he began tentatively.

She looked up, an agonised expression on her face.

Hugh leant across and took her hand. 'Fleur,' he said softly, his vision suddenly clearing, allowing him to see the situation in a different light. To view it almost impersonally: and face reality. 'What we had was wonderful, I'll never forget it. But.... I realise now it wasn't a marriage. It was a beautiful love affair.'

Fleur frowned. 'What do you mean?'

'I mean that we were married, but we never lived a normal married life together. We never had a quarrel. We met and loved each other in frantic passionate snatches.'

Her eyes remained glued to his face.

'Would it have lasted into peacetime?' he queried.

She said nothing. Just stared bleakly at him.

'Perhaps it would,' he sighed. 'But we'll never know.' He got up and walked towards her.

Fleur flung her arms around his neck and burst into tears. 'Hugh, I've dreamed of meeting you again. And now I have.......'

'It isn't what you expected.'

She wiped her eyes with the back of her hand. He passed her a handkerchief. 'I don't know Hugh.' She started to cry again. 'I don't know anything any more.'

He eased her gently onto the sofa. 'We're both confused,' he said slowly, sitting down beside her. 'It's been a terrible shock, perhaps more so for you. I had two days to get used to it.' He paused. 'I knew you weren't living with your husband, and I thought we might start again. Carry on where we left off.' Without his being aware of it the word had slipped out, he had referred to her "husband", and he realised that in his mind their marriage was already in the past. He had admitted, had accepted the fact that Fleur was no longer his wife. She was married to another man.

Fleur nodded.

'But, darling, ten years is a long time. Too long to be apart: I realise that now. All this time I've been living with a dream. Now I seem to have abruptly woken up.'

'And the dream?' she faltered.

'The dream was wonderful,' he breathed. 'But once awake one faces reality.' He sighed. 'I think that's what suddenly happened to me. Coming here where nothing has changed... except us.' He paused.

Fleur appeared to be holding her breath, willing him to continue, to bring their dream alive.

'We're no longer the same two people,' he said gently. 'We're not the breathless young lovers we were when we married.' He drew her into his arms and stroked her hair. It still had that fragrance of fallen rose petals which had always intoxicated him, and he sighed. 'I only wish we were,' he said softly. 'It would be so simple to go back. But the years we've been apart have changed us.'

She looked up at him, her face streaked with tears. 'But can't we go back?' she whispered.

'Do *you* think we can?' he smiled.

She said nothing.

'I think it's too late,' he said, as Fiona's face once again rose in front of his eyes.

The little gold clock on the mantlepiece struck the half hour. The tinkling chimes seemed to bring her back to life, back to the present.

She slowly nodded her head. 'When I saw you in the hotel,' she said hesitantly, raising her eyes to meet his. 'When we sat together and talked, I was sure we could. Sure that we could go back and recapture those wonderful few months we had.' She paused, fiddling with the tassle of a cushion. 'I suggested we came back here because I wanted you to make love to me. I wanted to relive our honeymoon, to go back down the years and start again.' She looked at him, her eyes pleading. 'Why has that suddenly changed? This flat has so many memories for us, it should have made it simple to slip back in time.'

He eased her back into the deep cushions on the sofa, and dropped a kiss on her hair. 'I thought that too when we left the hotel. For years I've dreamed of holding you in my arms again. After I came back and discovered you had gone, I ached for you during endless sleepless nights. The thought of you was the only thing that had kept me alive in those terrible camps: otherwise without you I'd have given in. When we met this evening, I couldn't wait to make love to you. I really imagined we could recapture what we had.' He smiled sadly. 'But darling, as I said, we're no longer the same two people. I'm not the dashing young pilot you married. I'm an overworked doctor whose hair is going grey, and getting thinner on top. And I don't imagine you're still the unsophisticated young girl who blushed so easily.' He put his finger under her chin. 'Or do you?' he teased.

She smiled. But didn't reply.

'You're still as beautiful, Fleur,' he whispered, 'even more beautiful. But you've suffered too, and suffering changes people.' Hugh put his arm round her and held her close as she nestled her head into his shoulder. 'We were so young when we married, weren't we? Now we've both grown up. What we had was a cameo of perfect love, something we'll always treasure. Don't let's spoil it by trying to ressurect it."

And once again they sat in silence. But there was now no embarrassment. It was the comfortable silence of two old friends who had once been lovers. He held her tightly and she leant against him, her eyes closed. 'I'm pleased we met again,' she said softly.

'And laid the ghosts?' he smiled.

'Perhaps.'

They sat locked in each other's arms, and an immense peace swept through Fleur. She felt as if a heavy weight, which she had not even been aware she was carrying had been lifted from her shoulders, and the knots which had tangled in her brain had finally been untied.

'What will you do now?' she asked at last.

'I think I'll go to New Zealand,' he said thoughtfully. 'My father joined my sister and her family in Auckland when he retired. I visited him last Christmas and did a tour of the large new hospital there. They had all the latest equipment, I was most impressed. Then last week I unexpectantly received this amazing job offer from them. Head of the Obstetrics Department. It's very tempting, I'd have to wait years before reaching that goal at Tommy's. Charlie Williams, my boss is only ten years older than I.'

'What made you choose obstetrics?'

Hugh smiled at her. 'It was you, Fleur,' he said softly.

She frowned.

'When I was in training I met many women who longed for children and couldn't have them. And others who had great difficulty conceiving or carrying a baby to term.' He absently stroked her hair. 'I understood then the deep desire most women have to bear a child. And I realised how I must have hurt you. I suppose to make up for that hurt I wanted to help them.'

Fleur gave a puzzled frown. 'Hugh,' she stammered. 'What hurt?' She took his face in her hands. 'I don't remember you ever hurting me,' she said softly.

He removed her hand and played idly with her fingers. 'Do you remember that last night we were together. In that little hotel in Scotland?'

She nodded, and her mind wandered back down the years. They had been so in love.

'You begged me for a baby, and I refused. All the time I was a prisoner, and ever since that memory has haunted me. I've *always* regretted not giving you the baby you longed for.' He took both her hands in his, squeezing them tightly. 'Can you forgive me?'

Once again, Fleur's eyes filled with tears. 'Hugh, there's nothing to forgive.'

Suddenly something clicked in Fleur's brain. She wasn't sure what it was, but it seemed as if the last piece of a jigsaw puzzle had finally fallen into place.

'I've been hesitating about accepting the position in New Zealand ever since the letter arrived,' Hugh went on. 'But.... meeting you again seems to have decided things for me. I'll wire my acceptance to the hospital authorities to-morrow. I could be on my way in a couple of months.' He grinned. 'Maybe John and Ruth will end up emigrating too.' He looked down at her.

'And you Fleur? Will you go back to your husband?'

She sat up slowly, and wiped her eyes. 'I don't know.' Like Hugh, she now realised that they couldn't go back. Couldn't recapture those wartime moments. They had changed: everything had changed.

'I'd like to think you'll be happy,' he said gently.

She smiled up at him, and in spite of himself his heart leapt. 'And I want *you* to be happy too,' she whispered. Her fingers played absently with his tie. 'Perhaps,' she began. Then stopped.

He looked at her enquiringly. 'Perhaps *what?*' he probed.

'Perhaps,' she said hesitantly. 'Perhaps there's someone in New Zealand waiting for you?' She looked up at him.

'Perhaps,' he said softly, returning her gaze as Fiona's face rose and blurred his vision. 'Perhaps..... one never knows.' He took her back in his arms and held her close. The fragrance of her hair filled his nostrils and her perfume enclosed them in a floating cloud 'Oh Fleur darling,' he said hoarsely, gazing down at her. 'This is where we came in.' he smiled. 'We've come full circle.' He dropped a kiss on her hair. 'I'm glad we've rounded everything off.'

They remained locked in each other's arms until the clock tinkling the half hour brought them back to earth. Hugh released her and clasped his hands behind his head. 'My father said something to me when I was in despair that Christmas I returned and found you'd gone.' he said thoughtfully. It didn't make sense at the time.' He smiled to himself. 'But somehow it does now.'

Fleur looked at him enquiringly.

'Dad has a deep Christian faith. He doesn't talk much about it, he lives it. It's an every day thing with him.'

'I know,' Fleur interrupted. 'He was wonderful when you went missing, so positive and encouraging. He faced reality, but never gave up hope. I didn't see much of him, but he telephoned frequently to ask how I was.' She sighed. 'Arthur's deep faith seems to keep him always on the crest of the wave, not going under like I did when disaster strikes,.' She looked at Hugh, and he noticed that her face expressed a deep inner sadness. 'After the telegram arrived, he was really the only person who was able to help me. He shared my pain.'

'I know what you mean. Dad helped me too, though I didn't realise it at the time.'

'What did he say to you?' Fleur asked quietly.

Hugh frowned. 'He quoted the Bible. Though I've no idea from which book, or whether it was from the Old Testament or the New. He said "He will give you beauty for ashes". The ashes of my life I suppose. Though I was more than sceptical at the time.' A slow smile spread across his face. 'I think that is what has happened to us. Out of the ashes we've met.... and the beauty is that we're parting friends.'

She nodded. But didn't reply.

A conversation he had had with Fiona came back to his mind. They had been discussing the helplessness they both felt when faced with suffering, and premature death. She had mentioned Jesus, but he had been embarrassed and quickly changed the subject. Now her words, like his father's suddenly made sense: and he discovered that he wanted to know more. Was that the secret of Fiona's serenity, he pondered. That aura of peace which seemed to surround her, and draw people to her?

Slowly the curtain parted. And he knew that Fiona was the answer to all his longings. He smiled thoughtfully at Fleur. 'I think,' he said softly, 'that this evening we have both finally found not just each other but something we've been searching for for a long time.'

She looked up at him, her eyes shining. 'I think we have,' she whispered.

'No regrets?'

'No regrets,' she smiled. And deep in her heart she knew it was true. Meeting Hugh again and the few hours they had spent together had wiped out all the regrets, all the pain and anguish she had felt during the years they had been apart. And only the sweet memory of their love remained.

He threw an arm around her shoulders as they walked towards the door. 'Go to the window and wave to me like you did that night we became engaged. It will set the final seal on our perfect love.'

Drawing her to him, he gave her a long lingering kiss. 'For old times sake,' he whispered.

And he was gone.

Fleur crossed to the window. She saw him leave the building, run down the steps and hail a taxi cruising along Oakley Street. He knew she was there. And turned and waved.

She waved back, blowing a kiss as the taxi door closed behind him. She watched as it headed towards the Embankment, then dropping the curtain in place flopped fully dressed onto the bed. She was exhausted. Not only because of the heavy week she had had, but from all the emotions meeting Hugh again had aroused. Yet she couldn't sleep. Her mind was in a turmoil. But she wasn't unhappy. In fact she felt more at peace than she had done for a long time. Lying wide-awake, reliving the evening, Hugh's words came back to her:

"I always regretted not giving you the baby you begged me for."

And suddenly the completed jigsaw puzzle sprang to life. For a moment she felt giddy. She wanted to laugh out loud. The nightmare which she hadn't realised had been haunting her evaporated and the veil of bewilderment which had been shrouding her life vanished, liberating her from the torment in her head, the jungle of tangled thoughts which had held her in their grip, confusing her, preventing her from entering fully into her marriage with Arvind. She now understood why she had inexplicably refused to give Arvind the child he longed for. Subconsciously she had still been hoping to carry Hugh's baby.

'Papa was right,' she reflected. 'I've been living all these years with a ghost. Leading a double life. Loving Arvind, yet waiting for Hugh. Refusing to grow up and face reality. She gave a deep sigh. But it was a sigh of relief. The tapestry of her life which until then she had only seen from the underside flipped over, concealing the knots and revealing only the completed work. As the fragmented pieces of her life slowly slotted together, a feeling of intense happiness swept through her. 'I'm so lucky,' she murmured, 'to have been loved by two such wonderful men.'

A silvery grey dawn was creeping around the edge of the curtains. She remembered the midsummer dawns she and Arvind had watched in Norway, where the fading twilight mingled with the awakening day, and suddenly she longed for Arvind. Longed to feel his strong arms around her, to hear his voice speaking softly in her ear, soothing her, comforting her, reassuring her. Telling her everything was going to be all right. And she didn't understand. She was in this room which held so many memories of Hugh, yet she felt Arvind's presence more strongly than she had done for a long time. Remembering his touch, Fleur suddenly had an overwhelming longing to cradle Arvind's baby in her arms.

Almost without realising what she was doing, she picked up the telephone beside her bed and asked for the number. She glanced at the little jewelled watch Arvind had given her on their first wedding anniversary. Twenty past three. Yet despite the hour, Fleur had never felt so wide awake. Her mind crystal clear.

The call came through remarkably quickly. She heard Arvind's sleepy voice on the line.

'It's Fleur,' she announced.

'Fleur?' he stammered incredulously.

She could hear him fumbling for the bedside clock.

'It's half past four in the morning!' A note of anxiety crept into his tone. 'Is everything all right?'

Fleur laughed happily. 'Everything is *wonderful*,' she trilled, 'I couldn't wait to call.' The words tumbled over each other in her excitement. 'I promised to telephone you once the conference was over and give you an answer.'

He caught his breath. 'Ye..es,' he answered uncertainly.

She detected a note of fear in his tone. And her heart went out to him in a great wave of love.

'I'm taking the first 'plane in the morning to Copenhagen.'

There was an abrupt silence. For a moment she thought he had hung up.

'Arvind....' she cried.

'Arvind, are you there?' She heard a quick intake of breath.

'You're..... coming *back*?' he gasped. 'Oh Fleur..... my darling Fleur.'

Fleur burst into tears, but they were tears of joy and relief. The long agony was over. The torment released. 'I'm coming *home*,' she said softly, her voice still choked with tears. 'To *you*.'

END

Made in the USA
Charleston, SC
10 May 2015